SHERLOCK HOLMES AND FRANKENSTEIN'S DIARY

SHERLOCK HOLMES AND FRANKENSTEIN'S DIARY

Barry Grant

This first world edition published 2013
in Great Britain and in the USA by
SEVERN HOUSE PUBLISHERS LTD of
19 Cedar Road, Sutton, Surrey, England, SM2 5DA.

British Library Cataloguing in Publication Data

Grant, Barry.
  Sherlock Holmes and Frankenstein's diary.
  1. Holmes, Sherlock (Fictitious character)–Fiction.
  2. Wilson, James (Fictitious character)–Fiction.
  3. Switzerland–Fiction. 4. England–Fiction.
  5. Detective and mystery stories.
  I. Title
  823.9'2-dc23

 ISBN-13: 978-0-7278-8218-9 (cased)

All Severn House titles are printed on acid-free paper.

Severn House Publishers support The Forest Stewardship Council [FSC],the
leading international forest certification organisation. All our titles that are
printed on Greenpeace-approved FSC-certified paper carry the FSC logo.

Typeset by Palimpsest Book Production Ltd.,
Falkirk, Stirlingshire, Scotland.
Printed and bound in Great Britain by
MPG Books Ltd., Bodmin, Cornwall.

For Mother,
who tells a good tale

'Power tends to corrupt, and absolute power corrupts absolutely.'

Lord Acton

'If you pick up a starving dog and make him prosperous, he will not bite you. This is the principal difference between a dog and a man.'

Mark Twain

'Many people seem to think that animals cannot develop their own faculties, and have no power of making observations, or of drawing conclusions from their own experience.

I am not one of those people, and I believe that animals, wild as well as tame, have eyes to see with, ears to hear with, and understanding of the same kind as we men, if not in so high a degree.'

Fridtjof Nansen

ONE

For England

I should have guessed that Sherlock Holmes – ex-boxing champ at Cambridge, fencing master, single-stick expert – would be very good at driving a modern car. What I did not expect was that his handlers at Scotland Yard would supply him with an Aston Martin.

'Do slow down, Holmes!' I suggested, trying not to sound breathless.

'Can't, Wilson!'

'Try lifting your toe.'

He sat upright, arms straight out, beige driving gloves. The silvery Chinese dragon danced and winked on the key chain. Wind ruffled the top of his driving cap and made me think that at any moment the cap would vanish.

'A bit dodgy on that last curve, Holmes!' I said, clinging to the armrest.

'I dare not lose her!'

I held tight as we went into a four-wheel drift, came out of it, accelerated up the next sharp incline. The auxiliary exhaust flap opened and the throb of the V12 became a guttural roar. I was pressed back in my seat and began to feel slightly giddy. Overhead the merry sun danced like a ball on the mountain tops; on either side the landscape blurred and shredded in the corners of my eyes. I was not at all sure that Holmes could hold the car on the road at this rate. The smell of pine hit me like a wall as we shot into a forest of flickering sunlight. I had given up hope that we were even close to our quarry. Hadn't seen her for miles.

Then I spotted the cycle, black, strangely small, tilting round the next curve.

Gone.

In view again.

Gone.

'You're gaining, Holmes!'

'We'll not lose her now!'

A straight stretch opened ahead. Holmes stepped down hard, I was flung back. A shimmer ahead, as of a mirage, and the cycle quivered at the curve and soared straight ahead, seemed to climb an invisible road into empty sky. A moment later I was thrown forward as we squealed to a smoking stop and froze at the very edge of the cliff, in roils of dust.

The girl rose from the cycle, seemed to float. Her black helmet flew off, long red hair flowered on wind, a square white laptop drifted upward as if she'd tossed it. Four objects – helmet, cycle, girl, laptop – flew up and up, slowly arced and swooped downward toward the sparkling water.

And vanished far below.

'I think you've lost her,' I said.

The crunch of gravel under my shoes seemed very loud.

Holmes walked to the edge and squinted down. Put hands in his pockets. 'Finished,' he said. 'Nothing we can do.'

I have always admired his sangfroid.

Another car stopped. The driver called on his mobile phone while the young lad in the back seat got out quickly and, paying no attention to the tragedy, came straight to our silver Aston Martin and touched the bright red leather upholstery. 'She's a six liter!' he said.

A third car stopped. The driver climbed out, horrified. She walked cautiously toward the edge, hand covering her mouth. 'Mon Dieu!' she cried.

It was a sheer drop down a rock face to the water – no way to climb down from where we stood.

Holmes was already back in our car.

'She hasn't come up,' I called, squinting at the sheet of glittering water.

'She likely broke her neck, or her back. Or knocked herself out and will drown,' said Holmes. 'Nothing can be done.'

He was right, of course.

'Excuse me, sir,' said the lad, pointing to the console screen in the sleek little Volante DBS. 'Is that a GPS?'

'It is,' said Holmes.

'How fast will this car go, sir?'

'About a hundred and ninety miles an hour,' said Holmes.

'Ohh!'

Holmes let the little Volante slide back onto the roadway. A moment later we were flashing up the mountain toward Chamonix.

'Wrong way, isn't it?' I said.

'Curiosity calls.'

'Surely our duty is to head back down to Martigny and tell her lover what has happened.'

'Perhaps,' said Holmes. 'But you and I have very little time in Switzerland. It occurs to me that we are near the laboratory of Dr Jan Droon. Duty, as well as curiosity, compels me to visit him.'

Holmes slipped Droon's business card out of his shirt pocket. 'His coordinates are on this – please tap them into the GPS, Wilson.'

I did.

A map whirled onto the screen and a voice began to speak. We followed our virtual will-'o-the-wisp along the Gorges du Trient, and before very many miles we were turning off the main road onto a tarmac drive just beyond the mountain village of Finhaut. We wound upward through trees and emerged in an open area dominated by a very large chalet. Most of the building was obscured by a twelve-foot-high stone wall. At the scrolled black iron gate we stopped. A voice demanded our business. Holmes gave his name, the gate immediately opened, and we drove through like royalty.

TWO

A Modern Frankenstein

Dr Droon emerged from the chalet with that same cheerful gusto he had exhibited as he had emerged, the previous week, from a dumpster in a London alley. On his broad porch he greeted us with genuine enthusiasm. 'My dear Mr Holmes!' he cried. 'How very good of you to visit my humble laboratory!' He embraced Holmes, then shook my hand. 'So good to see you again, Wilson – I always admire a warrior, truly I do.'

'That was years ago,' said I.

'Riding in Humvees, seeing the Afghan countryside, watching people explode – it must have been most interesting. No, no, my dear fellow, I am speaking seriously. I am not a one-dimensional man. I can see the charm of war . . . for a warrior. For civilians, of course . . . another matter.'

He was a handsome man of medium height. His curly hair, dark and slightly graying at the edges, made him look boyish. His slightly prissy manner made him seem sophisticated. And his know-it-all tone made him appear rather like one of those academic bores who are just ever so slightly out of touch with the world, and with themselves.

He led us into the massive house, saying, 'Come in, Mr Holmes, Mr Wilson – you gentleman know the purpose of my research.'

'World peace through biology,' said Holmes.

'Precisely, precisely!' said Dr Droon. 'How good it is to communicate with a truly scientific mind such as yours, Mr Holmes! A wide-ranging mind, a close-observing eye! You are, my dear sir, the quintessence of scientific purity. Others misunderstand me, you will not misunderstand me – Klebbing! Klebbing!'

We were in a large sitting room, decorated in the modern mode, with a painting by Mondrian on one wall, a painting by Dali on another. The paintings surprised me.

'Originals, I assure you,' said Droon. 'I collect them. As a Dutchman, how could I be anything but moved by great painting! Klebbing!'

A man appeared in the doorway. Something odd about him, but I couldn't be sure what.

'We'd like some drinks, Klebbing. Scotch on ice for Mr Holmes – Balvenie Doublewood, if we have it. And an American Martini for Mr Wilson: Boodle's gin plus French vermouth – Noilly Prat – very dry, on ice, with a squeeze of lemon.'

'Excellent memory, Dr Droon!' said Holmes.

'Memory is the essence of science, Mr Holmes – detailed memory of close observations, plus a poet's imagination to lift a theory into orbit.'

He was so full of himself, so energetic in his wish to please, that I scarcely noticed he had not been tactful enough to ask whether we actually *wanted* drinks. 'I'll have my usual,' he called, and the servant vanished.

Droon waved us into chairs by a picture window that offered a stupendous view of mountains.

By and by the servant limped into the room, giving a little grunt at every other step. He rocked as he walked, and stood at an angle, as if one leg were shorter than the other. I thought he might drop the tray. He looked a bit as if he were put together with random body parts. One side of his face was twisted into a leer, and the other side had been erased – evidently by nerve damage – into a blank stare. Hatchet-cut dark hair hung over his ears. I felt rather sorry for the fellow.

'Sherlock Holmes, James Wilson,' said Dr Droon, 'may I introduce my able assistant, Klebbing Hackfelt.'

Hackfelt muttered something unintelligible. He hobbled away and vanished. But a moment later he reappeared in the doorway and held up what appeared to be – to my astonishment – a cat-o'-nine tails, that infamous whip used to flog seamen in the days of the old sailing ships.

'Not yet, not yet!' said Droon, impatiently. 'In twenty minutes – you know the schedule, Klebbing!'

Klebbing Hackfelt bowed his head submissively and vanished again.

'I keep to a very strict schedule, Mr Holmes. You have come at a fortuitous moment, for my experiment is about to begin. Three o'clock sharp. It would do me honor if you would watch, Mr Holmes, and give me your frank opinion of my methods, and your suggestions as to how I might improve them. I don't ask this of many men but you, sir, are one of the truly scientific minds of the last several centuries – you are an exception.'

'I am most happy to oblige,' said Holmes, lightly. 'Tell me, who are the subjects of your experiment? Is Hackfelt one of them?'

'Heavens no, Mr Holmes! He is, as I said, my able assistant. The subjects are K47, a male gorilla, and X2, a female chimpanzee, and also X3, a male chimp. They have lived in near proximity to each other for a year, and have become good friends. And they hate me, so the situation is perfect for my experiments. I think I have described to you my theories.'

'I do understand your theory,' said Holmes.

'Oh, yes, well, from your tone I gather your unstated meaning, my dear Holmes. You are skeptical, and I entirely understand – I *want* you to be skeptical! But the truth is that the human race is a tribe of vicious monkeys. We murder each other century after century, war after war after war. In a thousand years there has not been the slightest sign of improvement in our natures. Philosophy is powerless. And the chances that we shall ever *evolve* into peaceful animals are remote to the vanishing point. Therefore we must abandon philosophy, abandon hoping for evolutionary miracles. We must instead *do something* to change our biology. My quest is to create a new man, a new life form! And the first step in that process is to understand what portion of our brains is responsible for kindness, for sharing, and for loving thy neighbor as thyself. That, my dear Holmes, is the step I am attempting to take. Drink up, gentlemen, drink up! The time approaches. We must not disappoint our subjects – they will be awaiting us. I do these experiments twice a day, punctually at ten in the morning and at three in the afternoon. Punctuality is absolutely necessary in this line of research.'

Dr Jan Droon leapt from his chair and led us through the huge house, down dark corridors and through a massive steel door with a wheel lock; he locked the door behind us after we had passed through. Two turnings later we entered a gloomy room that smelled of monkey. The lights came on, and to my shock there stood a huge gorilla behind massive iron bars, looking in the sudden glare a bit like King Kong. In another cage, right next to his, were two chimpanzees. To the left of both cages was a huge sliding barn door, twice as high as a man. A hatchet with a blue handle hung on the wall near the door. Klebbing Hackfelt took down the hatchet and, using the hammer end, knocked open the bolt lock. Then he slowly, laboriously, pushed open the creaking huge door, whereupon a panorama of mountains appeared. Gusts of fresh air seemed to motivate the captive apes – the gorilla shook the bars of his cage and roared, and the chimpanzees looked both fearful and angry. The chimpanzees had been grooming each other when the lights first went on, touching each other lovingly. Now they both were standing, knuckles touching the floor, looking very much like apes always look, a little primitive – but much more elegant that Klebbing Hackfelt, who stood panting nearby, with the cat-o'-nine-tails drooping from his hand.

'That gorilla is strangely mottled,' said Holmes. 'What happened to him?'

'He's been burned,' said Droon. 'He'll be all right. Apes can stand a lot of pain. They don't really feel pain as we do, you know.'

'What makes you think not?' asked Holmes.

Droon ignored the question.

'As I explained to you at the Dorchester Hotel, Mr Holmes, I have inserted electrodes and a tiny radio receiver into these animals' brains. When I send a signal from my computer – the computer there on the table – the electrodes stimulate a certain part of the brain with electrical pulses that short-circuit, as it were, the cerebral cells responsible for anger and aggression, while simultaneously stimulating those cells responsible for love and kindness. Watch.'

'Opening that cage might not be a good idea,' I said.

'It would be a fatal idea, except that my able assistant is standing by the computer switch, and I have this . . .' Droon lifted a blowtorch off a wall hook where it had hung by the hatchet. He lit the blowtorch with a lighter. The torch flared. A fierce hissing plume of flame appeared. The gorilla roared and backed away from the cage door. Dr Droon entered, burnt the ape's arm with the torch, waved the flame in the creature's face, burnt him again. As the ape howled, Droon shouted, 'Hit the switch, Klebbing!'

Whereupon the ape began suddenly to show submission to Dr Droon. The gorilla opened his hands, and lowered his head – and still the doctor burnt him.

'You see!' cried Dr Droon. He emerged from the cage with K47 following five paces behind him in a submissive posture, as if begging for affection. Droon slammed the gate on him but left it unlocked. Droon's face was rosy with the heat, and with a strange kind of ecstasy – obviously he had enjoyed this experiment.

Now it was Klebbing Hackfelt's turn. While Droon manned

the computer keyboard, Klebbing Hackfelt entered the chimpanzee cage. The animals showed anger and aggression as he
began to lash them with the cat-o'-nine-tails, and for a moment
I thought that the larger of the two was going to succeed in
grabbing Hackfelt and making an end of him – but at that moment
Dr Droon hit the switch, whereupon the two chimps, despite the
flurry of blows descending on them, began to crouch submissively
with downbent heads.

'Point proved,' said Dr Droon.

Klebbing Hackfelt lashed X2 and X3 while each crouched and
reached out as if requesting forgiveness.

'If the point is proved, then stop him from hitting the creatures,'
said Holmes.

'Oh, Klebbing needs his fun, Mr Holmes – I'm sure you
understand!'

'I'm sure I don't,' said Holmes.

'My experiments, Mr Holmes, are a mingling of techniques
that are very practical and crude, with others that are very delicate and sophisticated. I have isolated the precise parts of the
brain that need to be changed if men are ever to become truly
peaceful.'

'Obviously you regard torture as merely a necessary means to
a beautiful end,' said Holmes.

'Very well said!' cried Droon. 'I knew you would understand,
Mr Holmes. Other minds, lesser minds than yours, entirely
misunderstand me. Which is why I have been driven to conduct
my experiments in this mountain fortress. Illegal experiments,
they call them. But all the great ideas of mankind have been
called illegal, or immoral. Nonetheless, it is depressing to be
ostracized as I have been by the common people. I am a man,
after all. Do I not sting when unfairly criticized? Do I not hurt
when mocked? Do I not need approval, need encouragement –
need *love*, even? It is heartening to know, Mr Holmes, what a
truly superior mind, such as yours, thinks of me.'

'Ah, but I hope you *do* know truly what I think,' said Holmes,
softly.

'I think I do, Mr Holmes,' said Droon, with a warm and almost
beatific smile. 'I think I do. And I thank you for being so good
a friend.'

'I think,' said Holmes, 'you are the maddest man I've ever met – and I intend to put a stop to you.'

Droon stared.

Tact was never Holmes's strong point.

THREE
Midsummer Mystery

I am quite aware that the genial Dr Watson – whose talent for telling a tale surpasses even my grandest aspirations – never began a narrative *in medias res* in quite the way I have just done. I can only say that when I asked Holmes if I should chance such a beginning, breaking tradition with his famous nineteenth-century biographer, he laughed at my query, and waved his hand through the air dismissively. 'New times,' he cried, 'require new styles of telling! Have at it, my dear Wilson! If I am trying to become a new man, adjusted to the new age – the Age of the Instantaneous, as I call it – then surely you must strive to present me in a style that suits my aspiration! Do as you will, and as you think best.'

'But I want to make clear to you, Holmes,' said I, 'that I will be doing rather the same thing that you used to accuse Dr Watson of doing – sensationalizing, to a degree. Trying to attract the reader's interest at the outset.'

'And why not? Sensations are the essence of life. Carry on, Wilson! Spending almost a century in a glacier changes one's view of sensations. I now relish them, however unrefined they may be. Sensations, even the brassiest and crudest of them, stimulate thought. And if you can stimulate your readers to think about my methods, and perhaps to learn from them – what more could I wish?'

And so, with Holmes's approval, I embark on this terrifying tale that began long ago in the jungles of south India and that caught up with Sherlock Holmes and me on the morning of June 21st of this year, 2012, as I was sitting in my favorite chair, reading the morning newspaper. Holmes burst through the front door of our flat and cried, 'I've been hacked, Wilson! I feel an utter fool!'

I set down my coffee cup in surprise. 'Being hacked is a hazard of modern life, Holmes. I doubt there is a man alive who hasn't been hacked – may I get you some coffee?'

'Tea.'

'Tell me what happened, my dear fellow. And try to relax.'

He flung himself into a chair. 'Last evening I received a most unexpected email from Dr Coleman, saying he had discovered something curious in the clothing I was wearing when they found me frozen in the glacier. You will recall that after they thawed me out, and resuscitated me, Coleman returned all the personal effects he had found in my pockets – my penknife, watch, and so on. But the clothing itself he put on display in that lovely little museum at St Bart's Hospital.'

'A most interesting display it is, too. Your wax image is astonishingly lifelike.'

'Coleman thought he had emptied all the pockets of my clothes, but evidently he had missed one object in an inner vest pocket. He said he wanted to return it to me. I went to the hospital this morning to collect it. Coleman was in surgery, so I spoke to his nurse – you may remember the gorgeous Miss Devon.'

'I remember her very well – but I confess, Holmes, I am surprised that you noticed she was gorgeous.'

'When I told her I had come to pick up the item, she clapped her hand to her mouth and said, "Oh, but it was picked up earlier this morning . . . by your friend, Mr Swingle."'

'I told her I knew no Mr Swingle.'

'Nurse Devon was astonished. She showed me an email that appeared to have been sent by *me* to Dr Coleman. The email informed Coleman that a friend of mine named Alistair Swingle would pick up the item for me. Of course, the email was not mine. Someone, my dear Wilson, has hacked into my email account – that seems the only possible explanation. And then this person hurried to the hospital ahead of me this morning, and he picked up the item before I arrived.'

'And what did this person steal?'

'A Tewkesbury Dragon. Nurse Devon described the item to

me minutely, and there can be no doubt what it was. Fortunately, neither Dr Coleman nor Miss Devon handled it roughly – or we might have been lamenting not merely a theft but a death. It is a silver Chinese dragon on a silver chain. Until this morning I had completely forgotten it existed. How odd to have forgotten such a thing!' He rubbed his temple, and shook his head.

'After almost a hundred years, one is likely to forget certain minor matters,' said I, and I stood up and looked out the window where I could see no sign of my friend, Bucky Boudreau.

'I remember,' said Holmes, 'putting that little dragon into my inner vest pocket before I began my journey to see the Czar in 1914 . . . I say, Wilson, no word yet from your American friend?'

I turned away from the window. 'Afraid not. He was supposed to have arrived at Heathrow at seven, and I am surprised he has not called. He is most eager to meet you, Holmes. He has been a fan of yours all his life . . . but this Tewkesbury Dragon – I'm curious. In what way could a piece of jewelry be dangerous?'

'What a subtle piece of death it is!' cried Holmes. 'It was designed in 1898 to murder a man with a bizarre psychological disorder, and it first came to my notice in the oddest sort of—'

The door chime sounded, interrupting him.

Sir Launcelot jumped to his feet, tail wagging, and gazed at the entryway.

Holmes glanced at his watch. 'Must be Sigvard Kipling. He is punctual.' Holmes bounded toward the door.

The chime sounded again, impatiently.

Sigvard Kipling was a tall man of sixty-five or so, courtly in manner, with intense blue eyes and a firm grip. His voice was plummy, forceful, resonant, and full of soothing vibrations. He might have been an actor. His large face and high forehead gave him a presence. He was, in fact, a handsome man. He took a seat in the easy chair by the window, scratched Sir Launcelot between the ears, and accepted a cup of tea. 'It is very good of you to see me on such short notice, Mr Holmes.'

'And most considerate of you to arrive so punctually – particularly as I observe that you had difficulty finding your sports jacket this morning, had no time for breakfast, drove down from St Albans in heavy traffic, and were forced to park several blocks from here.'

'I am familiar with your methods, Mr Holmes,' said Sigvard Kipling, with a laugh. 'And although I am eager to know how you deduced all that from merely glancing at me, I confess I am even more eager to tell you my tale. You need no demonstrations to convince me that you are the greatest detective alive – undoubtedly the greatest who ever lived. That is the commonest of common knowledge.'

Holmes seemed a bit disappointed that he could not display his wares and reveal his method, but he was obviously pleased at the compliment. He pulled his chair closer. 'Proceed, my dear sir,' said he, almost trembling with interest, 'and, pray, omit no details.' Holmes gazed intently at our guest as he began to speak, watching every shadow of expression on his face, every subtle shifting of his body.

'For many years,' said Kipling, 'I was in business in the City. Ten years ago, at the age of fifty-five, I retired to my horse farm in Kent. There my wife Vera and I have lived ever since, enjoying ourselves and smiling at the usual bumps in the road of life. But yesterday we hit a pothole that has disturbed us greatly. My dear sister, Sylvia Swann, died. At first the manner of her death, though unusual, seemed explicable. But the more I thought about it, Mr Holmes, the more I came to feel that there was something very odd about how she died. That is why I called you late last night, and why I have come to you so early this morning. The police call it murder and they think they know who did it. But I am certain they have gotten hold of the wrong end of the stick altogether, and are off on a merry chase after an innocent person. I dare say I am an excellent judge of character, both of horses and of men. And I know it is quite impossible that so lovely and thoughtful a girl as Isabel Rocamora could murder anyone. But let me not get ahead of myself. I have read your cases, sir, and I know you like an orderly presentation of background information, followed by a clear presentation of the facts. So, let me try.'

'You have my full attention,' cried Holmes.

'My sister Sylvia's husband died earlier this year, in the very same room as Sylvia died – almost in the same spot. He was David Swann, the famous animal rights crusader. You may remember the stir caused eight years ago when he gave up his distinguished career as a television journalist in order to devote his full energies to saving animals from slaughterhouses and science laboratories. For years David was in the news because he was embroiled in legal battles with the billionaire Gerald Gurloch, who owns most of the newspapers in this country, and also a number of slaughterhouses. When David died, Sylvia took up his cause. She served as president of the notorious Rabbit Underground that David founded, and she continued his legal battles against Gurloch. And now suddenly she too is dead, in rather peculiar circumstances – and all this has set my mind aflame with suspicions, and rather perplexed me, Mr Holmes.

'I must tell you that David and Sylvia were very unusual people – radicals, really. Not ordinary. They met in 1969 at the Woodstock Festival in New York. Both had just completed a Grand Tour of America. Sylvia was travelling with an English pointer named Toby whom she had found as a stray in San Francisco, and David was travelling with a Volkswagen Beetle called Edgar. They were both twenty-one. According to family legend, Sylvia took her famous trip into inner space on the day she met David: she danced on a deserted stage to the tune of LSD, pulled down a banner of some sort, and generally made a happy fool of herself. We have an album of pictures revealing that momentous occasion. When she came down from her LSD cloud, Sylvia and David agreed to be married. Alas, while she was dancing on that stage and waving that banner, her English pointer was stolen. She was haunted for years by the hours that followed her LSD trip, hours spent searching for Toby. They finally found Toby in somebody's campsite, took him back by force, then went through the tedious process of bringing Toby into this country. They celebrated their nuptials on Midsummer Night's Eve of 1969, and did so while ascending in a large helium balloon – David's wild idea, of course. In the basket of the balloon were David and Sylvia, my wife and I as witnesses, the pastor, the pilot, and Toby the dog. When we landed in an alfalfa field the balloon basket bounced on a bunny, broke its leg, and David insisted on taking the little creature to the vet – maybe that was the start of his crusade on behalf of animals.

'I am rather old-school, I confess – even as a young man I was a bit of a stick-in-the-mud. David, by contrast, throve upon the Age of Protest. He was ever in the thick of Vietnam protests, ban-the-bomb rallies, all that sort of shenanigans. And Sylvia was never happier than when she was leading a group of earnest young radical vegetarians carrying signs emblazoned with the Rabbit Underground logo, that big blue R and U followed by a small red 'n' – the RUn brigade, as they called themselves. She loved to march at the head as they protested in front of factory farms, shops that sold fur, or Gerald Gurloch's newspaper offices.

'In their marriage Sylvia and David had three children. Andrew is now twenty-six, Canyon twenty-four, and Amy twenty-two. It has been a family tradition to meet on the day of Midsummer Night's Eve to celebrate David and Sylvia's anniversary. So yesterday, the summer solstice, the family met at Sylvia's cottage near St Albans. We arrived in the morning, had Midsummer brunch about ten, and then six of us retired to the bottom of the garden where we set up house in the gazebo and played tennis from twelve-thirty until four in the afternoon. The six tennis players were Andrew and his girlfriend Jenny, Canyon and his girlfriend Victoria, and me and my wife Vera. The tennis courts are out of sight of the house, about a hundred yards away, just beyond the duck pond. While we were playing tennis, Amy was off riding her horse on the bridle paths, and the new maid, Isabel Rocamora, was in the house cooking our supper. Isabel had come to work at Sylvia's special request, and had reluctantly agreed to work until five. At about three o'clock Isabel walked down to the gazebo carrying a tray of drinks – sherry and rum punches. She mentioned that she had just brought a glass of lemonade to Sylvia, who was in the study working on her anniversary letters. Isabel said that Sylvia was nearly finished with the letters – letters that she wrote every year to all of her and David's close friends. She said Sylvia had promised to join us shortly. Then we would all go up to dinner.

'But Sylvia never came down to the tennis court.

'So at five o'clock Canyon and I walked up to the house and called to her to join us. She didn't answer. I knocked on the study door and tried to turn the handle but it was locked. This seemed odd. We walked around to the garden and looked in through the windows of the study. Through the glassy reflections we saw a heap of gold and green tablecloth lying on the floor by the couch. Then Canyon noticed a foot protruding from beneath the tablecloth. Needless to say, we were alarmed. Canyon smashed a window pane with a garden rock, swung the window outward, stepped through the window and down onto the window seat, and so entered the room. He pulled the cover off the body and glanced back at me with a look of horror on his face as he cried, "My god, Uncle, I think she is dead!"

'My poor sister was lying face down on the floor with blood on the back of her head. On the carpet near her feet lay a statue of Aphrodite about two feet high, an ancient statue which she and David had bought in Greece years ago. It had been atop the barrister bookcases near where she lay. On the carpet near her head lay a book. What instantly occurred to me was that my sister had taken a book down from the shelf and was looking at it when she was hit from behind by someone who had used the statue as a club.'

'What was the title of the book?' interrupted Holmes.

'Title? I can't say I know. Her Pelikan fountain pen was open on the desk next to the writing paper, and seven envelopes had already been sealed and piled neatly. Another letter was partly written. We carried the news to the tennis court and everyone came up to the house. Naturally, we were all very distraught. We retreated to the sitting room and comforted each other while awaiting the arrival of the police and the ambulance. Amy was still out riding her horse. About six o'clock, just a few minutes before the police arrived, Amy appeared and we told her the horrible news. The police then did their investigation. Sergeant Drub and his team of detectives went over the room very carefully. I must say they worked most efficiently. I had confidence in them. Yet there was something about the situation that struck me as very odd, Mr Holmes. So odd that even as the police were working, I thought of you. I can't say the police were doing anything wrong. But their conclusions did not add up.

'Let me reconstruct the situation. There are only three possible entrances to the study: the inner oak door from the house itself, and the two windows that open into the garden. The door can be locked and unlocked from within the room by a simple lever, but from outside only by a key. So far as we know, just one key exists. It is kept in the top drawer of the dining room china cabinet – the same cabinet where the tablecloths are kept. The oak door to the study was locked, the key was in the china cabinet drawer, and the windows leading to the study from the garden were locked. To get in, Canyon broke a pane, as I have said, and he then pressed down the lever, and swung the window outward so that we could climb through. There is no fireplace in the study, no other way of entry or exit.

'The police examined the room. They also asked each of us numerous questions. Soon the ambulance people arrived and took Sylvia away. My wife Vera and I then closed and locked the cottage – I have a key – and we went with Andrew and Jenny to stay at a nearby inn for the night. Canyon and his girl, Victoria, went home, for they live close by. Amy went to Hemel Hempstead where she lives in an apartment with her girlfriend. I was tired, but I was so bothered by the thought that something was wrong at the cottage that I returned there alone at about nine o'clock last night. I went into the study and looked about. Everything was precisely as it had been – except, of course, that Sylvia was gone. Then I received a shock – for I realized a painting was missing! It was a beautiful little painting, by the eighteenth-century painter George Stubbs, of an English pointer standing beneath a big green tree with a beautiful dark bay horse. Worth a bit of money. David bought the painting as an anniversary gift to Sylvia many years ago, in memory of Toby, for the dog in the picture really did look just like her Toby. It might have been his portrait. I thought it odd that we should not have noticed that the painting was gone. Perhaps in our frantic states of mind we simply did not pay attention to minor matters – that is what I reasoned to myself. And yet, upon reflection, it seemed almost unbelievable that we hadn't noticed that the picture was missing. This threw a new light on things. I considered various possibilities. For instance, there is a closet in the study. We did not look into it until the police arrived. I suppose it is possible that whoever smashed my sister hid in the closet, and was hiding there the whole time we were dealing with the situation. And then, perhaps, he somehow managed to grab the painting and sneak out while we were in the sitting room, perhaps right out the window through which Canyon and I had entered when we found Sylvia. But that scenario struck me as the sort of implausible sequence that writers often put into mysteries, scenarios that are theoretically possible but so complicated and improbable that they seldom, if ever, would occur in the real world. That was when I called you. I was sorry to call so late, to be so intrusive. But I was in a frantic state of mind. You were most gracious to agree to see me this morning. After calling, I sat pondering in the study for another hour, and then I went back to the inn.

'This morning Sergeant Drub met me at the cottage about seven-thirty. I showed him the space on the wall where the painting had been. He had suspected the new maid from the start, and now this possible motive for the crime made him more certain than ever that Isabel Rocamora was the murderer. Quite frankly, Mr Holmes, Isabel is one of the nicest young women I've ever met. She is Swiss, she is meticulous, and she is beautiful. She dusts books every three days and polishes windows after every rain. In fact, she has been a bit too energetic a housekeeper for my poor sister, who was forever admonishing her to "Please stop fussing, my dear – quite unnecessary – you are wearing me out." Admittedly, it can a bit tedious to see someone adjust every picture that is a millimicron off center. It was I who recommended Isabel to my sister, for I knew her family in Zurich. I lived in Zurich for several years while on foreign assignment. Isabel's father, Walter Rocamora, is a highly regarded bookbinder in Zurich. He bound a set of sporting books for me, in red Morocco, years ago. The only thing that can be said against Isabel is that she appears to be romantically involved with George Bentley, a pleasant young man of no substance, not at all reliable. But women, you know, well . . . they are not always practical, are they?

'The police theory is that Isabel struck Sylvia with the statue, took the painting, locked the windows, then went to the china cabinet and got a tablecloth and also the key to the study. With the cloth she covered the body, presumably so that if anyone looked in through the garden window they would not see it. With the key she locked the door from the outside. She then – say the police – put the key back in its place, and soon was picked up by George Bentley. Presumably those two then hurried away with their booty, never to be seen again. It seems to me a ridiculous theory in every way. But I would like your opinion on the matter. That is why I have come to you this morning.'

Holmes sprang from his chair. 'I am curious, Mr Kipling – you say David Swann died in that same room.'

'Six months ago.'

'How did that occur?'

'David had triple bypass surgery fifteen years ago. That cured him for a while. Then it got worse. He had a pacemaker. Died of a heart attack. We were shocked – one always is. But we were not surprised. He had been forced to restrict his activity. He died on the daybed in the study, next to where Sylvia was found on the floor. She was in Paris when he died, vacationing in a small apartment she owned in the Rue Jacob. David was alone when Sara found him.'

'Sara?'

'Sara Drumling. The family's maid for many years. To our surprise, Sara came into money shortly after David's death, and she left the household to open a curiosity shop in Brighton. Apparently that had been her lifelong dream. That is why I recruited Isabel as the new maid.'

'How long had Sara been with the family?'

'Donkey's years.'

'You say your sister kept a flat in the Rue Jacob. That requires a bit of money.'

Sigvard Kipling frowned slightly. He put his large and shapely hand to his forehead. He brushed his forehead with his fingers, and shook his head. 'And that's another problem. My sister has a sizeable estate and she trusted me to handle her business affairs. She and David planned to rewrite their will to leave nearly everything to the Rabbit Underground. I had set in train the process to get this done . . . and now that she has died, all my work is undone. My heavens – I have a task ahead.' He smiled faintly, took a deep breath.

'So as things stand at present,' said Sherlock Holmes, 'I presume the children will inherit—'

'Oh, yes, they will inherit all the money. But they know their parents' desires, and they will, accordingly, donate all the money to the Rabbit Underground. No difficulty about that. But it does make the whole affair more complicated than it might have been.'

The rattle of a motorcycle in the street interrupted us. Holmes glanced through the front window. 'A solitary cyclist,' said he.

I looked out.

'The motorcyclist has parked illegally,' said Holmes, 'and I suspect – yes, he is darting toward our building.'

The door chime sounded.

FOUR

Black Swan Appears

Our visitor was a dark-haired young man, lean and tall, who wore blue jeans torn at the knees, high-topped white tennis shoes smeared with dirt, a blue T-shirt emblazoned with red Arabic script.

'I should like to see Sherlock Holmes,' said he, tossing his head back to shake the dark lock of hair off his brow. He hurried past me and announced himself brashly, 'I am Andrew Swann.'

Holmes gave him an impatient glance and made what seemed a dismissive remark: '"The dog barks, the caravan passes".'

'You read Arabic, Mr Holmes!' cried the newcomer. 'Perhaps your reputation as a polymath is not exaggerated, after all.'

Sigvard Kipling lurched from his chair, mouth smiling, forehead frowning. 'Andrew, what are you doing here?'

'Where better to be than with my favorite uncle?'

'Good heavens,' cried Kipling. 'The boy is a phantom, Mr Holmes! He knows where we all are at all times. Sometimes he even knows what we are thinking. Not very sporting.' He shook his head.

'I have some things to tell you, Mr Holmes,' said Andrew, in a nasal voice that was a bit piercing.

'Have a seat.'

'Sorry, but I don't wish to be here when Lestrade arrives.'

'Lestrade?' said Holmes. 'What makes you think he is coming?'

'I happen to know,' said Andrew Swann.

'The lad is uncanny,' said Kipling.

Holmes whirled, held a finger in the air. 'Tell me, Andrew Swann, what do you wish to see me about – *exactly*?'

'Corruption in the Metropolitan Police, Mr Holmes.'

Holmes looked out the window, and he remarked, 'A red-headed woman just emerged from a white Citroen and she is taking your motorcycle, Mr Andrew Swann.'

I hurried to the window and saw a tall, statuesque young woman with long red hair straddling the cycle. I heard the throb of the engine. 'She is driving it away,' I said.

'Not to worry, gentlemen,' said the newcomer. 'She is my girlfriend.'

'Then her name would be Jenny?' said Holmes.

'Yes. But please indulge me, Mr Holmes. Is there someplace we might talk privately? I must be on my way, for Lestrade will be here in eight minutes.'

Holmes gave me a brisk look. 'We will be in the garden, Wilson. Tell Lestrade I will return in half an hour.'

Sigvard Kipling stepped quickly toward the door, ahead of Holmes and Andrew Swann. 'Will you be coming up to St Albans to investigate, Mr Holmes?'

'This afternoon.'

'Very good of you, sir!' said he, and as he stood there, tall and square-shouldered in the hallway, bluff and handsome and reserved, he seemed to me a picture of British solidity, the sort of man who had conquered continents and administered the Raj.

They all went out.

Through the front window I watched Kipling float away toward Gloucester Place in a swinging stride. Holmes and Andrew Swann passed through the black iron gate into the private garden of Dorset Square and vanished beneath trees.

Twenty minutes later Lestrade arrived. I told him Holmes would be back shortly. I offered him a cup of coffee, which he gratefully accepted. 'I seldom need a second morning cup,' said he, 'but I need one today. In fact, I could use a Martini.'

'Trouble in the force?'

'You can't imagine, Wilson. Looks like you expected three for breakfast.'

'I set a place for my Chicago friend, but he hasn't arrived. He is going to interview Holmes for a piece in the *New York Times*.'

'I am surprised Holmes agreed.'

'So am I. But when Holmes learned Bucky Boudreau had covered the war in Afghanistan with me, he not only agreed to the interview but suggested Bucky should stay in our flat and sleep on the futon.'

I stood with my hands in pockets, gazing down at the street where the Aston Martin gleamed in the morning shine. Two young lads appeared out of nowhere, ran over to look at the car.

'I don't feel entirely comfortable riding in that car, Lestrade – thrill though it be.'

'Don't blame you. If the economic crisis continues in Europe, we are going to see a lot more than just Aston Martins being attacked. We are going to see rallies, marches, riots. People no longer think it right for a few people to have mega-pounds while the rest of the country buckles and collapses.'

We heard a metallic click in the lock, a footstep in the entry hall, and suddenly there was Sherlock Holmes, stepping toward us briskly. His tan explorer shirt was open two buttons down from the collar, and against his chest lay a silver dragon on a silver chain. I had never seen Holmes wearing jewelry before. He might easily have been mistaken for an ageing hippy of the sixties era.

'Yes, gentlemen,' said Holmes, picking up the thread of our conversation, 'the public used to think it charming to have a rich and leisured class. Things have changed. The hoi polloi no longer find it amusing that one man should have income sufficient to let him sit on red leather upholstery in a car costing hundreds of thousands of pounds, contemplating his 540-horsepower engine, while another man sits on a curb out of work, wearing broken shoes, contemplating from where his next biscuit might be begged. It is a recipe for riot and revolution.'

'Riot training for police has been stepped up,' said Lestrade. 'But thank goodness, I won't be involved.'

Holmes flung himself into his easy chair. 'Alas, you will be in the thick of it, my dear fellow!' cried he. 'I know you, Lestrade. You can't resist!'

'Not this time, Holmes. They are putting me out to pasture. Six months from now I'll be gone from the force.'

Sherlock sprang from his chair. 'What!'

'They want me out,' said Lestrade.

'Want you out!' cried Holmes, incredulously.

'Certain irregular things are happening in the police force these days, things I refuse to go along with.'

'Illegal things, you mean,' said Holmes. 'Yes, I just heard about some of them from a young gentleman who studies such matters.'

'There are a great many people who do not like it that I do not go along. Unfortunately, they can do what they like with me. I am past the usual retirement age. Excuses can bc found. A senior individual named Nigel Greenwood wants me out, so out I'll be.'

Holmes turned his empty briar pipe upside down and nervously rapped it on the hearth – though it had never held a single shred of tobacco in its life. He nodded thoughtfully. 'Nigel Greenwood, you say.'

'There is nothing you can do to touch him, Holmes. Don't even think about it.'

Holmes's eyes tightened for an instant, seemed to flare. 'I wonder about that!' He took off his tan driving cap, sailed it onto the couch next to Lestrade. 'Have you ever heard, my dear Lestrade, of a man called Andrew Swann?'

Lestrade frowned. 'He writes a blog called *Frankenstein's Diary*, under the *nom de plume* Black Swann.'

'That's the man.'

'I'd very much like to get my hands on him, Holmes. He is one of the most dangerous men in England. We suspect that Andrew Swann, alias Black Swann, is, in fact, none other than the notorious computer hacker called Hacking Jack Hawes, captain of the Hack Magic Group.'

'Captain!'

'So he styles himself.'

'How interesting!'

'My dear Holmes, if you know anything . . .'

'I only know that, whoever he is, you just missed him. He drove away in a white Citroën two minutes ago. He said he does not feel safe in this country and is heading back to Switzerland where his family has a chalet – a chalet quite near where the Gurloch family owns a chalet. Why he told me all those details rather mystifies me. But I think he had a reason.'

'Switzerland.'

'In the Rhône Valley. Near Martigny.'

'I must be off!' said Lestrade, hurrying toward the door. He clapped his phone to his ear.

A moment later he was gone.

FIVE
Web of Danger

I opened my newspaper. 'You look like a hippy, Holmes.'

'So you've noticed.'

'You weren't wearing jewelry a half hour ago when you went to the garden with young Swann.'

Holmes unfastened the silver chain from around his neck, laid the dragon on the desk. 'I will keep it, henceforward, on my key chain.' He walked to the window. 'I was about to tell you a tale.'

'Yes.'

Holmes gazed out the window. 'In 1898 I attended a play, and while standing at the bar during intermission I was approached by a gentleman who introduced himself as Osmond Tewkesbury. "I recognize you, Mr Holmes," said he.

'"I am his brother," said I.

'He laughed – he was a big man with a hearty laugh – "None of that, sir," said he. "Your picture is in all the magazines. I know you are none other than Mr Sherlock Holmes himself!"

'"Very well, sir," said I, "If I were Sherlock Holmes, what would you want of me? I perceive you are a silversmith and a jeweler – perhaps your shop has been robbed?"

'"Nothing stolen, Mr Holmes," said he, "but something very curious was recently *purchased* from my shop." He drew from his pocket a velvet jewelry box. Inside were two silver dragons on silver chains, including this very dragon that a moment ago was hanging about my neck. As I sipped my Bass Ale, Osmond Tewkesbury told me a tale.

'He said that six weeks earlier he had been commissioned to

make three of these dragons by Violet Langley, a very petite woman of forty or so, from Norfolk. She had come into his Bond Street shop with bruises on her face, and had produced dainty drawings that outlined in detail the design of the hollow silver dragon she desired. She had ordered three dragons and had paid handsomely for all three in advance. She said she needed them all on the following Thursday. Osmond Tewkesbury was busy, however, and assured her that although he could undertake to deliver the first of them on Thursday, the other two would not be ready for three weeks. At this point I asked Tewkesbury what his tale had to do with me, and he replied that I would be interested to know what had happened recently in Norfolk. He said Violet's husband, Bert, had died a violent death of poisoning. I told him I still failed to see the point, and he replied that her husband also had failed to see the point, which was in the tail of the dragon. Tewkesbury said the lady had supplied him with a phial filled with a yellowish substance, and directed that this substance must be sealed in a cavity in each dragon. She had given him the strictest warnings that he must never let any of it touch his skin.

'Having told me all this as I finished my Bass Ale, Osmond Tewkesbury closed the satin jewelry box, handed it to me, and without a further word he hurried out of the theatre. Next day I tried to find his shop in Bond Street but there was no such shop. No silversmith named Tewkesbury. Curious, I went to Norfolk and inquired into the case of Bert Langley. He was dead, no question about that. And most people were quite pleased he was dead. He had been a habitual drunk who grabbed things from people, and whose favorite phrase was, "Gimme that! It's mine!" He was a bully who grabbed men's beer, grabbed men's gloves right out of their pockets, grabbed the reins of a man's horse as he was tying him up, grabbed baskets of food from ladies on shopping days.'

'Not a proper gentleman,' said I.

'I learned that Bert Langley had been found dead on the floor of his apartment, with a silver dragon clutched in his fingers. Violet had called the police, who had concluded that her husband had died of drink. They removed his body. The next day Violet Langley was gone. She had packed up what few items her husband had not snatched from her, and she had departed for America on the *Majestic*.'

'Murder?' I asked.

'It struck me as a possibility,' said Holmes. 'Bert Langley was dead, and his wife Violet was beyond reach. Back in London I examined one of the dragons closely, using a tweezers and a magnifying glass, and wearing gloves. The little dragon was constructed so that the tail broke off very easily – revealing a tiny sharp blade that would have easily gashed a grabbing hand. The liquid inside ran out freely when the tail came off. It poured into the dish on my table, just as it would have poured into the wound of anyone who had grabbed it.'

'Very subtle,' said I.

'Rather,' said Holmes. 'I kept the remaining dragon as a curiosity. And when the king sent me on my mission to the Czar in 1914, I thought it might prove useful on some unforeseen occasion. So I carefully wrapped the dragon, put it into my vest pocket, and took it with me. I had forgotten how beautiful it was until Andrew Swann returned it to me a little while ago, down in the garden. It was he who hacked into my email, he who sent a false email to Dr Coleman, he who hurried ahead of me to St Bart's and collected my property before I arrived. He also had a little conversation with Dr Coleman aimed primarily at discovering whether I was really Sherlock Holmes.'

'But why did he now give the dragon back to you?'

Holmes plucked from the right front patch pocket of his safari shirt a tiny digital recorder. He set it on the table, touched it – and suddenly the nasal voice of Andrew Swann was speaking:

'I don't want your dragon, Mr Holmes. I stole it merely in order to have an excuse for an interview with Dr Coleman. I hacked you, Mr Holmes, because my uncle was about to entrust you to investigate my mother's death. But I trust no one who works with the Metropolitan Police, the media, or the government. And I trust no one who claims to be Sherlock Holmes – so many make that silly claim. You were a three-time suspect, once for having a friend who is a detective chief inspector at Scotland Yard, once for rooming with an ex-journalist named Wilson, and once for claiming to be the greatest detective of all time. I have read the stories about your supposed revival after a ninety-year sleep in a Swiss glacier – but lies are easily told and easily believed. A tale in a newspaper is nothing to me but a tale, until I verify it for myself. And yet there was the outside chance that you were the genuine article. By writing Dr Coleman a false email I was able to arrange a meeting with him. In that brief meeting I became convinced that he had accomplished the resuscitation that everyone believed he had accomplished, and I could see that he was utterly convinced that you are the genuine Sherlock Holmes. Not a doubt in the world, he said. And suddenly it occurred to me that if this were so, you might prove the one person I could trust to help me in my mission – for you are a man with a worldwide reputation for honesty, a logical mind, a habit of winning, and a man who has few, if any, allegiances to the corrupt institutions of our present era. It occurred to me you might be the man to help me halt the biggest ongoing crime in Britain.'

'And what is that crime, Mr Swann?'

This was the voice of Holmes, high, almost piercing, yet oddly musical.

'The suppression of animal rights and the subversion of human democracy. You raise an eyebrow, Mr Holmes! You think I overstate the case?'

'That is the usual flaw of earnest young men.'

'On the contrary, I understate it. It is a colossal crime, carried out by so vast a cast of conspirators as to boggle the brain. I stumbled onto it when I took up a cause that my father had lost. My father retired from Fleet Street some years ago to devote his time to saving the non-human portion of our planet. He formed the Rabbit Underground, and through that organization he inflamed the enthusiasms of young people in their thousands, who joined him in bringing the attention of the public to the many ways that animals are abused. He set about crafting legislation to better the lot of animals in factory farms and laboratories. He managed to have his bill read out in the House of Commons. It should have passed easily, for it was neither far-reaching nor revolutionary. The prime minister supported it, the opposition leader gave assurances . . . but then something odd happened. In a twinkling, the bill lost all support. My father called people in the government to ask why. These people gave him roundabout answers, saying that the time was not right, that further debate was required – the usual unconvincing evasions. Obviously, something more was in play than anyone cared to admit. And that was where I entered the fray, Mr Holmes.

'You will remember, of course, that reporters for tabloids owned by Gerald Gurloch were recently caught hacking phones of private individuals to get news scoops. And then emerged a deeper story still: Gurloch's newspapers were hacking phones and computers of government officials and Scotland Yard. At that point we might have thought we had hit bottom, but we hadn't. For then emerged yet another story, one that even now the public scarcely dares believe – namely, that the newspapers, the police, and the government are in league to suppress human rights and, in effect, to subvert democracy in this country. Gerald Gurloch gives good press to politicians who enact the policies he prefers – and he destroys those politicians who spurn him. The police go along with Gurloch, and don't make a fuss, partly because politicians high up in government lean on them to lay off, partly because in order to get convictions the police want the same information that the newspapers illegally obtain. Gurloch's hackers listen in on phone conversations, the police use this illegally obtained information to make arrests, and the public imagine the police are terrifically competent when they see them solving so many supposed crimes. And everybody is happy.

'I went to my father's defense by hacking into the records of the Gurloch empire, then into the computers of the Metropolitan Police, and then into the computers at Number 10 Downing Street. I learned that it was Gurloch who had stopped my father's animal rights bill. Gurloch owns a number of slaughterhouses in the UK and does not want his profitable killing operations in any way encumbered. So he threatened to expose indiscretions of several members of the PM's party if they did not kill the bill. And poof! No legislation. Thus do the tabloids run this country while keeping the public pacified by throwing them a discredited politician or two on page one, and some tits and bum on page three. The mass of brilliant British readers are so benumbed by a constant diet of bull pudding that they haven't the faintest notion of what is really happening. Perhaps they don't care. They refuse to believe, for instance, that the numerous visits by Gurloch to the PM before the latest invasions in Arabia could have had any effect on foreign policy. But those visits did have an effect, of course. The PM will not go into a war, even with the United States as a prodding ally, without the approval of the man who buys ink by the barrel.'

Holmes leaned forward, touched the button on the recorder. 'Any word from your friend, Bucky Boudreau?'

'Nothing.'

'We'd best have a bite of lunch, then start for St Albans. Sigvard Kipling and the police will be expecting us –' he looked at his watch – 'in just ninety minutes.'

SIX

Runaway

Two incidents had led Scotland Yard to supply Holmes with the pretty little car we were enjoying this summer's day. The first was the curious case of the vanishing Aston Martin. The superficial facts of that incident were clear enough. Lord Beasley Buckram had been driving his DBS Volante in North London, had set the GPS system to an address in Hampstead Heath, and had followed the directions of his navigation system exactly. Yet he was led not to his new mistress's house, as he had hoped, but to a dead-end alley. Buckram had stopped his car in surprise, put it in reverse; that much he remembered. But apparently at that point he had blacked out completely. He awakened a half hour later sitting on a park bench about a mile away, holding a blueberry muffin in his left hand. His car had vanished and was never found.

The second incident, that of the bashed-in Aston Martin, occurred not long afterward. Lord Percy Parks was driving his new Aston Martin DBS Volante to a political dinner near Pinner in Middlesex. He was falsely led by his navigation system into a wooded lane that grew narrower and narrower. Suddenly the road ahead was blocked by a fallen tree. Percy was forced to stop. No sooner had he done so than an Oriental woman leapt out of the trees. 'Lord, she was quite good-looking,' said Percy, 'and I hoped she wanted an autograph!' Instead, the woman pulled a stiletto out of the bun of her hair, held it to Percy's throat, jerked the key out of his ignition. She flung the key into the trees. Lord Percy was then made to lie on the pine-needled ground while two of the woman's accomplices bashed his car with a sledgehammer. They also spray-painted it with revolutionary slogans. He saw neither of the accomplices, only heard them. 'Dreadful,' said Sir Percy afterward. 'I do wish modern British criminals would learn to spell before writing on a man's car. It's embarrassing. The criminal class is not what it used to be.' What they had spray-painted on his car was **Death to Captolists**.

Scotland Yard's theory was that if Sherlock Holmes drove an Aston Martin around London long enough, he would be targeted by the same criminals who had hijacked the cars of Lord Buckram and Lord Parks. This would put the world's greatest detective on the scene from the start, and so these cases might quickly be solved.

Holmes, however, doubted the logic of Scotland Yard's plan. He pointed out that although Aston Martins were rare, nonetheless hundreds if not thousands of them were on the roads around London, and the odds that the criminals would target his particular car were rather small. But he didn't press the point, for he quickly grew quite fond of his little Volante, which he drove enthusiastically and (it seemed to me) a bit recklessly. He was quite happy to go along with Scotland Yard's hopes – and with the plan that they had coyly dubbed Operation James Bond.

'I had no idea a car could be hacked,' said I, as we scooted up the road toward St Albans. 'It seems an extravagant notion.'

Wind ruffled the top of Holmes's driving cap and the little silver dragon danced on its key chain. 'It was news to me too, till in a pub the other day I met a chap who is a white-hat hacker. Interesting fellow. He explained the facts of life to me in a way I had not heard them before.'

'White-hat hacker?'

'A freelance hacker who hires himself out to businesses who want their products made hack-free,' said Holmes. 'His job is to try to hack into their television sets, their garage door openers, whatever. If he succeeds, company engineers set to work plugging the holes by which he sneaked into their apparatus. According to him, anything that receives a signal can be hacked. He has hacked into automatic garage door openers by sending the right signals from his mobile phone. He has hacked into navigation and guidance systems. He told me that pacemakers can be hacked, especially the new models that are designed so doctors can reset the pace by simply sending a signal. Artificial hearts can be hacked. Hospital equipment of all kinds can be hacked, including, I suppose, all those machines Dr Coleman hooked me up to in order to revive me. And, likewise, cars can be hacked, for there are many computer components in a modern automobile. As my pub acquaintance started on his second pint of lager, he explained to me that a modern automobile is a computer on wheels. Not only the navigation system, but the engine, the brakes, the lights, and most other components are controlled, one way or the other, by on-board computers. And every one of a car's computer-controlled components, he said, can be reverse-engineered in order to find a path back into the central computer system – and from there, as it were, a hacker can work his way back to take over the whole car. The Bluetooth in a car is one easy way in, according to my public bar friend, for it receives signals. He told me he has never broken into a car through a Bluetooth, but he knows people who have.'

'Perhaps I'll buy a 1914 Stutz Bearcat,' I said. 'No computers on board, no intrusion.'

'That was an American car,' said Holmes.

'The 1914 model had right-hand drive.'

Holmes sat rigid as a statue, concentrating on the sea of cars around us. He was a very alert and serious driver. Sweat beaded his brow as we crawled through London traffic. The sun poured down on us. I was relieved when at last we shot up onto the M1. Holmes cut in the afterburners. The thrill of wind and the giddiness of speed and the pressure of acceleration were very cheering – for a moment. But soon I found myself kibitzing.

'You just passed ninety, old chap.'

Holmes was frowning. 'Something feels quite wrong with this machine, Wilson.'

I laughed. 'You are a wonderful actor, Holmes. Your sense of the absurd is exquisite. But such coincidences never happen in real life.'

'My dear fellow, I am not jesting. Absurdly coincidental the situation may be, but I do believe someone is trying to take control of this vehicle!'

I saw the intense and frozen look on his face, and I realized something might actually be amiss. 'Could the cruise control be malfunctioning?' I suggested.

'I tried that already, old fellow – I switched it off.'

We were moving so fast that bright-colored automobiles appearing far ahead of us seemed to be blown backward toward us, then snatched away behind us as if by a giant hand. Landscape blurred in the corners of my eyes. Top speed of the Volante is nearly two hundred miles an hour, and we seemed to be headed for the top. I grabbed Sir Launcelot and pressed him down in the seat for fear he might blow away.

'Try turning off the Bluetooth, Wilson – I'd rather not look away from the road. We're at one hundred and twenty.'

'It's off!' I said, flicking the switch.

'No change. We're up to a hundred and thirty.'

'Try shifting out of gear.'

'Brilliant.'

He shifted, we began to slow. He hit the brake. With engine racing, we glided to the side of the motorway.

'Bravo!' I cried.

He switched off the ignition.

A moment later he switched it on again. The 540-horsepower engine came to life and we surged ahead, and we were back in traffic, and for a while everything seemed to work properly.

'The speed limit is seventy – you're doing a hundred,' I said.

'Lively little beast,' said Holmes. He touched the brake pedal and the big carbon-ceramic discs slowed us almost instantly to seventy – whereupon a blue Ford Focus shot by us.

Holmes swung into the left lane.

A Mini Cooper filled with hulking silhouettes swooshed by.

'Please take the next exit on the left, in one mile,' said a pleasant female voice. 'Please take the next exit on the left in three-quarters of a mile.'

'That's wrong,' said Holmes.

'Maybe you tapped in the wrong coordinates.'

'They were correct.' He handed the map across to me.

The girl in the navigation system kept insisting. 'Please take the next exit.'

'We've just been hacked, Wilson!' cried Holmes. 'A moment ago I thought maybe the acceleration was due to a defect, the floor mat or something of that sort. But this is unquestionably . . .'

'But who is doing it?'

'Perhaps the grey minivan that keeps changing lanes when I do, or the blue Ford that's slowed down to be behind us again. Who can tell? Hang on . . .'

The Volante DBS suddenly accelerated. Holmes cut without warning into the exit onto the A1. He slowed a little, looking into his rear-view mirror.

'What do you see?'

'The blue Ford is still on us . . . the grey minivan missed the turning.'

He slowed some more.

So did the Ford.

'You have made a mistake,' said the navigation system. 'Please . . .'

Holmes switched it off.

We shot into another exit ramp and followed small roads to a place called Cooper's Green. The Ford was right behind us. Holmes stomped down, drove fast, bearing always to the right. We made a loop back to Cooper's Green, passed through the village again. The Ford was gone. About a mile later we had lapped the blue Ford and we came up behind it and Holmes flashed his lights. The Ford sidled to the edge of the road, stopped. We stopped behind.

'What do we do?' I asked.

'Wait.'

We did not wait long. A man emerged from the Ford and began walking back toward us. He waved. 'You boys like to drive pretty fast,' he hollered.

'Bucky!' I cried.

I jumped out of the car and Bucky gave me a hug and I shook his hand. 'Long time.'

'Bucky Boudreau, Sherlock Holmes.'

'You look just like your pictures, Mr Holmes . . . maybe a little younger.' Bucky grinned. 'This twenty-first-century air must suit you.'

'I believe it does,' said Holmes. 'Glad to make your acquaintance, sir.'

Bucky's face was bright as ever. The same old shock of blond hair was falling over his brow. He was not a tall man, but compact and fit. At thirty-five he had seen more, suffered more, done more than many men much older. Yet there was a naivety about him, an aura of wonder, as if he'd be glad to be amazed at anything.

'I understand you chaps met in the Afghan war,' said Holmes, looking at Bucky with a genial yet penetrating gaze.

'We met when Wilson plucked me from the jaws of death, Mr Holmes. I was hit in the buttocks by a sniper. Younger men with rifles watched in astonishment as Wilson charged across open ground – bullets spitting all around him – and dragged me to safety. Old James then flung himself on top of me to make sure I stayed safe until the medic arrived.'

'Good heavens!' said Holmes, and he gave me a look.

'Oh, I *see*,' said Bucky slowly. 'Good old Wilson has not told you any of that story. You Brits are modest to a fault. Every British officer ought to have an American subaltern to do his bragging for him. I tell you Holmes, Wilson was magnificent, the way he moved across that ground, hauling me, weaving and bobbing.'

'A bit of luck,' I said.

'Is *that* what you call it!' cried Bucky. 'Anyway, I saw you two sliding out of Dorset Square and I tried to phone you, but my phone doesn't seem to work in this country. You were a little too quick for me. I almost caught up with you when you stopped by the roadside, but then you rocketed away again. I wondered why you'd stopped.'

'As it happens,' said Holmes, 'we are just on our way to investigate a death. Would you care to join us?'

SEVEN
The Sudden Death of Sylvia Swann

At Sylvia Swann's cottage near St Albans we were greeted on the porch by Sigvard Kipling. He led us into the study and introduced us to a slim policeman in a uniform, Maximilian Drub. Sergeant Drub leaned down and petted Sir Launcelot affectionately but did not appear terribly glad to see the rest of us. 'This is still a crime scene, gentlemen, so please just observe and touch nothing, nothing at all.'

'To observe is our only intention,' said Holmes.

A kidney-shaped walnut desk sat in the center of the room on a large Turkish carpet of floral design. The desk faced north toward two tall windows that looked out into the garden. All the other pieces of furniture – barrister bookcases, daybed, side table, wingtip chairs – were ranged around the sides of the room. Along the east wall stood a large and ancient black steel safe with the words Cox & Co. painted on the front in flowery gold letters. A white lace cloth covered the top of the safe and hung down on both sides. On this lace stood a slender vase of roses that had begun to fade. Several petals had dropped.

Drub called Lancy, told him to sit. Sir Launcelot dutifully obeyed.

'My condolences, sergeant,' said Holmes, 'to you and your wife. It is always very hard to lose a family member.'

'Thank you, sir,' said Drub. 'It was hard indeed, but we're
. . .' He broke off and stared in astonishment. 'I say . . .?'

Already Holmes had knelt on the floor by the richly embroi-
dered green and gold tablecloth. Being careful not to touch it,
he examined it with his old wooden-handled magnifying glass.
He next examined the marble statue of Aphrodite, slim and
unusual, which lay face up on the carpet nearby.

'I do not think that statue is ancient,' I ventured.

'Not a chance,' said Holmes.

'On the contrary, it is certainly ancient,' said Kipling, in a
voice so calm and assured, so resonant and plummy, so terribly
upper-class, that his voice alone seemed to settle the question
beyond all doubt.

Holmes examined the carpet near the fallen book, then the
book itself. Kneeling on the floor, peering at the book, he said,
'It's by a man called Henry Salt. *Animals' Rights Considered in
Relation to Social Progress.*'

Holmes got up quickly and walked to the desk, on top of
which was a white Apple laptop computer, an uncapped Pelikan
fountain pen, and a single sheet of gold-embossed stationery,
plus a box of that same stationery. On the sheet was written:

Dear Alice,
I'm dizzy . . .

And nothing more.

Beneath the box of stationery protruded the corner of a letter.
Holmes pushed the box aside with his finger, in order to read
the letter beneath, which was from David Swann to his wife
Sylvia.

'Here now!' said Drub. 'No touching, Mr Holmes!'

'No harm done,' said Holmes, calmly, and he read the letter
aloud:

Dear Sylvia,
*I hope to be with you for our next, but my heart beats
oddly. I've ordered our new Summer Solstice stationery
early, just in case – in remembrance of the golden days of
wine we've known since first you danced for me at*

*Woodstock, and tore down the banner in your delight. Accept
also this small hidden gift, my love, for old time's sake.
Hope you have a good trip!*

Happy Anniversary –
David

Holmes took a picture of the letter with his pocket camera.
Sergeant Maximilian Drub stood straight and stern with arms
folded. Sigvard Kipling stood with hands in his trouser pockets,
his tweed shooting coat fitting him royally, his large and impres-
sive head fringed in light, a look of command and contentment
on his face. 'The painting was there,' he said, pointing to a space
on the wall.

'It seems to me, Mr Holmes, nearly an open-and-shut case,'
said Drub, unable to restrain himself any longer.

'Oh?' said Holmes.

'Consider the facts, sir. The family were away all afternoon,
six of them playing tennis, one riding a horse. None of them
could have been involved. The six tennis players did not return
to the house until after the woman's death. The horsewoman did
not return until an hour after that. The only person known to be
at the house during the afternoon hours, other than the victim,
was Isabel Rocamora. We know that Isabel recognized the value
of the painting from a conversation she had with Mr Kipling.'

'Yes,' said Kipling. 'We discussed the painting once upon a
time, it is true. But that hardly means . . .'

'Nothing in itself means anything,' said Maximilian Drub
briskly. 'But many things added together generally *do* mean
something. Point one. Several days ago Mrs Swann and Isabel
Rocamora had a falling out, and Isabel gave notice. It was only
with difficulty that Isabel was convinced to stay on long enough
to help with the Midsummer's Eve party – and even then she
stipulated she must leave by five.'

'I didn't know that,' said Kipling.

'You did know it, sir,' said Drub. 'You were there when Mrs
Swann's daughter, Amy Swann, told us.'

'I didn't understand that she had actually given notice,' said
Kipling, slowly.

'Point two,' Sergeant Drub continued, 'the matter of Isabel's friend, George Bentley. He is heavily in debt after betting on the wrong stocks. And he is facing criminal charges for misappropriation of funds in his stock brokerage firm. Point three: Bentley dropped Rocamora off here yesterday morning, and she was heard to say that Bentley would pick her up at five. Point four: Isabel Rocamora is the last one known to have seen Mrs Swann alive. Point five: the only known key to the study was found in its proper place in the china cabinet drawer, but with Isabel's thumb print on it. Point six: both Isabel Rocamora and George Bentley have disappeared. We know they crossed the channel via the car ferry at Folkestone. Point seven: they have carefully left their mobile phones behind, so that we cannot trace them. We found Bentley's phone in his apartment – a most improbable circumstance. These days people don't leave their phones behind. And we found Isabel Rocamora's phone in weeds by the edge of the pond out back.'

Bucky Boudreau put his hands into his pockets and ventured, 'Have you considered that Isabel might be a victim . . . and might be in that pond?'

Sergeant Drub frowned.

'Just a thought,' said Bucky.

'And then where,' said Drub, 'would Bentley be?'

'I haven't the faintest idea,' said Bucky. 'Maybe he was the one who killed her.'

Drub said, 'We will drag the pond. I will be very surprised if we find anything.'

'Continue with your theory,' suggested Holmes.

'We believe Isabel Rocamora came into the study, hit Sylvia Swann with the statue of Aphrodite, then went to the china cabinet and got a tablecloth with which she covered the body in order to prevent anyone from seeing it if they happened to look in through the garden window. She lifted the picture off the wall and carried it out of the room. She got the key from the china cabinet drawer, locked the study door, put the key back into the china cabinet drawer. George Bentley collected her. And on their way out Rocamora flung her mobile phone toward the pond. It fell short of the water and landed in weeds. The two lovebirds vanished with their booty. They are at present, no doubt, somewhere in Europe. We have alerted Interpol.'

Holmes pulled a tape measure out of his pocket and measured the height of the barrister book cases. 'How tall is Isabel Rocamora?' he asked.

'Five ten, I suppose,' said Kipling. 'Tall girl.'

'Whose dog was Gigi?' asked Holmes, gazing at an urn atop the second tier of bookshelves. A collar encircled the urn, and on the tag was the word *Gigi*. A few dried flowers were sprinkled around the urn.

'Sylvia and David's dog,' said Kipling. 'A beautiful Briard she was. They had to put her down a year ago.'

'That safe is very large for such a room. Did they use it?' asked Holmes.

'Only rarely,' said Kipling. 'It was David's idea of decoration. Sylvia was upset at him for having dragged an antique safe in here. David was subject to whims.'

Holmes wandered to the barrister bookcases on the far wall and gazed up at the two shelves of photo albums. 'Might one of these contain photos from Woodstock?'

Kipling hastened to his side. 'All should be marked with the year . . . here, 1969 . . .' Kipling drew the album down and handed it to Holmes, and he glanced at Drub. 'This can't hurt, surely.'

'By all means, carry on!' said Drub, annoyed.

Holmes paged through the volume, and pointed. 'Is this Sylvia?'

'Sprightly Sylvia we called her.'

'Dancing on an empty stage,' mused Holmes. 'And holding a stream of material in her hand like a flag – what is that written on it?'

'I have often wondered, Mr Holmes. Can't tell. Some sort of banner? She was stoned, I suppose . . . so the story goes.'

'You know, Mr Holmes,' said Bucky Boudreau, 'I believe there is a way to lock this window from the outside. Let me demonstrate.'

Lightly Bucky stepped onto the window seat and in an instant was out the window and looking in at us from the garden. He adjusted the little lever on the latch, carefully pushed the window closed . . . and slammed it.

The latch fell into position and locked the window.

Holmes smiled, nodded.

I walked to the window to open it so Bucky could climb back through, but Drub stopped me. 'No more touching, gentlemen, please!'

Bucky walked around the front and came in through the door. Sir Launcelot, who had been sitting quietly on the carpet with his legs folded under him, hurried to greet him.

Drub hitched up his pants. 'I am curious, Mr Holmes. Do you see anything at all that might cast doubt on my theory of the crime?'

'Only that the windows are very tall,' said Holmes, 'and that this is the longest day of the year.'

Drub looked at him blankly. 'Sir?'

'Those facts might mean little,' said Holmes, 'except that the bindings of the books on the bottom shelf are blue.'

Drub frowned as if he had not heard correctly. 'The books are blue, that is certainly true.'

'A complete set of Robert Louis Stevenson in blue Morocco is quite valuable. I would pay attention to the blue books, Sergeant Drub,' said Holmes. 'They are suggestive. And the lace atop the safe is also a queer and curious detail.'

'Queer?' said Drub.

'You will notice that it is askew, hangs a little cockeyed.'

'A little, yes.'

Holmes turned briskly to Sigvard Kipling. 'I think that is all I can do at the moment. But I should like to meet the other people who were here when she died. Can you arrange that?'

Sigvard Kipling nodded his head. 'Certainly, Mr Holmes. I'll call Canyon and Amy. We'll set a time.'

Drub folded his arms. 'Mr Holmes, in this atmosphere where we all are spied upon so often, I hope you don't mind if I ask exactly how you became aware . . .'

'Of your domestic tragedy?'

'Yes.'

'Sir Launcelot and Gigi, told me,' said Holmes.

'Sir?'

'When you let us into this room you were most particular that we touch nothing, disturb nothing. Yet you allowed Sir Launcelot to come in without demur, and you even squatted down and petted him most fondly. You then stood and sighed, twisted your

wedding ring on your finger, gazed for a moment at the little urn
on the barrister bookcase, the urn of ashes surrounded by Gigi's
collar and tag. You then looked again at Sir Launcelot, put your
hands into your pockets, strolled to the window in an introspective
mood. When Sir Launcelot began to walk toward the fallen
tablecloth, you called, "Tommy . . . Pooch! Come here." Which
made me think you were used to calling a dog named Tommy.'

'I see.'

'And the dog told me the rest.'

'This dog?' Drub pointed to Lancy.

'Yes.'

'But this dog did nothing,' said Drub.

'That's what told me,' said Holmes.

'Sir?'

'He would have sniffed your pant legs if you had had a dog
in your house. He didn't, so you don't. I deduce you have not
replaced Tommy.'

'No. We haven't.'

Sigvard Kipling drew himself up very straight. He looked the
very picture of hale spirit and good health. 'Then what happened
to your dog, sergeant?'

'Kidneys went out on him,' said Drub. 'Died in a fortnight.
Poor little fellow.'

'"So quick bright things come to confusion",' said Holmes.

Which I thought, under the circumstances, a little cold of him.

That evening Bucky, Holmes and I had dinner at the Criterion
Restaurant. Bucky was alive to the richness of the place, its gaudy
luxury. But Holmes seemed remote. Afterwards we went back
to Dorset Square and played dominoes. Holmes beat us soundly
then suddenly got up from the table and went into the front room
and sat down in his chair, and for a long while he did not move.
Dim lamplight fringed his profile. He wore his old smoking
jacket, held his unlit pipe. By and by he got up and poured
himself a glass of water out of the pitcher on the side table.

'What were you pondering, Holmes?' I ventured.

'The letters on Sylvia Swann's desk,' said he.

EIGHT
World Peace Through Biology

The following morning Bucky Boudreau hurried off early to see London sights while Holmes and I lingered at our breakfast table, sipping coffee, reading. I was immersed in André Maurois's *Prometheus: The Life of Balzac*. Holmes was reading through his three morning tabloids. Suddenly he folded *The News of Civilization* back on itself and cried, 'Why, look at this, Wilson . . . heavens! Life only gets stranger and stranger!' He handed me the newspaper.

Bunnies Make Professor Hop
(Into a Dustbin)

Yesterday two leggy girls dressed in bunny outfits accosted a distinguished visitor to London, did a little dance about him, kissed him simultaneously on both cheeks, and clapped a chloroformed rose to his nose. Dr Jan Droon said he felt dizzy as the rambunctious bunnies tumbled him into the darkness and oblivion of a dumpster in a small alley off Park Lane.

He awoke an hour later and emerged to a crowd of newspaper and television reporters who had been alerted to his plight. Two officers of the Metropolitan Police helped Professor Droon out of his cage.

On the side of the dumpster were painted the words 'Psychology Experiment in Progress'.

'The girls cuddled me, befuddled me, and did me dirt,' said Droon. 'It seems to have been a very well-planned operation. They knew exactly where I had taken my morning walk the previous three mornings since I'd been in London, and they placed foam into the dumpster, evidently to prevent serious injury and to make me comfortable when I fell in.

But it was a frightening experience. To treat another human being in this way is outrageous.'

Droon, a medical doctor, professor of psychology, and international expert in animal consciousness, is in London to testify before government committees on the necessity for animal testing in Britain. Droon operates an independent research laboratory in Switzerland. A native of Rotterdam, he . . .

'What do you make of that?' asked Holmes.

'I cannot help but wonder,' said I, 'if those girls might have some connection with the Rabbit Underground, since they were dressed as bunnies.'

'I should like to have a talk with this man Droon,' said Holmes, as he produced his mobile phone. He disappeared into his bedroom saying '. . . Hello, Lestrade?'

When Holmes reappeared he was alight with enthusiasm. 'Droon is staying at the Dorchester Hotel. We will meet him for lunch – are you free?'

'Perfectly.'

'Lestrade will arrange it.'

'So quickly?'

''tis the Age of the Instantaneous!' cried Holmes.

By eleven thirty we were walking into an alleyway near Park Lane. We hurried toward a dumpster with the words 'Psychology Experiment in Progress' painted on the side in red letters.

'Give me a leg up, Wilson.'

'Surely you don't need to be quite this thorough, do you?' said I, as I locked the fingers of my two hands to make a stirrup for his foot.

A moment later he was up and into the bin, looking about in the dark with his pocket flashlight. Finally he was satisfied and he began to haul himself out.

I had a sensation of being watched.

I turned and encountered the unfriendly gaze of a big dirty man with a thick black beard, who stood behind me. 'You'll not find anything to eat in there, gents,' said he. 'They've cleaned it out.'

He held in his hand a plastic container of cold spaghetti. A hunk of bread and a piece of onion were strewn on top of the heap. He ate a few strands with his fingers. I helped Holmes out of the bin.

'Have some of this, if you're hungry,' said the stranger, offering Holmes the container.

Holmes now had smears of black on the front of his shirt. And a smear on his cheek.

'Thank you very much,' he said. 'I just had breakfast. You in this area often?'

'I know what you are driving at,' said the man, slyly.

'You do not need to play the game with me,' said Holmes. 'Here is a tenner, whether you tell me anything or not.' He slipped a ten-pound note out of his pocket and handed it to the man.

'Now I owe you,' said the man, looking a bit dumbfounded.

'You owe me nothing,' said Holmes. 'You are a fellow creature, you are hungry. I am not hungry. So it is I who owe you.'

'Funny way of thinking.'

'I have always been flattered as having a funny way of thinking,' said Holmes. 'It is how I make my living.'

'Then I'll tell you.'

'Only if you wish.'

'I saw the two bunny girls – like to have eaten them, myself.' He laughed a sly and yet pathetic laugh. 'Especially the American one.'

'Naturally enough,' said Holmes.

'Two lads came out of a car and helped the girls lift the poor sod and dump him into the bin. One of the lads painted the sign. Then all four got into a car and sped off like the devil's own.'

'What kind of car?'

'Mini Cooper. Blue.'

'And then?'

'Didn't want to get involved, mate. Thought they might have killed him. But by and by I ventured back, and I heard him groaning inside. Thought I should do something before someone dumped plaster and boards on him. Met a bloke out on Park Lane, asked him to call the police. He said he would. Funny. He did, too. Never would have thought it.'

'People surprise you sometimes,' said Holmes.

'Usually the wrong way!' Blackbeard laughed and his mouth

looked small and red and broken amidst the beard. 'But something else was funny.'

'What was that?'

'The bloke had scarcely put his phone in his pocket when the press arrived and began getting out cameras. Even before the police arrived. How did they know?'

Holmes and I left Blackbeard standing there with his meal in his big, dirty hand.

Holmes cleaned himself up as best he could in the public bathroom in the pedestrian subway beneath Park Lane. We then made our way to the Dorchester Hotel where Dr Jan Droon met us in the lobby. We accompanied him to the dining room. Holmes ordered roast beef, I ordered fish, Droon ordered veal.

Droon struck me as a very pleasant-looking individual, punctiliously dressed – almost to the point of being a dandy – in a light tan suit, pale blue shirt, dark blue tie. A silk handkerchief was fluffed in his lapel pocket. His horn-rimmed glasses and his curly dark hair, sprinkled with gray, made him look younger than he was. The wrinkles at the edges of the eyes, and in his neck, told a different tale than his spiffy clothes.

'I am so glad to meet you, Holmes – and you too, of course, Mr Wilson. What an honor to have so eminent a duo looking into my case!'

'Our pleasure,' said Holmes. 'I have read about your curious scientific quest with great interest. But I am still not certain exactly what you would like to accomplish.'

'Simply put, Mr Holmes, I have come to believe that no philosophy – neither Christ's nor Buddha's nor Socrates's nor Lao Tse's nor anyone else's – can ever deflect the human race from its vicious and murderous path, and lead it into the ways of kindness and caring. For millennia we have fought with each other, warred with each other, murdered each other, stolen from each other, raped and spied and deceived and generally come to blows at every opportunity. In five thousand years of recorded history there has not been the slightest sign of improvement in our natures or our manners. And the chances that we shall ever evolve into peaceful animals are remote to the vanishing point. Therefore we must abandon philosophy, abandon hoping for evolutionary miracles. We must instead *do something* to change our biology. My hope is to create a new man, a new life form! And the first step in that process is to understand what portion of our brains is responsible for kindness, for sharing, and for loving thy neighbor as thyself. To find that portion of the human brain is my mission, my quest.' He laughed. 'I have just given you the opening lines of the lecture I frequently give when I am called upon to explain my experiments.'

'And very eloquent you are, too,' said Holmes. 'But let us say you find that portion of the brain, and locate it exactly. What will be the next step? How do you propose to change the brain of every human being so that the kindness portion dominates?'

'A slow process, Mr Holmes. Obviously, I cannot operate on seven billion people, and readjust their internal wiring, even if I knew how to do it.'

'That occurred to me,' said Holmes.

'I believe that in the end the change must be made at the gene level. Change the gene structure of the human, and the human will be different. That is obvious.'

'Of course,' said I. 'But will people agree, even if you perfect the method of altering genes, that the human race ought to be altered? Change one thing, and you may end with worse. The history of science is replete with examples of experts standing up in white coats and assuring us of one thing, which later turns out to have been devastatingly wrong.'

'Oh, I think in the end people will agree to be changed . . . they must. Or we will all perish.'

'An extraordinary confidence!' said Holmes, glancing at me – and I thought he would wink. But he restrained himself.

'Oh, not so much, not so extraordinary,' said Dr Droon. 'Consider your own case, Mr Holmes. What a miracle of science has brought you back into the world of life! What a strange manipulation of cells, of regrowing and reconstituting! Amazing! Only a few years ago people would not have thought that possible. Now science has not only brought back Sherlock Holmes from a century ago, but is contemplating bringing a woolly mammoth back from a hundred thousand years ago.'

'I understand you are in London to testify on the necessity of animal testing,' said Holmes.

'Quite true. I have agreed to testify even though I am very

busy, and really haven't the time to waste testifying to this and that – for there is work to be done. But I could hardly resist when Fresh Farms Sausage and Bacon Limited offered to pay my expenses – expenses plus a good deal more if I would testify.'

'I believe that firm is owned by the Gurloch conglomerate, is it not?'

'It is, yes. You see, the bill being proposed to parliament deals with animal welfare generally, including not only animal testing but animal production and slaughter procedures. That's where lies the interest of the Fresh Farms Sausage and Bacon people.'

'What is your feeling about meat production?' I asked. 'I've found it can be a very harrowing experience merely to *read* about the suffering these animals are made to endure before they are finally slaughtered.'

'Life is not perfect,' said Dr Droon. 'And a man must eat.'

'But must he eat meat?' I said. 'I happen to eat meat, myself. But millions upon millions of people don't. Indians, for instance. So obviously eating meat is not a necessity, but merely a preference.'

'To be a vegan, you mean – that sort of thing?'

I shrugged.

'I'm as tender-hearted as any man,' said Droon. 'I have a dog, I feed the birds and the squirrels. But one can carry concern for alien forms too far. We humans are, after all, the master race. That is obvious.'

'I have always thought so,' said Holmes. 'But the more one thinks about that proposition, the more doubts creep into one's mind.'

'Doubts?'

'I doubt the idea that wherever I stand must be the center of the universe. Is that not what human belief in human superiority comes down to?'

'Sobering thoughts, sobering thoughts,' admitted Droon, and he sliced another forkful of veal, and put it delicately into his mouth. Then he paused as he chewed, and he looked at me quizzically. And he nodded, as if he understood my unspoken question. 'Oh, I know,' he said. 'I know all about how veal is raised. Calves are taken from their mothers very young, put in stalls so small the animals cannot even turn around, can barely move, are deliberately made anemic so their flesh is sufficiently white. And I realize the anemia makes them weak and sick, and that they never see a grassy field in all their short lives . . . I know all that. Still, there are worse fates in life.'

'And a man must eat,' said Holmes.

'Quite, quite so. Wisdom is knowing when to stop thinking.'

'And when to rethink,' said Holmes.

'It is always a guessing game, Mr Holmes. No absolutes. We scientific minds always hope for absolutes – but there aren't any.'

'Who do you think threw you into the dustbin?' asked Holmes.

'Without doubt those silly animal rights people, some group or other. Impractical people. They did half of what they intended to do: they frightened me. But the other half of what they hoped to accomplish they will never accomplish, and that is to stop me. I know my path, Mr Holmes. It is a glorious one, though there may be messy portions – mud holes and unfortunate encounters – here and there. But what I seek is the betterment of mankind. I shall never be deflected from that path. It is what we are here for, after all, isn't it? To help each other? The problem is that the animal rights brigade takes a narrow view of life.'

'They mean well.'

'Oh, I'm sure they do, Mr Holmes. But well-meaning people tend to go to extremes. They start with a pure idea, but cannot control it. The idea may be a fine one, an excellent one, a moral one, but that idea – just because it is so fine, so excellent and so moral – takes possession of them, turns them into fanatics, into perverts – and, in the end, their extreme good actions turn into extreme evil ones.'

'I think you are quite correct on that point,' said Holmes.

A solid man of about fifty approached our table. He was dressed in a blue blazer and grey slacks, and his beard was reddish brown. His eyes were a hard, glittering blue. His face might once have been handsome, but was now just slightly too fleshy. His barrel chest and wide shoulders proclaimed him to have been something of an athlete in days past. He looked down at us and said, 'Dr Droon, I presume?'

'I am Dr Droon.'

'I am Bedford Brock – I am a relative of Mr Gurloch, whom I think you know.'

'Why, yes!'

'Mr Gurloch would like to make certain that you are protected from further attacks and annoyance while you are here in London. He has asked me to look after you – may I sit down?'

'No, I don't think so, Mr Brock. I feel I am quite all right on my own.'

'Please, if you don't mind, I should like to explain our plan for keeping you safe.'

'No, thank you, sir. I do appreciate the effort, but I do not want to become involved with bodyguards. Never a good thing when a man needs a bodyguard . . . and I, if you don't mind my saying so, do not think I need one.'

'Ah, well, that is a matter of interpretation and opinion. If you don't mind, sir . . .'

'But he *does* mind,' said Holmes sharply. 'So if *you* don't mind, please leave us to our lunch.'

Bedford Brock looked down at Holmes with a startled smile. His tiny teeth showed very white, his blue eyes glittered strangely. 'And who are you?'

'And who are *you* to ask me who *I* am? I resent your presumption.'

'Here now, we need no trouble!' said Dr Droon, anxiously.

Brock gazed down at Holmes, nodding as if he'd like to take a swing at him. Then he turned and walked out of the dining room. As he passed out through the door I saw him slide a mobile phone out of his coat pocket and put it to his ear.

After lunch we parted from Dr Droon in the Dorchester lobby. Holmes made a quick phone call, then announced he must dart over to Bernard Quaritch Booksellers near Golden Square. It was a pleasant walk, though brisk, and involved darting across streets in Holmes's usual impatient style. One of the Quaritch staff admitted us through the locked door, and we entered the inner sanctum where multitudes of very expensive volumes filled whole rooms. Holmes purchased the book that he had called about, Henry Salt's *Animals' Rights*.

'Does that book have a bearing on the case?' I asked.

'I am interested to learn if it might,' he said.

'A very expensive volume,' said I.

'No doubt there are reprints to be had,' said Holmes, 'but I like first editions – they put me in the mood. They conjure up the ambience of that earlier world in which the author lived. I like to know that the first people who touched this book, who read it, were the author's contemporaries.'

'For you to hold such a Romantic view, Holmes, is most odd!'

'Yes, isn't it? I have often thought so myself.'

NINE
The Quiet Death of Lord North

We hurried from Quaritch Booksellers to our flat in Dorset Square, collected our overnight bags, and drove north to Stratford-Upon-Avon. Holmes was trembling with suppressed energy as we checked in to our room at the Falcon Hotel on Chapel Street, an ancient establishment within easy walking distance of the theatres. Months earlier he had purchased tickets for the Royal Shakespeare Company's new production of *Julius Caesar*, one of his favorite plays. As we changed into our theatre clothes I banged my head on a low overhead beam, but Holmes barely seemed to notice, for he was drawing parallels between the bloody politics of ancient Rome and the politics of the present day. We stepped out into the sweet evening air of summer, heading for a restaurant. Holmes was so energized that he seemed about to fly. He began quoting lines from the play, as if he could scarcely wait for the actual production to begin. '"The fault, dear Brutus, is not in our stars, But in ourselves that we are underlings . . ."'

But his phone interrupted him. He pulled it from his pocket, glanced at it. 'Lestrade, I'm afraid.' He turned on the speaker:

'Holmes, terribly sorry to bother. I know it is your theatre night out. But something disturbing has just occurred. Lord North died a short while ago at his home in Clifford Chambers, not five miles from where you are standing. Police are on their way and I'm sure they can handle it. But I'd feel much better if you would pop over there and have a look. North intended to deliver his committee's report on the phone-hacking scandal in the next few days. As chairman of the committee, he was going over the report one last time. And now this. He was an old man, it is true – nearly eighty, and he had an artificial heart, and lots of health problems. I suppose it is not shocking that he died. And yet . . . so many peculiar things are happening these days. He told one of his colleagues at Westminster yesterday that he was worried that his report might never see the light of day, worried that nothing is secure – "neither men nor messages," to use his phrase. And now he's dead.'

We walked quickly back to the hotel.

The Aston Martin swept us into the shaded main street of Clifford Chambers where a cluster of vehicles gleamed in the driveway of Lord North's grand thatch-roofed house. We were admitted to the house immediately by an officer by the name of Conrad Klept, a big man with bushy brows and worried eyes. 'Mr Holmes,' said he, 'come in, please come right in. Inspector Lestrade phoned me. I don't think we require your special talents in this case, but you are certainly most welcome to look about and—'

'Thank you,' said Holmes. 'When did the gentleman die?'

'Between one and two hours ago, sir. The gardener talked to him at four o'clock, his wife found him at five o'clock, and it is now a little after six. I can tell you a little about the man, if you like. I've just spoken with his wife.'

'By all means.'

'Lord North was a person of very regular habits. I have learned that he invariably secluded himself in his study at one o'clock in the afternoon, bringing with him a bottle of Perrier water and a bowl of fruit – today it was two pears and one peach. His habit was to work until four o'clock precisely, then descend the stairs to join Lady North. He always poured her a glass of sherry, and himself a glass of Scotch, and then they discussed the day's activities as he stood sipping before the fireplace, and as she sat sipping on the couch. Today he did not appear at four. At four thirty she became curious. At five she became concerned. She went up and knocked on the door.

He did not answer. So she went in with her key. She found him slumped over his desk. Dead.'

'Is it usual for him to lock the study door?'

'He did so to prevent grandchildren from bursting in on him while he was working. It isn't clear that he was working, however. No computer.'

'Not all people work on a computer.'

'True. It appears he was writing a letter by hand when he died. His wife said she is not certain that he brought his computer up with him from London. He had the computer carrying case, and she naturally presumed it contained the computer. But she did not actually see the computer. No sign of it now. Presumably it contains the famous Gurloch hacking report. Perhaps he left it in London for safety's sake.'

'May we see where he died?'

Klept labored up the staircase ahead of us, two flights, and led us into the study. The police photographer had just finished taking pictures. The body of Lord North was still slumped over his desk. They placed the little man on a stretcher and carried him carefully away. The expression on the dead man's face struck me as one of mild surprise – small mouth open slightly beneath the neat moustache, eyes blue and wide open. He wore a blue shirt with faint gold pinstripes, dark trousers, very shiny black shoes. Holmes looked curiously at the body as it was carried past him, then walked to the desk and gazed down at the letter that Lord North had been writing:

My Dear Overton,

The fastest way to spill a secret is to put it on a computer. Therefore I trust pen, ink, and the Royal Mail to communicate this afterthought to my somewhat longer message of yesterday – a message which I hope you have by now safely received. Dear friend, though we be old, yet we be bold, and are resolved. We will, I think, prevail as we have so often done before. Best towns to visit, you ask? Here is my advice. I believe you will find the journey very much worth the effort: Kabul, Skopje, Muscat, Windhoek, Astana, Dili, Sana'a, Belgrade, Taipei, Barka, Vientiane, Cairo, Kuala Lumpur, Al Hudaydah, Yaoundé, Raysut, Bamako, Asunción,

Kampala, Ankara, Tallinn, Moscow, Bratislava, San Salvador, Addis Ababa, Nairobi, Havana, Riga, Kiev, Quito, New Delhi, Oslo, Valletta, Buenos Aires, Wellington, Phnom Penh, Tegucigalpa, Baghdad, Amsterdam, Asmara, Hanga Roa, Maseru, Dublin, Ljubljana.
   All very best wishes,
   North

Holmes took a picture of this queer missive with his pocket camera. He turned to Klept, 'Did anyone enter this room after Lady North found him?'

'No. Lady North's daughter and children were downstairs and never came upstairs. Lady North waited downstairs until we arrived. No one else was in the house.'

Holmes darted to the open window and looked down into the garden. I looked out the window too: below were sills and shutters of the window on the first floor, and sills and shutters of the window below that. Also a drainpipe. A few vines. Sheer brick. No trees near the house. 'No one could have come in or out this window,' I said.

Holmes was already on his knees, looking into the wastebasket. 'How odd,' said he, and stood up.

'Odd, Mr Holmes?'

'Only one pear core in the wastebasket – and nothing left in the fruit bowl but a peach. Then where is the second pear core?'

'Thrown out the window, perhaps?'

Holmes picked up the mobile phone that lay on the desk, touched the screen a few times, set it down.

'Shouldn't do that,' said Klept.

'I know,' said Holmes.

Downstairs we found Lady North sitting in a chair, fanning herself, trying to look calm. She was a thin and fragile old woman who once must have been the pixyish and energetic sort. Her daughter stood near her, and also her daughter's husband and their two young children.

'Lady North,' said Holmes, 'I just read the last text message written on your husband's phone. It was to Overton, and it said this: "Do not phone or text me. When we were boys, we knew where the real secrets were hid."'

'Oh, my!'

'Have you any idea what that might mean?'

The old lady stared as if she had not heard the question. Then her eyes opened wide in surprise, as if suddenly she saw something. 'Why, yes! As boys they were good friends, you know.'

'I did not know,' said Holmes.

'Bunny and Edward were very good friends. And afterward they were at Oxford together. Yes, and they were both Fellows of the Royal Geographical Society – my husband and Bunny Overton were very close friends all their lives.' She laughed. 'Oh, they had many a secret – boys will be boys, you know!'

'Did they have a secret hiding place?' asked Holmes.

'Of course! In the big old oak tree.'

'Oak tree?'

'At Bailey Cliff. Bunny still lives there, Bailey Cliff.'

'Can you tell us where the tree is?'

'It's at Bailey Cliff – that's in Hertfordshire, you know. You know the place? Just forty miles from London, not far. Oh, heavens! I don't know if the tree is still there! But, of course, oak trees last longer than men.'

'Usually,' said Holmes.

She raised her thin finger in the air. 'By the north bank of the duck pond is a large oak tree. Just below the crotch is a hollow hole. The boys hid a little hamper of lunch there once, from Harrods. They surprised us girls. Wine, too. We weren't supposed to have wine then, at our age.'

'Have you noticed anything unusual in this neighborhood today?' asked Holmes.

'It is always very quiet here,' she replied.

'Nothing ever happens,' agreed the daughter, a blonde woman of almost middle age, the bland and calm sort. Her name was Agnes.

'Then you would have noticed if anything unusual had occurred,' insisted Holmes.

'I am sure we would have,' said Agnes. 'Why do you ask, Mr Holmes?'

'When a man dies suddenly, a man of your father's standing, who is in the midst of an important investigation, one cannot help but look closely at the circumstances surrounding his death.'

She nodded her head slowly, as if she understood. 'There were many whom he has upset, Mr Holmes – but none, I think, who would do him harm. He was very respected, even by his political enemies. And he had no personal enemies. And nothing at all unusual has happened today, neither in the house nor out of it, so far as I am aware.'

'Pepper ran away,' said the little girl. She was perhaps seven.

'Pepper is the cat,' explained Agnes.

'Ah!' said Holmes, immediately bending down to the child. 'I had a cat once. Did you find Pepper?'

'Under the furniture van. I chased him out. Then he ran home.'

'When was that?' asked Holmes.

'A little while ago,' said the child.

In a sudden fit of shyness, the little girl turned and clung to her mother's leg.

'Where was the furniture van?' asked Holmes.

'At the corner, sir.'

'Thank you all,' said Holmes briskly. 'Now I should like a word with the gardener.'

Inspector Conrad Klept led us out of the house and we found the gardener carrying a spade and a bucket. 'I'm Sanford Searle,' said he.

'I'm Sherlock Holmes.'

'He's with me,' said Klept.

'Of course,' said Searle, a little bewildered. 'Sherlock *Holmes* did you say?'

'Did you notice a furniture van near here today?'

'I did, sir. It was parked up at the corner for a short while. I think the driver was lost. I saw him reading a map.'

'Can you describe the vehicle?'

'Certainly. A green medium-size panel truck, it was. With "Grosvenor Square Furniture" painted in yellow on the side.'

'You are very observant!' cried Holmes, delighted. 'What time did you see it?'

'Just after Lord North spoke to me – perhaps a little after four o'clock.'

'What did he speak to you about?'

'He appeared at his study window, Mr Holmes, and called down to me. I was in the back garden working on the trellis. He wished to know if I had accomplished an errand he had sent me on yesterday.'

'And may I ask what errand that might have been?'

'I would rather not say, sir.'

'Ah!' said Holmes. 'Lord North asked you not to say, I presume.'

'Yes, sir.'

'But can you tell me if the errand involved making a delivery?'

'It might have done, sir,' said he. 'But I'd rather say no more.'

'Did you see anyone else today while you were working?'

'I saw a very small child in a green hat running along the River Stour behind the house – worried me, till I saw there was an adult with him. Children ought not to be allowed to play alone near water.'

'Can you describe the adult?'

'Couldn't really, sir – as you will observe, there is a lot of shrubbery between here and the river.'

Holmes strode away to the back of the property and walked slowly along the path by the river, looking carefully at the ground and occasionally glancing at the back of Lord North's house. 'Ahh!' he cried, and suddenly stopped.

'What is it, Holmes?'

'Look here, Wilson: three indentations in the soil, just by the side of the path. They form a triangle. See?'

'As if a tripod had been set up here.'

'Precisely.'

'And there is a pear core!' said I.

'I noticed that,' said he.

'What do you make of it?'

'It doesn't look good, Wilson. Strange things have taken place here today.'

Inspector Klept was waiting for us by the house. We said our farewells, hurried to the Volante, and returned swiftly to Stratford-Upon-Avon where we managed to swallow a couple of sandwiches before hurrying to the play – a play that we both enjoyed enormously.

Afterward, in our hotel room, Holmes dialed Lestrade and asked directions to Bailey Cliff, Lord Overton's residence in Hertfordshire. When Holmes hung up he looked a bit strange.

'What is it?' I asked.

'Lestrade just got word that Overton was admitted to hospital this afternoon, in a critical condition. Evidently he got into an automobile accident of some kind.'

'That cancels our trip to Bailey Cliff,' said I.

'On the contrary,' said Holmes, 'it makes it urgent that we visit Bailey Cliff as quickly as possible.'

'It is almost midnight,' I said.

'And we cannot accomplish our mission in the dark. We'll wait till first light.'

The following morning we found Bailey Cliff easily enough. The large stone house sat amidst Hertfordshire hills and swales, plain and solid, looking slightly abandoned in morning shadow. We idled through the grounds until we came to a duck pond lying far out of view of the house, hidden in a tangle of woods. Mallards dragged V-ripples across the sheen surface as we made our way through the sedges at the edges of the pond. A crow protested with raucous squawking as we arrived at the massive old oak. Holmes grasped a ragged limb, hoisted himself up, and with surprising speed he rose to the gaping hole below the crotch. He reached his arm in. 'I have it!' he cried.

Down he came, breathing heavily. In his hand he held a package wrapped in dark plastic.

'This is absurd, Holmes!' said I. 'This is a boys' adventure tale.'

''tis exactly how the world used to be, my dear Wilson, before it began to collapse from constant communication.'

'Collapse?'

'True civilization is made of individuals, and individuals cannot exist without solitude.'

We made our way back around the margin of the pond. Breeze whispered through leaves overhead and rippled the surface of the water. A crow cawed. For a moment I felt delightfully isolated.

Then Holmes's mobile phone began to tweedle.

TEN

An Indian Tale

Holmes and I shot back toward London in his favorite little rocket. Our radio boomed huge on the wind as we listened to a BBC reporter give statistics on the astonishing flotilla of satellites floating overhead in the summer sky – tons of machinery fired up into space over the decades, a celestial junkyard. Yet amongst the flotsam and jetsam, said the earnest reporter, were more than a thousand satellites not yet junk, satellites alert and operative, busily snapping pictures, making videos of the earth's surface, relaying streams of data, sensing sunspots, tracking rockets, sending navigation signals or mapping storms.

'Big Brother is watching, no doubt of that,' said I. 'Orwell was right.'

'Everyone talks about Orwell,' cried Holmes. 'I must read that man.'

'He lived in the century you missed, Holmes,' said I. 'But you should read him, that's true. He certainly sensed where society was headed. But even Orwell could never have imagined the details – surveillance cameras on every corner, in every bus, in every train. People walking zombie-like through streets while gazing at little objects in their hands that have worked a spell upon them. Whole continents of creatures in thrall to screens that make them ravenous for ephemeral images that may or may not be truths. Multitudes of addicts in bondage, unaware that they are entangled in a web in which they can be tricked and tracked, hoaxed and hacked. Not even Orwell – brilliant as he was – could have imagined all this. Sometimes I think, Holmes, that we can't imagine it ourselves. It is so huge a truth, so omnipresent, that it vanishes. We are too used to it. It has become so common it has ceased to exist. We have become numbed.'

We floated into our parking space in Dorset Square and Holmes astonished me by managing to leap out of the car without opening the door.

'Always wanted to try that,' he said. He grabbed his package and darted away up to our flat.

I went to Mrs Cleary's flat, collected Sir Launcelot, and took that energetic little one-eyed dog for a long walk in Regent's Park. As I was returning to Dorset Square I encountered Lestrade, who looked very grim. 'Overton is in a serious condition,' he said. 'I was just on the way to your flat to see Holmes.'

'You mentioned Overton had been in an accident.'

'I have now learned it was no ordinary accident. He was attacked. Same scenario as before. Someone decoyed him into a dead-end street while he was driving his Aston Martin. Overton was still behind the wheel when an Asian woman appeared out of nowhere, pulled a stiletto out of her hair bun, leaned into the car, snatched the keys out of the ignition. She flung the keys away into a sewer grate. She threatened Overton, holding the stiletto to his throat. She ordered him to lie face down on the ground. Unfortunately, Overton – who once was a rugby three-quarter, and is still a large, hale and vigorous individual – did not obey. He fought back. She stabbed him, and he may not live. He was barely able to tell us what happened, and he is now in a coma. He could hear her accomplices bashing the car with sledgehammers, and we found the vehicle spray-painted with the slogans "DEATH TO PLUTOCRATS!" and "REVOLUTION NOW!".'

'What puzzles me, Lestrade, is why have you involved Holmes in this sting operation? Surely he is fit for better uses than to be used as mere bait. I don't approve.'

'Nor do I. But Aston Martin want Holmes on the case. This sort of publicity is hardly helpful to the company. Influential people have talked to the commissioner. And the commissioner, knowing Holmes is an old friend of my grandfather, and therefore inclined to listen to my requests, has instructed me to enlist his help.'

'I am disappointed.'

'So am I,' said he. And he looked a little hangdog.

'You are putting him in needless danger. Being mere bait is not his *métier*!'

'But you must admit that Holmes always does seem to land on his feet.'

'He does seem to,' I admitted.

'I know I've done the wrong thing,' said Lestrade. 'I am sorry for it. I am damned sorry for it.' He looked pretty miserable.

'I suppose it will work out all right,' I said.

'I came to deliver a manual about the GPS system in the Aston Martin. Holmes wanted it.' He handed it to me. 'I also came to get the Lord North Report. I am instructed to take it from you.'

'Holmes is reading it – has been reading it for the last hour and a half. I've been walking the dog.'

'They told me I am to bring the report to headquarters, unread,' said Lestrade.

'*They*?'

'My superiors.' Lestrade looked nervous. He rubbed the back of his neck. 'Is Holmes still in your flat, Wilson?'

'Yes.'

'Are you quite sure? Because once that report vanishes into the bureaucracy above my head, I am not certain it will ever be seen again. By anyone. So I ask again, are you absolutely certain that Holmes is still in the flat – you've been out walking the dog. How can you be sure?'

'Are you saying what I think you are saying, Lestrade?'

'I am just thinking that Holmes might have left the flat while you were gone. He might be reading the report in a pub somewhere.'

'That is quite possible,' I said, nodding slowly. 'Indeed, I would not be surprised if that is what he has done.'

'Then I will come round for the report in the morning. I don't intend to chase all over London trying to find Holmes.'

'I'll tell him to have it ready for you.'

'And tell him also,' said Lestrade softly, 'that if he wants a copy of that report for himself, he'd better make one.'

Lestrade climbed into his black automobile.

A moment later I was in our flat telling Holmes what had happened to Lord Overton.

About seven that evening I made some sandwiches and set two of them near Holmes, together with a glass of wine. He ate, sipped, continued reading. By and by he sprang to his feet as

if electrified. He walked in a circle around the edges of the
room, then plunged back into his easy chair. He put his elbows
on the arms, pressed the tips of his ten fingers together below
his sharp chin. He stared at something far away. He grabbed
the Lord North Report again. He let its hundreds of bound
pages droop in his hand as he held it up. 'Tremendously detailed,
Wilson. Tremendously interesting!' he cried. 'Filled with
intriguing characters. Hacking Jack Hawes is mentioned – the
same character Lestrade mentioned to us the other day.
Apparently his Hack Magic Group is particularly devoted to
creating massive rogue programmes that will bring down
electrical grids, airplane navigation systems, water and sewer
systems, industrial plants . . .'

'Including uranium processing plants, I presume, such as has
happened in Iran?'

'Lord North's expert advisors assure him that the Hack Magic
Group are now developing malware programmes much more
complex and deadly than the Stuxnet worm that brought down
Iran's centrifuges. Nothing is clear in the cyber world, but the
suspicion is that Gerald Gurloch is financing the Hack Magic
Group. And this group are developing catastrophe-inducing
programmes, cyber-world bombs that, if launched, will cause
whole sections of the real world to crash and burn.'

'But why would Gurloch do it? What could be his motivation?
Surely he has so much power and stake in our society that he
would be the last person to want to destroy it.'

'I wonder if that is true,' mused Holmes. 'In Lord North's
report I have found sections dealing with Gurloch's early life.
Gurloch's autobiographical writings are particularly intriguing.'

'I confess I don't know much about him, other than that he
is from New Zealand.'

'India, actually. New Zealand came later. His early years in
India seem to have had a profound influence on his life. His
father owned an English language newspaper in Cannanore, in
Kerala state, in the south of India. As a young boy Gerald swept
the newspaper office, ran errands for his father, read books under
a tamarind tree. His favorite author was Poe, and his favorite
Poe story was *The Murders in the Rue Morgue*. Later he was
fond of *Oliver Twist*. In short, he had a literary bent. At seventeen

he was sent to England where he read English literature and psychology at Cambridge. At university he gained a bit of notoriety for gambling and rude behaviour. His fellows regarded him as provincial, which galled him. According to some of his classmates he was brilliant but crude. "Gerald did not fit in," wrote one, "and I wasn't sure that he wanted to fit." The young Gurloch wrote essays about the toxic effects of Britain's upper classes, and these were much praised in some quarters. He graduated with honors, went back to India for a short while, watched his father sink into bankruptcy. Then, by financial legerdemain not quite fully illuminated in the Lord North Report, young Gurloch moved to New Zealand and started his own newspaper. There began the part of the story everyone knows. He acquired media outlets in all the old British dominions, acquired enormous influence over the masses through his tabloids, and by this means he at last became the confidant – some would say the *master* – of British prime ministers. He became, according to Lord North's opinion, the man who not only reports government policy, but makes it; the man who not only reports on wars, but begins them. His present life is the part of the story everyone knows, or thinks they know. But the ending of a story generally goes back, in some fashion or other, to the beginning. And I have begun to wonder, Wilson, if Gurloch's motives, and the whole mainspring of his life, may be discovered in his early life. What made him do all that he has done, is doing? "What food does Caesar eat that has made him grow so great?" Was his desire the simple lust for power, such as any man might have? Or was it, rather, some little thing that happened to him when he was young – some seemingly insignificant event that scorched his life and drove him to such extremes?

'Included in the report are a few examples of the column that he wrote for his New Zealand newspaper when he was twenty-nine or so. His column often was autobiographical. Two of these autobiographical columns I find particularly interesting. The first is called simply "My Monkey". It tells of how when he was a child of seven he and his best friend, an Indian boy called Pasha, spent long days training Gerald's pet monkey, a creature called Baba. At a gesture of the hand, Baba would climb a tree with amazing speed, throw down a coconut, then descend and sit dutifully on the ground waiting for his leash to be snapped back on him. The boys taught Baba to skitter up the front of Gerald's house, pop through the window, find a book in the room, and bring it down to them. Unfortunately, Baba occasionally got loose and decided to go up the front of the house next door, which was Colonel Winter's house. In through the colonel's window went the monkey, and he would steal whatever suited his fancy – a book, a picture, a muffin, a mirror. The colonel, who was not a patient man, warned Gerald's father to keep the monkey out of his house. One day Colonel Winter appeared in his white uniform, wearing a pith helmet, and in the privacy of the court-yard he went after the defenseless rhesus monkey, Baba, with a cricket bat. Pasha flung himself in front of the animal to protect it. The colonel cried, "You little nigger" and threw Pasha to the ground. He then swatted Baba, and killed him . . . here's the passage: "I never recovered from that," writes Gurloch. "My best friend was humiliated, and the creature I loved most was killed. My feelings about the Raj, and the glorious British Empire that supported it, can well be imagined."

'The other column was titled "Lies". In it Gurloch briefly told the complicated story of how his father was sued for defamation by the governor of Kerala state. His father was convicted, lost his newspaper, eventually went bankrupt, and was disgraced. And here –' Holmes paged through the report – 'is the passage that ended that column: "I remember standing in a hot room, watching fans turn slowly overhead. My father had told the truth in his newspaper article. But it was not a truth approved by the British authorities. My father stood in the box looking shocked and defeated as the judge rendered his verdict. Not long afterward we left India. So quickly is a fairyland destroyed – and all the sweet-ness of a remembered childhood. From that day onward I became a man. My father always said that truth is beautiful. I never disputed my father, who was the only thoroughly good and honor-able man I've ever known. But from that day onward I knew that truth, though it may be beautiful, is not enough."'

ELEVEN

Two Floozies and a Wolf

Not far from the oldest medieval belfry in England is a St Albans pub where high-voltage political people drink, dine, date, and do deals – or so it was described to us by Sigvard Kipling, who had arranged for Holmes and me to meet there with the rest of the people who were present on the afternoon when Sylvia Swann died. At about six we arrived at the pub and joined Sigvard and Canyon, who were already convivial.

The bibulous and magniloquent Sigvard Kipling was glowing and in high form. His voice boomed a welcome. Canyon Swann proved to be a handsome young man of twenty-four, with a solid jaw, light brown hair, twinkling blue eyes. His small mouth frequently became very wide and very bright as he broke into smile – as he did now. 'I cannot believe it was Isabel,' said he. 'It just doesn't make sense, Mr Holmes. You don't smack someone with a statue in order to run off with a painting. Where would she sell it? She is an intelligent girl – she couldn't possibly imagine she could get away with such a thing. No, Mr Holmes, it was an accident, a queer and terrible accident. Of that I am convinced. My poor mother reached up to look at Gigi's ashes, or perhaps to open one of the doors in the tall stack of cases to get a book, and in so doing she may have wobbled the bookcases – I know those cases were piled too high and wobble easily. The statue has a narrow base, and it would not take much to wobble it and tip it. Something like that is what happened. Some years ago Mother had a CAT scan that revealed what might have been a small aneurysm in her brain. She never followed up on the finding, for the doctors said it was so small that it might have been absolutely nothing at all. But maybe it *was* something, and perhaps it had something to do with her dying so quickly from a crack on the skull.'

'And the painting?' said his uncle.

'I think my sister Amy may have it,' said Canyon.

'Amy!' Sigvard Kipling looked shocked.

'Mother told her last week that it was hers, rightfully and sensibly hers, since Amy is so fond of horses, and since Stubbs was famous for painting horses. So mother told her to take it. Amy wouldn't take it. So I told her, "Take it, you silly goose." And she said she would – and maybe she did. I think perhaps she took it yesterday before mother died, and put it in her minivan before she went riding, and we just didn't notice it was gone.'

'Then why did she say nothing about it?'

'Why should she?' said Canyon, opening both hands. 'Does she even know the police think it has been stolen?'

'Perhaps not,' said Kipling.

'There it is,' said Canyon. 'Anyway, we can ask her when she turns up. She said she'd try to be here.'

'And what,' asked Sigvard Kipling, 'about the cloth that was covering your mother? You surely don't propose, dear boy, that she toppled the statue onto her own head, and then covered herself with a tablecloth.'

'That is a bit of a mystery,' admitted Canyon. 'I am counting on Mr Holmes to solve it.'

At that moment a beautiful – I may even say gorgeous – redhead came to our table and looked down at us expectantly. Canyon rose quickly, as did we all, and he introduced her as Victoria, his girlfriend. Victoria shook Holmes's hand, then mine, and she sat down very prettily – and she promptly took over the conversation.

'My father thinks he may use me as a presenter for his new film noir channel.'

'Who better!' said Canyon.

'I love film noir,' she said.

'Love is all we need,' said he.

'It has been my hobby for years. Turner Classic Movies has Robert Osborne, Gurloch's Film Noir will have me.'

'Gurloch?' said Holmes.

'My father is Gerald Gurloch, yes,' she said, saucily. 'He is not as bad as people say, Mr Holmes.'

'Few people live up to their notoriety,' said Holmes.

She laughed. 'What did you say your name was?'

'Sherlock Holmes.'

The girl had begun to disturb me: she reminded me of someone. I struggled a while, then remembered. 'Do you ride a motorcycle?' I asked.

'No more. I used to ride everywhere. I used to be quite daft about motorcycles. I won races, even. But I had a little accident that scared me, and I haven't ridden since – and I have sworn never to ride again! My sister Jenny still rides, and I tell her she is crazy. She'll kill herself one of these days.'

'Victoria lost control of her motorcycle four years ago,' Canyon explained, 'and slid a ways. Lost some skin. That was in Switzerland, where our family has a chalet very near Victoria's family's chalet. Andrew and I begged our parents to buy one there, so we could be near the girls.'

'Perhaps I should take a stage name: Victoria Shadows, Mistress of the Noir.'

'Two days ago,' said Holmes, looking at Canyon, 'I examined the study where your mother died. I am told your father died there also.'

'Yes,' said Canyon.

'I thought it curious,' said Holmes.

'Well, it *was* odd, in a way,' he said.

'In what way?'

Victoria laughed, a bit histrionically. 'There was nothing odd about it, Canyon,' she exclaimed, brushing a strand of hair from her brow. 'Let us talk about something else. Let us talk about your many talents.'

Canyon smiled his bright and toothy smile. 'Why not just talk about my good looks?'

'You look just like your father,' said Victoria, gazing at him tenderly.

'My father had heart problems, we all knew that,' said Canyon. 'Even so, there were certain things surrounding his death that bothered me.'

'Such as?' said Holmes.

Victoria laughed again. 'He imagines things, strange things,' she said, turning her pretty face toward the rest of us, conspiratorially, while simultaneously caressing Canyon's shoulder as if to fondly shush him.

'Perhaps I do,' said Canyon, genially. 'Even so, the matter of
Sara leaving so quickly, and apparently having suddenly come
into money . . .'

'Sara, the maid before Isabel?' said Holmes.

'Yes. She was my parents' maid for many years. Soon after
father died, she left. And not merely that, the surrounding circumstances were a bit strange.'

'Circumstances?' said Sigvard Kipling. 'What circumstances?'

'Sara said some odd things . . . before she went silent,' said
Canyon.

'Darling, don't torture yourself!' cried Victoria. 'Your poor
father died . . . that's all.'

Canyon Swann grew suddenly reserved. He gazed at his drink.
'I don't know . . . I'd talk to Sara Drumling, if I were you, Mr
Holmes. She has a shop, now, in Brighton.'

'Oh, please!' cried Victoria. And she got up from our table
and hurried to the bar, and began talking to the barman, as if she
needed immediate attention.

'I've never been convinced that Dad died of a heart attack,'
said Canyon. 'There was more to it.'

'Such as?'

'I haven't the faintest idea, Mr Holmes.'

Sigvard Kipling followed Victoria to the bar and began talking
to her, and then they both returned to the table.

'Might your brother Andrew or your sister Amy be in any way
involved?' Holmes asked Canyon.

He shook his head. 'Impossible, Mr Holmes. Oh, I know the
old saying – that you never really know your own family until
the will is read. But neither Amy nor Andrew have the least
twinge of greed or unkindness in them. They are not that sort of
people. Andrew is carrying on my father's work, in fact.'

'Carrying it on in rather a different direction, I should say,'
said Victoria.

'Not really. Just by different methods. The aim is the same.'

'Andrew is an extremist,' she insisted.

Canyon ignored her. 'All of us children are aware that the
will was about to be changed so that the Rabbit Underground will
get nearly everything. But we were all happy with that. Nobody
objected.'

'Where is Amy?' asked Holmes.

'She is making funeral arrangements,' said Canyon. 'She hopes she can make it here.'

Bucky roused himself from the trance-like stare with which he had been observing the scene, and he looked at Canyon and Victoria. 'How did you two meet?'

'We have known each other since childhood,' said Canyon. 'We met in the playground.'

'We're like an old married couple, almost,' said Victoria.

'And to make matters even more clannish,' said Canyon, 'my brother, Andrew, lives with Victoria's twin sister, Jenny. Andrew is two years older than I.'

'Jenny likes older men,' said Victoria. She laughed. 'Isn't Canyon an Adonis! I tell him he should go into films. He looks like his father, who actually *was* in films at one stage of his career – wasn't he, Canyon?'

'My father did act in a few pictures as a young man. My parents lived in Hollywood for a while – which is why I was born at the rim of the Grand Canyon. A badly-timed vacation. But after a brief burst of trying for stardom, my father decided to return to England. I was very young. We moved to St Albans, and there we met the Gurloch girls . . . the rest is history.' He laughed.

Sigvard Kipling lifted his chin, as if to point with it. 'Look there, coming in the door. The prime minister and Maureen Gripp.'

'Why, I believe it *is* the PM,' said I, startled by celebrity.

'Maureen Gripp,' explained Sigvard, 'is Gurloch's chief editor. She is very good friends with the PM.'

'Of course she is,' said Victoria. 'It is natural she would be.'

'Is it *natural*?' said Kipling. 'Or is *conspiratorial* the better word? Ah, and there is your father, coming through the other door . . . with a couple of floozies on his arm.'

'High-tone floozies, though,' said Canyon. 'Strictly high-tone.' He laughed.

'Oh, please!' said Victoria.

Gerald Gurloch, the famous newspaper magnate, walked to the table where the PM and Maureen Gripp were already ensconced and chatting as happily as if no one else existed in

the world. Gurloch stood there a while, nodding affably, a girl
on each arm. At last he signaled the girls to be off – shook them
loose, so to speak – and he sat down with the PM and his chief
editor.

'Look closely at that table,' said Sigvard Kipling. 'You are
looking at the people who run Britain. The only one missing is
the police commissioner.'

The two floozies, as Kipling called them, looked a little
shocked, bewildered, when Gerald Gurloch cut them loose. They
shrugged at each other and, for an instant, glanced our way. To
my surprise, Sherlock Holmes gestured toward them. The two
girls conferred with each other for a moment, laughed as at a
private joke, and headed our way. Very long legs. Very short
skirts, made of a swinging silk-like material. High heels.

Holmes stood up. 'Welcome, ladies,' said he.

'Hey, now!' said one – with an American accent.

'You know Mr Gurloch well?' asked Holmes.

'Well enough,' said the other. Her English working-class accent
was close to cockney. 'We do little stunts for Mr Gurloch.'

'Trade shows, that sort of thing.'

'We dress as bikers . . .'

'Or spark plugs . . .'

'Or turkeys . . .'

'Whatever.'

'Robots, once . . . remember, Jill, the little blond fellow who
said he didn't want a mechanical screw?'

'I don't remember . . .'

'There were so many.'

'You ought to be in movies,' said Holmes, taking a puzzling
interest in them.

'You know anybody who could help us?'

'If Gurloch can't, I can't,' said Holmes.

'Bingo!' said Sasha, the Brit, and she put her hand on her hip,
as if about to dance.

'Can you dance?' asked Holmes.

'Who for?'

'Who do you usually dance for?'

'Whoever pays,' the Brit replied.

'It's the way of the world,' said the American.

'I'm paying for drinks,' said Holmes.

'Now, that's more like!' said the American.

And they pulled up two more chairs, and I wondered what Holmes was after. I had seldom seen him so genial. Holmes has always been an actor, and many is the time he has adopted the genial manners necessary to influence whomever he needs to influence, be it doormen, street people, baronets or floozies. The girls grew giddier and giddier the more they drank. I must say, I grew to like them both very much, the longer we talked. Each had, when you looked at her face long enough, a pretty weakness about her that made a man sympathetic, and made him want to . . . to *do* something for her. Sasha was from East London, had aspired to be a dancer with a major ballet company, but I could see that she had already given up, although she pretended she was just doing these odd jobs temporarily. And Jill, the American, despite her many charms, seemed frightened that she had already missed most of life.

'Have you ladies ever ridden in an Aston Martin?' asked Holmes, suddenly.

'We don't know anybody with an Aston Martin,' said Jill.

'You know me,' said Holmes.

'If we did, we'd be all over him!' laughed Sasha, and she sucked off the rest of her gin with a ladylike gesture.

'I have one,' said Holmes.

'You?'

'You mean you don't think I'm that sort of a chap?' said Holmes.

'I didn't mean that,' said Sasha.

'Come, then, and learn truth, my dear girl!'

'I think he's serious,' said Jill.

'There is room for all three of us,' said Holmes. 'Though it might be a bit cozy.'

'Cozy is our favorite thing,' said Sasha.

The three of them got up and made for the door. 'Now, you mustn't be kidding us,' said Jill. 'I hope you really do drive an Aston Martin – really and truly.'

'Of course I do,' said Holmes. 'What kind of a man do you think I am?'

TWELVE
Lord North's Last Scribble

Holmes never returned to the pub.

Bucky and I drove back to London and stayed up late, talking about old days in Afghanistan. It was nearly midnight before Holmes appeared suddenly, like a phantom, materializing in the dark entry hall and tossing his driving cap onto the coat tree peg.

'You are walking with a very light step, Holmes,' said I.

'They showed me things I'd never seen before,' said Holmes.

'I'll bet they did,' said Bucky.

'Learn anything useful?' I asked.

'Those two charming ladies,' said Holmes, 'required me to do a great deal of roaring about the countryside. They cajoled me into buying them a number of bottles of booze – which I insisted they *not* fling into hedges. And finally, having come to conclude that I was a *bit of fun*, they decided that I could be trusted to share *their view* of the world, and they admitted to me that they had been the bunnies who dumped Dr Droon into the dustbin.'

'As you suspected.'

'Gurloch had instigated the whole caper, they said, in order to make the Rabbit Underground appear in the worst possible light – attacking an honored scientist. The question Gurloch debated was whether to have them paint the Rabbit Underground logo – RUn – on the dumpster, or not. He finally decided not. He felt that it would be more plausible that the RUn would *not* sign their own crime. Also, he felt that the news would be more intriguing if there were some mystery involved, some uncertainty as to whether the RUn had actually done it.'

'Whatever else Gurloch may be, he knows how to grab the public's attention and wring the most out of little,' said Bucky. 'A brilliant media strategist.'

'The Machiavelli of media,' said I. 'That's what they call him.'

'Gurloch paid Droon a very large sum,' said Holmes, 'to testify against legislation that would cost Gurloch big money. Then he had Droon attacked to make the good professor seem a more sympathetic and moderate witness.'

'Well,' said Bucky, 'there have been newspaper magnates that have started wars in order to turn a profit.'

'That may even be true of Gurloch,' said I. 'He is hand-in-glove with the PM, isn't he?'

'That probably cannot be proved,' said Holmes.

'Which is what allows, thank god, the public to maintain a few of its illusions,' said I.

'And to carry on pretending all is well – or, well enough,' said Bucky.

'It is an imperfect world,' said Holmes.

'It is getting late,' said I, 'and I grow weary.'

'Me too,' admitted Bucky.

'Help yourself to your beds, gentlemen!' cried Holmes. 'I cannot sleep, for I am tormented by the murder of Lord North and the theft of his computer.'

'Murder, Holmes?'

'Without question, my dear fellow. I am convinced that many of the answers we seek will be found in the strangely coded letter that North wrote to Overton –' he held up a copy of the letter he had printed from his camera – 'if I can but break the code.'

I looked again at the letter.

My Dear Overton,

The fastest way to spill a secret is to put it on a computer. Therefore I trust pen, ink, and the Royal Mail to communicate this afterthought to my somewhat longer message of yesterday – a message which I hope you have by now safely received. Dear friend, though we be old, yet we be bold, and are resolved. We will, I think, prevail as we have so often done before. Best towns to visit, you ask? Here is my advice. I believe you will find the journey very much worth the effort: Kabul, Skopje, Muscat, Windhoek, Astana, Dili, Sana'a, Belgrade, Taipei, Barka, Vientiane, Cairo, Kuala Lumpur, Al Hudaydah, Yaoundé, Raysut, Bamako, Asunción, Kampala, Ankara, Tallinn, Moscow, Bratislava, San Salvador, Addis

Ababa, Nairobi, Havana, Riga, Kiev, Quito, New Delhi, Oslo,
Valletta, Buenos Aires, Wellington, Phnom Penh, Tegucigalpa,
Baghdad, Amsterdam, Asmara, Hanga Roa, Maseru, Dublin,
Ljubljana.
  All very best wishes,
  North

'I suppose the code must lie in the town names,' I said. 'For
surely they don't indicate a sensible travel itinerary.'

'I would agree,' said Holmes.

'It is curious that most are capital cities,' said I. 'Then again,
the capital city is often the prime tourist site in a country – Paris,
London, Madrid.'

'Even more curious,' said Holmes, 'is that *almost* all are capital
cities, but *not quite* all – and the towns are not arranged in a
logical order.'

'Logical, Holmes?'

'If you were giving me a list of towns to visit, wouldn't it be
natural to mention places in one region of the world, then another,
then another? To mention, for instance, towns in Europe, then in
the Middle East, then Africa – something of that sort? But he
jumps all over, almost randomly.'

'I cannot see where that thought will lead you.'

'Neither can I,' said Holmes, and he darted to his feet in a fit
of nervous energy. I could tell he was in for a sleepless night.

'Good night,' said I.

'Good luck,' said Bucky.

The following morning I heard Holmes leaving before I arose.
When I looked out the window I saw him in his Aston Martin
just disappearing round the silent corner into the mist of morning.
After breakfast Bucky and I prowled about London. I showed
him Dickens's House, the National Gallery, Tate Modern. We
ended our day at a little restaurant in St Martin's Lane. When we
returned to Dorset Square we found Holmes sitting in a pool of
lamplight reading the copy he'd made of the Lord North Report.

Shortly afterward Lestrade appeared in our hallway. He swept
into the room without ceremony, stood before us in that quietly
commanding way of his. 'Holmes,' he said softly, 'if you worked
for me I'd put you on report.'

'I thought I *did* work for you!' cried Holmes, standing up quickly.

'You might as well know that I am disgusted with you. You broke our agreement.'

'I had to,' said Holmes. 'There was no other way.'

'You were supposed to call us, not try to handle everything alone.'

'There was never any great danger.'

'You might have been killed, man!' said Lestrade. 'I begin to wonder about your judgment.' Lestrade turned to me. 'I could use a drink, Wilson.'

'Certainly.'

'Holmes is impossible.'

'Perfectly impossible,' I agreed.

I mixed an American Martini for Lestrade, just as he liked it, complete with lemon. I handed it to him. 'So,' I said, 'is this a secret between you two, or are you going to tell the rest of us?'

'He hasn't *told* you!' cried Lestrade, getting more and more agitated.

'We are in the dark,' said Bucky.

'Minor incident,' said Holmes.

'Holmes was attacked on the Brighton road!' cried Lestrade.

Holmes strolled to the sideboard and poured himself another splash of wine. 'They were merely school children, Lestrade. They live in a slum. Before I gave the young man a karate chop to make him drop his ax, he shouted, "Democracy in this country is a sham!" And from what I've been learning lately, he may have a point. They were youngsters working for someone else, but probably they really wanted to make their political statement, and probably they imagined someone was paying them to make that radical point. I doubt they realized they were being used.'

'Do spare us the defense of the indefensible,' said Lestrade. 'It is not like you, Holmes. I'd be more interested in hearing your version of events. I've read your preliminary report, of course.'

'While driving on the road to Brighton to see Sara Drumling,' said Holmes, 'I noticed a red car following me. I also noticed that something strange was happening with my GPS unit. I quickly—'

'When did they hack it?' asked Lestrade.

'I haven't the foggiest,' said Holmes. 'I presume someone hacked it a few minutes before the GPS started going dodgy. I saw the false directions coming through on my screen, so I simply followed those false directions, and they led me into an alley outside of Brighton. I had been there but an instant when the girl appeared. She approached me smiling, as if to ask if she might help me – and then she produced the stiletto from her hair bun, threatened me with it. Very quick she was. She leaned down and grabbed the key out of the ignition . . . instantly she howled with pain, and dropped to the ground.'

'Whatever it was in that little dragon,' said Lestrade, 'almost killed her. The doctors think she will probably come out of her coma – though perhaps with brain damage.'

'Let us hope she recovers,' said Holmes. He held up his key chain and the silvery dragon. 'Drained of its deadliness, it is now but an ornament. I regret that the mastermind behind these attacks is not suffering, instead of some misguided young girl.'

'Your sentiments are admirable, Holmes. But I wonder if she is such an innocent as you suggest.'

'When the girl went down, one of the boys dropped his sledge-hammer and knelt by her and began shaking her frantically. The other young man then appeared, holding his spray can in one hand and his ax in the other. He began howling epithets against England. He took a swing at me with the ax. He swung wild, and I dropped him with a karate chop to the back of the neck. And that, my dear Lestrade, is when I called the police.'

'The plan, my dear Holmes . . .!'

'I know the plan, my dear fellow. But it occurred to me that since both the newspapers and the police in this country find it so easy to hack into telephones, this group might have hacked into mine – in which case, if I had called you they would have been alerted, and would have aborted the ambush.'

'I see your point,' said Lestrade. 'Anyway, Operation James Bond has been a success and now we can close it down.'

'Alas,' said Holmes, 'I think not! We have learned almost nothing, Lestrade. We have captured the foot soldiers only. We have captured a few kids from the slums. We still don't know who the real crim-inals may be – the mastermind, the hackers themselves. And still mysterious is the method by which they hacked into my car. There were no hacking devices in the red car that the attackers drove. We need more data. And perhaps, having attacked me once unsuccess-fully, they will try again, and give us a chance to acquire that data.'

Lestrade waved his hand impatiently. 'You are an amazing fellow, Holmes.' He took a sip of Martini, waved his icy glass through the air. 'An old man takes on two burly eighteen-year-olds, plus one Mata Hari style seventeen-year-old girl, and defeats them with the greatest of ease.'

'A bit of luck!' said Holmes gaily.

'And a bit of pluck!' added Bucky Boudreau.

'The Tewkesbury Dragon did for the girl,' said Holmes. 'When she was hurt, the first young man could do nothing but sob over her prostrate body until the ambulance and the police arrived. As to the chap with the ax – few men are practiced in the use of an ax as a weapon, nowadays.'

'Not since the fifteenth century or so, I suppose,' grunted Lestrade.

'Has the chap recovered?' asked Holmes.

'Not bloody likely. You broke two vertebrae and he is unable to move his head.' Lestrade strolled to the mantel and lifted down the Lord North Report. He slipped it into his briefcase.

'Before you give that report to the bureaucracy,' said Holmes, 'I suggest you read it. Did you know that Gurloch tried to buy the Aston Martin company, twice? And failed each time?'

'I did not know that.'

'It is all in that report.'

'I have been instructed not to read the report.'

'Following instructions undermines character,' said Holmes.

'Yes, I've noticed that you've been trying to improve your character recently. But I'm being rather severely watched, Holmes. I have the feeling someone is tracking me. Nerves, I suppose.'

'Stay here and read it.'

'I could, I could . . . By the way, today Scotland Yard issued me a new key card. So maybe they expect me to be around for a while yet.'

'What was wrong with the old key card?' asked Holmes quickly.

'Nothing I know of.' Lestrade shrugged. 'I guess the new policy is to change them occasionally. For security.'

'Have they ever done this before?'

'No. Must be something new. By the way, what did you learn from Sara Drumling in Brighton?'

'I learned that a little before David Swann died of a heart

attack, a gentleman came to the door and asked Sara whether this was the address where the furniture was to be delivered. She assured him it was not. The man then inquired whether this was the residence of David Swann. Sara said it was. The delivery man then asked her to check with Mr Swann about the furniture. She knocked on the study door, learned that Swann knew nothing about any furniture, and she reported this to the man at the door, who gave his apologies and drove away in a green van. On the side of the van were the words "*Grosvenor Square Furniture*". Shortly afterward David Swann had a heart attack.'

'Well, then the connection is obvious!' I said, and I was about to say more, but Holmes shushed me. And he did something rather odd – odd even for him. He walked to his desk, drew out two sealed envelopes from the top drawer. On one was written '*Lestrade*', on the other '*Wilson*'. He handed them to us, almost furtively.

'Open these tomorrow,' he said quietly, casting a significant glance in each of our directions.

'What . . .?' began Lestrade.

Holmes put his finger to his lips.

Lestrade shrugged, put the envelope into his inner coat pocket. I put my envelope on the mantel.

'My superiors have demanded that you turn in your Aston Martin,' said Lestrade. 'What should I tell them?'

'That I am not finished with it.'

'The vehicle is still in pristine shape. I hope you will keep it that way.'

'I am a very responsible chap, Lestrade!'

'News to me, Holmes! I can't see that you have ever been even minimally responsible, in either of your lives. You have become obsessed with solving crimes and problems, and therefore you are *dedicated*. But *responsible*? I wonder! Beating corpses with a stick, playing dead for two years while your dear friends grieve, testing poisons on your own body, driving a hundred and thirty miles an hour. Please be good enough to restrict yourself to two-digit speeds from now on – and no four-wheel drifts.'

'I will drive so slowly that even insects will be safe,' said Holmes.

'Insects?' Lestrade frowned.

'Have you seen today's edition of *Frankenstein's Diary*?'

'I'm afraid not.'

'Evidently the Rabbit Underground are now taking up arms for insects' rights.'

'I hope you are joking,' said Lestrade.

'I have here a verse written by Black Swan. You shall judge!' cried Holmes, and he brandished the paper in the air, stood by the window, held his script at arm's length, and declaimed in his most dramatic, poetical style:

I'm drawn to bugs, lovely creatures
   Men would crush: they have such beauties –
      Bright on dung, tiny on an arm, or singing,
Stinging, winging, according to their natures.
   Most go their way (no cowrin', tim'rous beasties
      They) and ask but little of the clanging

Human crowd that fills the hills with crams
   Of cars, concrete, and condos in huge heaps –
      Ask only freedom to splat a windshield, whizzing,
Sail small in the sun, track crumbs
   Of somebody's bagel, leap in brittle hops
      For a sweet suck of someone's garbage, while buzzing

Softly a drowsy summer music I miss
   In winter when bleak streets are soundless in sun
      Save for fluff of pigeons and footsteps of sparrows
And old folks puffing breathless. The cold mass
   Of winter stillness is solace for a while, but when
      I stroll I prefer to see a beetle in the furrows

Of a field or garden, see a spider ascend
   The empty air, more glorious than a spire –
      More full of god than all the saints in the sea.
I await, in winter's freakish silent land
   That startling moment when, through whispering air,
      The first sweet fly of spring will sing to me.

'They've gone daft,' said Lestrade, shaking his head.

'I like dragonflies,' said Bucky.

THIRTEEN
Greyfriars

Holmes was already gone when I awoke the following morning. I saw the envelope lying on the mantel, opened it:

Wilson,
Meet me in the Greyfriars Garden at precisely 11:05 this morning. Do not contact Lestrade. Have no electronic equipment of any kind on your person – no mobile phone, iPod, tablet. Nothing. Walk to the Baker Street Underground, take Bakerloo to Oxford Circus, Central Line to St Paul's. Walk west along Newgate to King Edward Street. I will be in the garden.
Holmes

Though I had passed by the ruins of Greyfriars Church many times over the years, I knew nothing about the place. I Googled it and learned that the Franciscan Monastery and Church of Greyfriars were established in 1225. The church had been destroyed in the Great Fire of 1666, rebuilt by Christopher Wren, destroyed again during the Blitz in World War II, and never rebuilt after that. In 1989 a rose garden had been laid out on the site.

Bucky left at nine o'clock for a day of sightseeing. At half ten I descended into the Baker Street Underground and a half hour later I climbed back into the bright world at St Paul's. I walked along Newgate Street and soon was gazing up at the one grim remaining wall of Greyfriars church. The beds of roses were a warm contrast to the baleful stare of the wall. I sat down on a garden bench.

Lestrade appeared. 'What's this all about, Wilson?'

I shrugged.

He glanced at his watch. 'We're a minute and a half early.'

Ninety seconds later Holmes appeared from the shadows, strolled briskly toward us, and sat down between us on the bench.

'We are birds on a wire,' said Lestrade.

'What's this all about, Holmes?' I asked.

'Secrecy,' said he, and he drew from his little brown briefcase a folded paper. 'I have here the message from Lord North to Lord Overton.'

He unfolded the paper, held it in his thin hands so that all three of us could look at it. On the paper were two columns of names, with lines drawn across the sheet at intervals, thus:

Kabul	Afghanistan
Skopje	Macedonia
Muscat	Oman
Windhoek	Namibia
Astana	Kazakhstan
Dili	East Timor
Sana'a	Yemen
Belgrade	Serbia
Taipei	Taiwan
Barka	Oman
Vientiane	Laos
Cairo	Egypt
Kuala Lumpur	Malaysia
Al Hudaydah	Yemen
Yaoundé	Cameroon
Raysut	Oman
Bamako	Mali
Asunción	Paraguay
Kampala	Uganda
Ankara	Turkey
Tallinn	Estonia
Moscow	Russia
Bratislava	Slovakia
San Salvador	El Salvador
Addis Ababa	Ethiopia
Nairobi	Kenya
Havana	Cuba
Riga	Latvia
Kiev	Ukraine

Quito	Ecuador
New Delhi	India
Oslo	Norway
Valletta	Malta
Buenos Aires	Argentina
Wellington	New Zealand
Phnom Penh	Cambodia
Tegucigalpa	Honduras
Baghdad	Iraq
Amsterdam	Netherlands
Asmara	Eritrea
Hanga Roa	Easter Island
Maseru	Lesotho
Dublin	Ireland
Ljubljana	Slovenia

'What is it?' asked Lestrade.

'My decryption of a once-removed geographical acrostic,' said Holmes.

'Never heard of such a thing,' said Lestrade.

'Nor have I,' said Holmes.

'The first column seems to be the list of towns in North's letter,' said I.

'Exactly,' said Holmes. 'And the second column lists the countries in which each of those towns is found. Kabul is in Afghanistan, Skopje is in Macedonia, and so on.'

'I don't see the message in all this,' said Lestrade.

'I tried first,' said Holmes, 'to find an acrostic in the original list of cities, taking first letters: KSMW etcetera. But those seemed to mean nothing. Then I pondered the fact that most of the cities were capital cities – but not quite all. Which seemed odd. The third city in the list is Muscat, capital of Oman. The tenth in the list is Barka, merely a city in Oman. Likewise, the seventh city is Sana'a, capital of Yemen, but the fourteenth is Al Hudaydah, merely a city in Yemen. Why this insistence on cities in Oman and Yemen? That thought prompted me to write the list of countries that corresponded with the cities – and, *voila*! It was obvious: the first letters of the countries spell the message. And the reason Oman and Yemen appear so often in the list, when every other country appears but once, is that Oman is the only country in the world that starts with "O" and Yemen the only country that starts with "Y". Lord North needed several "O's" and several "Y's" in his message, therefore had to use those countries several times. To obscure the code, he used different cities to call up those countries the second or third time.'

'A cumbersome method of encrypting,' mused Lestrade.

'But effective for short messages – and easily encrypted and deciphered by two old Fellows of the Royal Geographical Society.'

Lestrade read the message, slowly. '*A monkey stole my computer. Seek clue in Manchineel . . . is*? It seems unfinished.'

'*I S* for island. Manchineel Island,' said Holmes.

'Never heard of it,' said Lestrade.

'It's a small island in the Windwards of the Lesser Antilles,' I said. 'Part of the Grenadines.'

Lestrade laughed. 'Wilson, you always amaze me.'

'I poked about in the West Indies a good bit in my younger days. Never been to Manchineel Island, but I know where it is.'

From his case Holmes pulled out a map, folded it open. 'I just came from Stanfords in Long Acre,' he said, 'where I purchased this map of the Windward Islands of the Lesser Antilles.' He pointed. 'Here is St Vincent, and . . .'

'There's Bequia,' I said. 'I've been there. Look to the east of Bequia and you will see some deserted islands, Battawia and Balliceaux, and to the east of them should be Manchineel Isle . . .'

'Manchineel Isle is no longer deserted, if ever it was,' said Holmes. 'But the queer thing is that it does not appear on this map, or on any of the newer charts.'

I pulled the map toward me slightly. 'I'm pretty sure it should be right about there . . .'

Holmes took out a pencil and made an 'X' in the blue sea where I had touched. 'You are right, Wilson. That is where the island is shown to be on the older maps. I have found it on charts at the British Library, and on a map published in the seventies that I discovered in a used bookstore.'

'Mapping companies seldom make errors of that sort,' said Lestrade. 'I can't believe the island is really there if . . . could it be that Manchineel blew up, vanished? That has sometimes happened to small volcanic islands.'

'The island definitely existed in the sixties,' said I. 'I've known people who visited it. I went halfway there myself. I've heard people talk about it.'

'The island certainly exists,' said Holmes.

'Then where has it gone?' asked Lestrade, tapping the blue sea with his finger.

'Suppose,' said Holmes, 'that a hacker managed to get into the files of a mapping company, and managed to alter the map by erasing the island. Suppose that the intrusion was not observed. Suppose, also, that the omission was not noticed when they reprinted the map.'

'Do you think that is what happened?' asked Lestrade.

'What I know is that the island did not vanish,' said Holmes. 'I also know that Gerald Gurloch bought the island in the sixties. And I know that Gurloch has the Hack Magic Group working for him, led by the notorious Hacking Jack Hawes.'

'But why would he want his island to vanish from the maps?'

'I don't know,' said Holmes. 'But under the circumstances – and on a dead man's recommendation – I think perhaps we ought to try to find out. Unfortunately, I cannot leave London at the moment.'

Lestrade looked at me. 'Well, Wilson. You've been there.'

'It certainly is a very pleasant part of the world,' said I.

'Settled, then!' cried Holmes, delighted.

'Did I volunteer?' said I.

'I thought you might have.'

'If I may ask,' said Lestrade, 'why are we meeting in this strange place?'

'In hopes of not being overheard,' said Holmes, and he began folding the map smaller and smaller.

Lestrade leaned forward and rested his forearms on his knees as he watched the map shrink in Holmes's hands. 'Who might be listening, Holmes?'

'Gurloch, for one. He must be aware that I am on his case, and that I am investigating his connections with Dr Droon, the Swanns, and Lord North. Scotland Yard, for another. And perhaps even Lars Lindblad, who seems always interested in my movements.'

'Some of my superiors at New Scotland Yard may well be monitoring you, or trying to,' said Lestrade. 'You are the man they fear most. But I doubt Lindblad is tracking you. Why would he? The refreshing thing about Lindblad is that he is the most old-fashioned criminal in the world, simply in crime for the money. He'll only track you if he plans to rob you.'

'But Lindblad is also in it for the sport,' said I. 'He said so himself, if you recall, during our little Shakespeare Letter adventure. The world's greatest thief against the world's greatest detective – that's how Lindblad sees it.'

'The man is slightly mad,' said Lestrade. 'Who knows what he might be doing. But this message you have decoded, Holmes. What's this business about a monkey stealing a computer? What does that stand for? It appears to be a code within a code.'

'I take it literally,' said Holmes. 'I take it that a monkey stole his computer.'

'Come now!'

'Read Lord North's report and see what you think, Lestrade.'

'Maybe I should.'

'I believe a monkey was involved, and that Gurloch has Lord North's computer. Fortunately, North did not trust computers as much as he trusted paper, so he made a paper copy for Overton just one day before his computer was stolen. Any news of Overton?'

'Still critical.'

'Wilson will want a false identity for his journey, can you arrange it?'

'No problem. I still have a few trusted friends in the department. Also in MI5.'

'I'm not sure I need a new identity!' said I.

'When travelling, it never hurts to be someone else,' said Holmes.

At that moment an old man came walking slowly along the garden, so we stopped talking. The old fellow limped, was carrying a newspaper under his arm. He stopped in front of us, leaned to sniff a flower, then shuffled on and vanished at the corner.

'Look there,' said Holmes, nodding toward the street.

A green Grosvenor Square Furniture van passed slowly along King Edward Street.

'How can that be!' said I.

The van glided out of view.

'Scotland Yard gave you a new key card, Lestrade – may I see it?' said Holmes, much agitated.

Lestrade slipped the key card out of his wallet and handed it to him.

Holmes held it up to the sunlight, squinted at it curiously, then held it in his palm as if to weigh it, before handing it back. 'Could it be a transponder of some sort? A beacon for a homing device?'

'That card is giving out no signals that I know of,' said Lestrade.

A moment later Holmes bounded across the path, fell to his knees amongst the roses, searched, then stood up and flung something sidearm into the street.

'What are you doing, Holmes!' said Lestrade.

'That old man who passed us a minute ago stopped limping before he vanished round the corner.'

'Stopped limping?'

'Fatal mistake for an actor. At Cambridge old Jessup always admonished us amateur thespians, "Stay in character, gentlemen, until you are well offstage!"'

'So somebody knows where we are?'

'The old man dropped a microphone in the roses.'

'The furniture van again,' I said.

'The van may mean nothing,' said Lestrade. 'There *is* a Grosvenor Square Furniture company. I checked this morning. They specialize in Queen Anne furniture, both genuine antiques and modern imitations. They have a fleet of ten vans in London.'

'How long has the company existed?' asked Holmes.

'Two years.'

'So brief a time? Who owns it?'

'The more I looked into that question, the murkier the answer became. What queer goings-on, Holmes! I am baffled at every turn.'

'This old church may have never seen queerer goings-on than it has seen today,' said I. 'Bugs in the roses, limping old men, forces of evil, codes and whispers.'

'My guess,' said Lestrade, 'is that this old wreck has seen plenty of queerer days than this, considering it has been here for hundreds of years.'

'Since 1225,' said I.

Lestrade gave a soft whistle. 'Your historical knowledge astounds me.'

'Don't be too impressed,' said I. 'I Googled "Greyfriars" before setting out this morning. Read its history on Wikipedia.'

Holmes grasped my arm. 'You Googled? Then there is our answer! That is how they know we are here.'

'What has Googling to do with anything?'

'Surely you are joking, Wilson!' said Holmes. 'Google knows your every whim and curiosity. Make a query about Bellweather Umbrellas or Underwood Soap on Google, and ads for Bellweather Umbrellas and Underwood Soap appear every time you read your email or read a newspaper online.'

Lestrade looked mystified. 'But how could someone so quickly learn of his queries about Greyfriars?'

'Google computers can be hacked like anyone else's,' said Holmes.

FOURTEEN
The Frangipani Hotel

Sherlock Holmes, Inspector Lestrade and certain other gentlemen having asked me to write down – on paper, not a computer – the particulars of my adventure to Manchineel Island, I take up my pen in the year 2012, in the Beau Rivage Hotel in Nyon, Switzerland, to begin a narrative which I will perhaps later incorporate into a complete presentation of the Swann–Gurloch affair . . . and I go back to that morning in June exactly one week ago when, still unaware of the seriousness of the movement to subvert democracy in Britain, I boarded a plane at Heathrow airport, bound for Miami. I traveled not as James Wilson, writer, but as Ernest Farley, accountant. My new identity had been supplied to me by MI5 and by the Metropolitan Police, and it took the form of false papers and new luggage. The passport in my possession was several years old, peppered with

passport control stamps from countries where the phantom Mr
Ernest Farley had presumably traveled – Thailand, China, the
US, Canada, and so on. I hoped MI5 had not bumped off a
genuine Ernest Farley in order to set me up in his place –
a prospect that flashed through my mind as not quite a serious
possibility but yet, in these days of rendition and torture by
western democracies, not quite as pure fantasy either. For years
I had been used to travelling with a small backpack and no more
than twenty pounds of luggage, and I had wanted to follow this
semi-hippy tradition of mine, but my 'handlers' would not allow
it. Such equipage did not fit the character of Ernest Farley, they
said. Instead, I toted a small carry-on bag with wheels, plus a
briefcase with a gold E.F. monogram embossed discreetly on the
top edge. The briefcase contained a number of balance sheets
for the St Ripon Paper Company, a number of business letters
to and from Ernest Farley, and £20,000 in cash in a hidden
compartment. It also contained a few articles of spy gear,
including a small camera, a life-sensor that chimed if a living
creature came closer than twenty feet to me, and a tiny disposable plastic pistol that would kill a man at thirty yards. The
disposable pistol was good for three shots before the barrel melted
out of shape, and I had no confidence in it. Since they thought
I needed a pistol at all, I requested a real weapon, preferably the
same I had carried in Afghanistan. Lestrade denied me, explaining
that this three-shot plastic pistol was designed to be scanned in
airports without showing up. Then he laughed and added – with
uncharacteristic humor – that on this mission I was authorized
to kill no more than three people anyway. The case also contained
Ernest Farley's mobile phone. My own mobile phone Holmes
had put in the boot of the Aston Martin so that anyone who tried
to track my whereabouts by homing in on the phone would be
utterly deceived.

In Miami I caught a flight to Barbados. I arrived late in
Bridgetown, stayed the night there at a luxury hotel, and the next
morning boarded a LIAT prop plane bound for St Vincent. I
prefer small airplanes, and as the little craft moaned upward out
of the cloudy island into bright air, I was thrown back to that
summer of 1968 when, on a day just like this, I had first flown
this route. I had been a young man then, full of hope and

expectation, and today I felt just exactly the same as I had felt in that earlier time – full of curiosity and ready for unexpected wonders. From the air Barbados looked exactly the same as it had on my first trip so long ago – like a broken cookie lying flat in the sea, a bit disappointing. Tiny lines of white breakers crawled slowly toward its shore. Here and there could be seen the white blip of a boat at sea.

By and by St Vincent appeared. Its Soufrière, wreathed in cloud, made the island as mysterious and intriguing as a Caribbean island ought to be. We swooped down to the runway, the door opened. As I stepped onto the tarmac I felt as though a hot wet towel had been thrown over my head. Crushing heat. I drifted through customs, caught a taxi. The old vehicle darted through Kingstown and down to the docks, and that was where I realized with shock how much things had changed. Forty-four years earlier I had been carried to Bequia on a little blue motor launch with wooden seats in a wooden cabin. Waiting for me now was a huge steel ship that accommodated both passengers and cars. I went up the gangplank feeling disconcerted. Inside the ferry one might have been anywhere in the world, for we were hermetically sealed. The journey was swift. We rounded the point into Admiralty Bay. The mountains surrounding the harbor had shrunk, it seemed to me. Could memory be so defective? Then I realized that I was standing on a high deck, several storeys above the sea, whereas on my first journey I had been sitting a bare twenty inches above lapping waves. Today the beautiful little harbor was overloaded with boats at anchor – a thriving scene . . . but no longer picturesque. A massive jetty had been built. We clanged to rest beside it. Skipping black seamen threw down the hawsers.

I debarked.

The Frangipani Hotel was much the same as it had been long ago, small and wooden and neat, like a sea captain's house. It still had a patio bar which was just a short stretch of sand away from the lapping bay. Alas, the effect of intimacy with the sea had been spoiled by a little stone walkway that had been built along the edge of the bay. That little walkway, civilized and convenient, obliterated the gentle touching of sand to sea that once had been so charming.

I took the same sort of basic room as I had years earlier, in the old part of the hotel. Toilet and shower were down the hall. The room had been freshly decorated, everything bright and lovely, and was complete with Wi-Fi to connect me with the world if I should care to go back from whence I'd just come. But I had no desire to do so, and, anyway, I had been instructed not to use a computer lest I be sensed and attacked by spiders of the Web. '*Incommunicado*, that's the watchword,' Lestrade had warned me. 'Pen and ink, my lad – nothing else!'

The desk clerk seemed dubious when I told her I was looking for someone who would take me to Manchineel Island. 'It is a private island,' she said. 'Landing there is not allowed. You will have a hard time finding anyone to take you.'

'I once landed on Battawia and Balliceaux,' I said. 'And I've taken the mail boat through the rest of the Grenadines down to Grenada. But I've never seen Manchineel Island.'

'Manchineel is far beyond Battawia and Balliceaux,' she said. 'But you might try Dougie Huggles. He's the only one I know who might take you. You might find him over in The Nook. He drinks there when he is desperate and out of work.'

I found Huggles just where she predicted he would be, slouched in a corner of The Nook. He was nursing a rum. But it appeared he was not quite so desperate, after all. 'It's too far, mahn,' he said. 'You don't want to go to Manchineel.'

'But I do.'

'No, mahn! Bad business, mahn . . . I'm booked tomorrow. Maybe next day.' He was a short man in a dull red shirt, big-shouldered, arms almost as long as his legs. Glittering eyes in a black face, black beard sprinkled with grey.

I walked out into the easy air and strolled, talked to several boat owners. They all turned away when I mentioned Manchineel Island. At supper I spoke with the desk clerk again. She suggested that perhaps, if I were willing to pay, I could induce someone to fly me over the island. 'You won't see much of Manchineel from the sea, in any case, for it is all cliffs and rocks and trees. Flying over might give you a better view.'

I was surprised to learn that Bequia had an airport. In 1968 it had had no airport, no electric lights. In that year I had sat typing a novel in a little house on Friendship Bay. I had used a Tilley lantern for light at night, and I had kept my food in a refrigerator run by a kerosene flame. It had all been quite idyllic. I was disappointed that Bequia was now accessible by air. But I decided to go to the airstrip in the morning to see if I could finagle a flight. What I really needed to do, though, was to get onto Manchineel Island, a prospect that seemed more and more unlikely as the day wore on.

After supper I walked along the beach where once I had bought delicious fresh home-made bread from an old woman. Beach-made bread, rather. In those days she had baked it in a makeshift sheet-iron oven heated by charcoal, right on the sandy beach. But now the old woman had been replaced by upscale restaurants. The bay was full of pretty boats. I thought perhaps I might learn where the rich yachtsmen hung out, go there, strike up conversations, and try to induce one of them to sympathize with my plight and to volunteer, in a gallant gesture, to take me to Manchineel Island. But after supper that night something occurred which made that plan unnecessary.

I sat drinking rum punches on the veranda of the Frangipani for a long while, talking with a succession of strangers – people from Muscatine and Manchester, Chicago and London, Cincinnati and São Paulo. Couples, mostly. Old and young. As the night grew older the breeze freshened and splashes of rain began to fall. Then more rain. Palm trees thrashed wildly. I suddenly realized I was alone on the thatch-covered patio. Or so I thought. A shadow in the corner got up from his table and came over and introduced himself. He said his name was Dunstable Smith. He was a tall, slender man with a slouch. He offered me a rum punch and I accepted. He went to the outdoor bar to order it. I was surprised when the waitress came carrying four of them – 'Just in case,' said Smith, 'for they will be closing the bar soon.'

She set the four glasses on our table.

'Merci, sweet wench!' said he.

'Yes, sir,' said she, and hurried away.

The palm trees clashed overhead, the wind blew hard. Then the lights went out on the island.

My companion was in his late twenties or early thirties, dark-haired, stubble-bearded, and he slouched in an easy manner. He wore a flamingo shirt and a red headband with Chinese writing on it. British accent, yet with an American tinge. I plied him with questions and he was quite willing to speak only of himself. He said he had a sloop in the bay. 'That's my craft there,' he said, 'the one with pretty lines and a blue dolphin painted on the prow. You can see it in the flashes of lightning.'

Flickering lightning lit and unlit the bay like a bad bulb. In one of the flickers I spotted his craft.

Smith said he had worked his way through Oxford University as a circus performer in America. He said he went sailing to 'get sane occasionally' and that he had sailed down from Antigua. On the sloop, he said, was his pet boa constrictor. 'I throw her a live chicken once or twice a week and that keeps her happy,' he said. He told me he had spent time on Haiti and was conversant in the art of voodoo. 'I can make people vanish,' he said.

At that point I knew I was talking to a crazy man, or a very drunk man. I gave a non-committal laugh.

Dunstable Smith seemed alarmed. 'But it is true!' he said.

'How do you make them vanish?' I asked.

'You'd be surprised,' he said.

'I imagine I would.'

'I throw salt behind them . . . what brings you to the Caribbean?'

I told him I was down here on a sentimental journey, hoped to see the Grenadines that I had missed forty-four years ago. I told him I wanted to see Manchineel Island.

'When do you want to go, then?'

'Soon as I can find someone to take me,' said I.

Smith sipped his drink, pushed his empty glass away, started on his standby drink. 'If you are that keen, I will take you,' said he, wiping his lips with his wrist, 'But you may regret it.'

'Why would I regret it?'

'Most people do.'

'You know where it is?'

'Got a pretty good idea.'

His reply did not give me confidence.

'Meet me right here at this table tomorrow at six in the morning, old chap, and we'll have a go,' said he.

We drank the rest of our drinks.

'Tomorrow at six,' he said.

'I'll be here,' said I.

He stood, shook my hand. 'Good to meet you, Farley.'

Dunstable Smith drank the dregs of his rum, set the glass on the table. He turned and walked down to the shore. I heard a burble of sound as his small outboard started and began to putter. The last I saw of him he was in his dinghy purring through black waves that seemed about to swamp him. The moon reappeared in a ragged sky. Masts of the anchored yachts waved in moonlight like thin-armed men who were drowning.

I hurried upstairs to the silence of my room. Already the island seemed asleep . . . lulled by rain that now beat steadily against the panes.

FIFTEEN

Storm

At a little before six o'clock the following morning I was on the patio, waiting. The rain had stopped. The sky looked strange, streaked with light and chunked with heavy cloud. By six-fifteen Smith still had not appeared. I began to suspect he had forgotten me amidst the rum punches of last evening. But time flows at a different pace in the West Indies, so I did not give up hope. I walked to the gurgling, sloshing shore and looked across Admiralty Bay in search of the sloop with the blue dolphin on the prow. It was not to be seen.

A clatter of palms. Fresh breeze blew my shirt. A voice behind me said, 'I'll take you.'

Dougie Huggles wore baggy shorts and a dull red shirt and his toes looked huge in his flip-flops.

'Hello,' I said.

'Some mahn, he cancelled. I can take you, mahn.'

'Excellent.'

'Only to look. Just to circle Manchineel and look, then to come back.'

'I understand.'

'Can't land there, mahn – not allowable.'

We haggled price. Then ate breakfast. By the time we had finished eating it was raining softly but steadily. 'You sure the weather's OK?' I asked.

'No problem, mahn.'

We got into his skiff. He rowed it slowly but with sure stroke across the chop of Admiralty Bay. We labored past all the sleek white boats that rode and dipped at ease on the fretted water. Then I saw the sloop he was aiming for, a half-painted craft that looked like a scow compared to the others. He must have known what I was thinking. (Sherlock Holmes isn't the only one who can read a man's thoughts.) 'These white gulls good for show,' said Huggles, 'but my old boat, she will weather the heavy storm.'

'It looks,' said I, 'like she already has weathered a few.'

The diesel engine on Huggles's sloop took a while to start but eventually it did and we chugged between the moored boats and out round the point, and the sea was getting heavier all the time as we left the protection of the bay. Huggles seemed a quick and competent sailor. We pulled up the sails together – for I had done a bit of sailing in my youth – and the wind bit in and the mast strained, and we were under way with good speed. For half an hour it seemed as though this would be a jolly cruise. The prow was lifting and falling, bashing the waves gracefully, and we were holding our course due east. I sat outside on deck. But by and by the rain increased and I went into the wheelhouse. Dougie offered me a paper cup of rum. I told him I never drank rum till noon. He thought this a very strange notion, and poured himself another.

My precise purpose in travelling to Manchineel Island was vague. Lord North had encountered numerous references to the island, and it was a matter of record that Gerald Gurloch had bought it in 1965, and that for years Gurloch had frequently visited there. Little else was known about the place. There had been a small resort hotel on the island before Gurloch bought it. Also a few houses, evidently owned by the anonymous wealthy that always own getaway properties in the remote places of the earth. In the nineteenth century whaling boats from Bequia had used the island as a base, and, according to Lord North's report, freighters from ports of call in India now frequently landed at the deep-sea jetty that had been built on the north side of the island. Sherlock Holmes, Lestrade, and the few others privy to my journey, had asked me simply to scout the place as best I could, to determine what, if anything, was going on there, and to make a quiet exit before anyone could discover I was a spy. My plan was to play the role of one of those hapless and somewhat elderly travellers who don't really know what is going on, but who blunder into things they think curious and then blather on about them.

I could only do what I could do, trusting to luck and improvisation. If I learned nothing of importance on the island, I would at least have had a journey and a small adventure. But there was always the chance that I might stumble on to whatever it was that Lord North had imagined might be happening on Manchineel Isle – something evidently so startling that he found it necessary to use an elaborate code to recommend to his friend that the island be investigated.

Huggles clung grimly to the wheel as the winds grew stronger. A net full of melons rolled about the deck up front. Huggles told me that the melons belonged to his brother in Carriacou. By and by he lashed the wheel and went below, and came back with a bottle of rum. He poured himself another paper cupful. Perhaps he saw the concern in my face, for he said, 'No problem, mahn! I always sail best on rum, no problem.' Then he pointed, and I saw we were passing two islands, both dim in the rain.

'Battawia and Balliceaux?' said I.

He nodded.

We continued on and Huggles kept assuring me, 'It will pass, mahn! It will pass!'

'But when?'

'Ahh, that is the question.' He laughed. 'Relax, mahn!' Took a sip.

Quickly it became obvious to me that this voyage had been a mistake. Huggles was getting drunker, the seas were getting higher, and the vessel was tilting dangerously. I suggested we go back.

Huggles shook his head. 'Can't turn her now, mister. Got to ride it out.'

As he spoke, the prow rose toward the boiling and vaporous

sky and came down with a thunderous crash, and the whole vessel shuddered and seemed to come to a stop. I clung to the rail. In that instant I realized that the voyage was over and that we'd go the rest of the way on foot, so to say. The boom had hit the water. We were wallowing. Another wave hit, the shock stunned me, water came boiling over the deck. The deck was now so tilted that I thought one more wave would capsize us – and no sooner had I thought the thought than I was in the sea, swimming and thrashing to keep my head above water.

'Stay with the vessel!' cried Huggles.

He shot feet first into the sea and vanished in a turmoil of water. Those were the last words I heard him speak.

I was underwater and I saw what seemed to be a whale, or giant fish, and this confused me. Then I realized it was the bottom of the boat. I was already forty yards from it, and being carried further away every second. I found I was entangled in the net of melons. I clung to it. I had made the mistake of swallowing seawater while gasping for breath, and I coughed and gagged like a drowning man. My raft of melons carried me toward the rocky shore. Shore? I was astonished, confused. I had no idea where I was.

I seemed to lose consciousness for an interval. At the same time I was perfectly aware of my body being lost in a chaos of wind and water. The rocky shore drew near. I could see I would soon be battered on the rocks, but I could not think of a single thing to do about it. I was too weary to struggle – even the best swimmer in the world could not have swum against those mighty seas. In the event, I was simply lucky. A peculiarly large wave bore down on me, dwarfing the others that had come before, and it lifted me and hurled me in a whirl of foam over the line of rocks and slammed me face down on the flat black sand. Succeeding waves tried to drag me back into the sea, but I clung and crawled, and eventually I escaped the fingers of water that kept grabbing at me. I reached higher ground. Looking down on the rain-blurry scene I saw melons smashed and split. They made me think what might have happened to my head. I did not feel grateful for having been spared, only confused. And amazed. Nothing seemed real. As if I were watching a movie, yet part of it – acting in it without volition of my own.

I clambered slowly up out of the reach of the sea. I found myself in grass atop a low cliff. Where could I be? I could only conclude that I had been washed onto Manchineel Isle. We had passed by Battawia and Balliceaux an hour or so before – could it be an hour? It seemed obvious that I must be on Manchineel Isle. But nothing is obvious when you are on a strange shore alone in a storm. I might have been standing on a shore of Bequia, or St Vincent, and been none the wiser. I had been told there was a deep-sea jetty built on the north side of Manchineel Isle, and presumably some kind of settlement would be there. But which way was north?

The rain still fell and the wind still blew and vaporous clouds darkened the sky. The rising sun was hidden. We had sailed pretty much due east to reach this place. So it seemed to me likely that I had been washed onto the first shore we would have come to, the western shore of the island. If so, the shortest way to the north shore would be to walk clockwise. This I did, keeping the sea on my left. I had wisely put my passport and money in a plastic bag in my flap pocket, but I had lost my bag of lunch. As I walked I began to feel hungry. This seemed odd, for I had had a big breakfast.

At the first little cove I encountered I looked down to my left and saw something on the rocks. A body. I recognized the red shirt. It was Huggles. Water washed over him and he did not move. For a long while I stared. I convinced myself he must be dead. There was no obvious way to climb down to him. I was too exhausted to even think of it. Even if, by some miracle, I managed to get down to him, and even if I found him alive – what then? We'd both die there. I could never get back up.

I walked on.

It seemed to me that this island's perimeter could not be more than about five miles. I calculated that two miles of walking should bring me to the jetty. But the storm was getting stronger. I felt myself being pushed by buffeting wind toward the valley on the land side. I slid down an embankment. By sheer luck I was blown almost to the entrance of a cave. An opening as high as a man stood before me, dark and welcoming. I entered. Ten paces later, miraculously, I was out of the storm. The dirt beneath

my shoes was dry. I must have been very weary. I lay down on
the dirt. I squirmed to get as comfortable as I could. I fell asleep
almost instantly.

SIXTEEN
Monkeyshines

I opened my eyes.
Sun blazed beyond the cave entrance.
'What are you eating?' I asked.
The monkey gazed at me. He touched a long black finger to
his nose. He nonchalantly put another morsel into his mouth and
scampered off.

I got to my feet feeling wonderfully rested. My clothes were
dry. I reached into the deep pouch pockets of my trousers and
found that my journal in its plastic bag had never got wet. Neither
had the camera, the life-sensor, or the plastic pistol. All were
safely in their plastic bags. I was surprisingly intact. I walked
out into sunshine and saw that the cliffs at this point tapered
down to sea level. The cave was in the last significant hill that
marked the rise of the cliffs. Beyond me – in what I supposed
must be a northerly direction – lay a black sand beach. It was
late afternoon, already four o'clock according to my watch. To
my right lay a little valley, and far down the valley there appeared
to be a structure of some kind rising above the trees. I set off
walking in that direction on a small but well-worn path. I confess
I felt a bit like a fearless nineteenth-century explorer, as if I were
about to discover El Dorado or the source of the Nile. When I
made the final turn and emerged from trees I felt, instead, like
Alice in Wonderland – for there, straight ahead of me, was Tower
Bridge! A little to the right of Tower Bridge rose Nelson's
Column, a full-scale model of it. I felt for a moment I was actually in Trafalgar Square. I rubbed my eyes; but when I opened
them again, both Tower Bridge and Nelson's Column were still
there. Stranger still, they were swarming with monkeys, hundreds

of them. Climbing and sitting. I heard a sound on the path behind me. A creature loped by – I recognized him as the monkey from my cave, with his torn ear. He must have been following me. He joined his companions, skittered to the top of Nelson's Column, sat on Lord Nelson's hat, and calmly continued eating whatever he had been eating.

More facts, as Holmes would say, were required. No use theorizing. I returned along the valley path to the shore and then turned north along the black sand beach.

I was by now very hungry. Along the edges of the sea-blown shore, where black sand met the firmer soil, little trees grew, bearing fruit. I was tempted. But I knew these must be the poisonous manchineel, for which the island was named. I had been warned about manchineel trees years ago, on my first journeys to the West Indies. Never go near them, people said, nor even sit beneath them. The fruit is poisonous. The juice of the manchineel, if it drips on skin, will cause blisters. If eaten, the manchineel fruit will cause wracking pain and perhaps even death.

A half hour's walk brought me in view of the jetty. A sleek motor launch was moored alongside it. A white path ran from the jetty's end across the black beach and up into dense trees. I walked onto the jetty and gazed out over the calm sea.

'Hello there!' said someone.

A man appeared on the deck of the motor launch. I walked toward him.

'Can I help you?' said he, with a note of suspicion in his voice. 'You look a mess.'

'My vessel broke up in the storm,' I said. 'I washed ashore on the south-west side of the island.'

'Good god, man! On the rocks?'

'I was lucky,' I said.

He leapt, a bit stiffly, off the deck of the launch and onto the dock. He came toward me. His unusual face, narrow, with eyes too close together, and yet oddly handsome, was by now widely known, for it had appeared on all the front pages of the world.

'You remind me of someone,' I said, pausing as if puzzled. 'Are you Mr Gurloch?'

'I am.'

'If you don't mind my asking . . . where are we?'

'We are on my island,' he replied. 'Where did you think you might be?'

'I haven't the foggiest,' said I. 'I chartered a boat in Bequia to take me to Battawia and Balliceaux. By the time we reached those islands, the storm was at full blow, and my captain was drunk. We were forced to sail on. Eventually we capsized. Captain Huggles is on the rocks – dead, I fear. I couldn't get down to him.'

He put a finger to his lips, gazed at me as if considering my tale. At last he seemed satisfied. He took a brisk breath, motioned vigorously, and said, 'Come along, lad. Let us get you some food and a place to clean up. You look like you've been sleeping in dirt.'

'In a cave.'

Gurloch wore white cotton trousers, white deck shoes, a blue-and-white striped pullover shirt. An old but vigorous man in bright clothes. I followed him to the end of the jetty and onto the white stone path that led uphill through the trees.

'On the charts this is Manchineel Isle,' said he, 'but I call it Monkey Island.'

'I can see why. I've never seen so many monkeys!'

'Oh!' he said, with some alarm. 'Did you venture up a valley?'

'I did. I noticed some structures rising above the trees, and I hoped they indicated civilization. Imagine my surprise when I came upon Tower Bridge and Nelson's Column – both covered with monkeys.'

'I built them as a playground. You see, Mr . . .?'

'Farley, Ernest Farley.'

'. . . Mr Farley, this entire island is a monkey refuge. I founded it a decade ago. My mission is to save the unwanted monkeys of India, give them a good home in a natural setting. You may have heard of the monkey overpopulation problem in India.'

'I have. Rhesus Macaques are filling the cities, accosting people and demanding their bags of bread. Even snatching their food. And no one can stop them because the monkey is sacred to the Hindu.'

'Terrible problem,' said Gurloch. 'People suffer, monkeys suffer. I'm doing my small part to alleviate the misery. Of course, it is a problem that can never really be solved.'

'Too many monkeys,' I said.

'On the contrary, Farley. Too many people. Seven billion and counting. Where *would* monkeys go but into the city, when people have chopped down their forests? We have built cities on their land – is it not so? And where would tigers go, when villagers have chopped down their habitat, other than into those villages?'

'You have a point,' said I.

'The world is sinking under the weight of people. Even if six billion people were eliminated tomorrow, that would still leave a billion, which is far too many for a healthy planet . . . ah, but here we are.'

Just ahead loomed a large and freshly painted Victorian house, with gables and peaks and very steep roofs. Gurloch hurried lightly up the front steps onto the boat-deck porch. He waved his arm as if to comprehend the whole place. 'Built in 1850 by Captain Arnold Blakeney, refurbished by yours truly in 1980. A desolate wreck when I bought it. I trust you will find it comfortable here, Farley, until we find a way to get you back to Bequia. One of my men is due here with his boat later this evening, and tomorrow he goes back to Antigua. I expect that he will be willing to deposit you in Bequia on his way north.'

'Most appreciated,' said I.

The silence of the trees was astounding. 'Are there no monkeys at this end of the island?' I asked.

'Mostly they stay near Tower Bridge. That's where they are fed.'

'When I awoke in the cave I was greeted by a monkey with a torn ear. He was gazing at me as if I were a strange form of life.'

'That would be Charlie.' He laughed. 'He's a roamer.'

'No research is done here, no profits made?'

'You talk like a true businessman, Farley! But this island is dedicated not to any business but monkey business. I love these little creatures. I have found that research of any sort leads always to more research, and somewhere along the line – if not immediately – it leads to making the subjects of the research uncomfortable, intruded upon, deflected from the normal channels of their lives, and, in most cases, dead. This I will not stand for. I want my monkeys happy – queer though it may sound for a man like me to say so.'

'It sounds to me not queer, but kind.'

'This is the sitting room. You are welcome to make yourself completely at home here until supper time, my friend. Meanwhile, I have duties to attend to. There are shelves of books, as you can see, just help yourself – now come up these stairs and I will show you to your bedroom, and how to find the bathroom.'

The bedroom featured a four-poster bed with vanilla-colored canopy and a grand white mosquito net that was bunched at the top and hung down beneath the canopy in a white mist. Victorian dresser and high mirror, two cane-bottom chairs, side table with what might have been a genuine Tiffany lamp on it. Two windows looked out into a deep ravine. The ravine was filled with trees and vines, gloomy green, swimming in bubbles of light, its silence pierced by occasional whistles of birds. The deep ravine ran down toward the sea and I could see, beyond the green tangle, a slice of blue water. A massive smooth-barked tree reached one limb toward my window, as if to beckon me out.

Gurloch again urged me to make myself at home, and he said, 'Super at six?'

'That would be wonderful.'

'Meanwhile, I'll have the girl bring you something to nibble on.'

I went down the hall and took a bath to wash off the sea salt and cave dirt. I was disappointed that I had no fresh clothes to step into afterward. My khaki pants were dry but grubby.

When I returned to my room I noticed an oddity: the bedroom door could be bolted from the outside. I wondered if old Captain Blakeney had had a mad wife, or an insane brother, or something of that sort, whom he had locked in my bedroom. It was a curious old house.

On the table in my room I found a plate of cheese, crackers and fruit. Also a wine glass and a bottle of Chambertin, a whisky glass and a bottle of Hankey Bannister Scotch, a water glass and a pitcher of water with lemon slices. Whatever else might be said of Gerald Gurloch, he was an excellent host.

He also proved an intriguing conversationalist. At six I descended to the dining room. Gurloch sat at one end of a long mahogany table, I at the other, and on each side of the table places were set for three. I wondered who the other six guests might be. A young woman appeared and set our plates before us – lamb cutlet, mint jelly, boiled potatoes with parsley, green beans almandine, all very nicely presented. Also a salad.

'Thank you, Ambrosia.'

'Yes, sir,' said she.

'I hope you like lamb chops,' said Gurloch.

'Very much,' said I.

'Lamb from my own flock in Scotland,' said he. 'A breed I have developed myself. This lamb on our plates was slaughtered less than a week ago.'

'Excellent!' I said.

Gurloch went on to talk about his farming operations – his cattle operations in Scotland and Australia, his poultry plants in Poland – and then, quite naturally, he began to talk about his slaughterhouses, and how he was attempting to make them efficient so that even the poor could afford the best cuts of meat. 'But this monkey refuge is more pleasure to me than all my meat money,' he said, and he laughed a strange laugh.

'I am a little puzzled,' I said. 'I have read that you are accused of operating slaughterhouses that are peculiarly cruel and in defiance of animal welfare codes – but, having talked to you, I can scarcely believe it.'

'Not *peculiarly* cruel, Farley – merely ordinarily cruel. There is no slaughterhouse that is anything but cruel, whatever anyone may tell you – kindness makes no profits.' He laughed a stern laugh.

'But don't you see something of a contradiction here, Gurloch? You go to great expense to save and care for monkeys, but you . . .'

'Oh, certainly, certainly!' He waved his arm brusquely. 'I minister to monkeys but I carve up cows?'

'Yes.'

'Human nature, Farley. If you think about it, you'll notice that same contradictory trait in nearly every human you meet – full of flowing kindness for their pets, which they treat like family, while simultaneously supporting the meat industry by eating beef or lamb or pork seven days a week – and what they are supporting is cruel, believe me. We jam our animals into a whirlwind of death. They are frightened, terrified. Animals are not stupid, Farley. They smell death, hear death, know it is coming. I do not delude myself. The great majority of mankind live in delusions of all sorts, pretending not to know what they really *do* know. But I choose to look at my nasty nature – my cruel, human, and selfish nature – to look myself straight in the face . . . my face in the mirror. I am of the same vicious nature as all the other vicious little monkeys of our breed – except (though I brag a little to say so) I am more honest than most.'

The topic was depressing me. I wished I had not brought it up. I was no longer enjoying my lamb very much.

'But I presume your mass media holdings remain your main money-spinners?' said I.

'That is where my power lies,' said he.

'You are to be envied.'

'I wonder,' said he. 'I wonder if I am to be envied. But it is certainly true I have great power. Perhaps too much. Many say I have too much, Farley. And they may be right. But if so, it is not my fault.'

'No?'

'Fault of democracy itself. Politicians are bought and sold. That's the game. I didn't make the rules.'

'No.'

'What would you have me do, Farley – let someone else buy off these politicians, let some other big-money buyer call the shots? No, thank you very much! Why should I? I am not a terribly smart man, Farley. But it has always been my belief that I am about as smart as the next fellow.' He laughed again. 'That is what everyone figures, don't they?'

'I imagine they do.'

'There isn't a dolphin in the sea who doesn't think he is as smart as every other creature on earth.'

'He may be right, if he's a dolphin.'

'You like the wine?' He tipped the glass to his lips.

'Excellent. It is all most excellent.'

He nodded, waved a hand dismissively. 'So I figure that my influence and my mad ideas may as well prevail as some other jackass's. I suspect my ideas are about as good as anyone else's – and my ideas make me happy.'

'Makes sense. Then you don't see it as blackmail?'

'Nonsense. It is no different with me than with any other

cockroach in the kingdom. Except that my money amplifies my voice.'

'Your money and your newspapers.'

'Quite true. It is a matter of neither influence nor blackmail, but of discussion. Discussion is the foundation of democracy, is it not?'

'So they say.'

'Look, Farley. If I tell some politician – the PM, for instance – my view of what his policy in a certain area should be, he can do what I suggest, or not do it. As he pleases. And if I agree with what he does, it is my duty to support him. But if I disagree with what he does, it is equally my duty to refute him, and boot him, if I can. Isn't that fair?'

'It sounds fair,' I said.

He gazed at me intently. He slowly put a forkful of lamb into his mouth, chewed. He shrugged. 'Yes, but you are right. Too much power. I've overdone it, no doubt. I am subject to hubris, to delusions of grandeur. A lot of tommyrot is wasted on proving what we know in advance is false. Still, what to do?'

He went on in that vein, humble one moment, assertive the next. We touched on many a topic, but I was unable to learn anything further about this island and the secrets which I felt certain must be hidden here. Gurloch several times mentioned servants, and also mentioned the servants' quarters. Evidently those servants' quarters were located somewhere in Tower Bridge valley. I wondered what duties the servants performed, and how many there were. But always some awkward twist in the conversation prevented me from asking. I was grateful that he seemed so incurious about my own life. Only once or twice was I called upon to make up plausible lies about the life of Ernest Farley.

He must have noticed me glancing from time to time at the empty place settings and empty chairs on either side of the table, for by and by he said, 'You are curious, Mr Farley?'

'I am, a little.'

'My friends will be coming shortly. I only invite them for dessert – I hope you enjoy them.'

'I am sure I will,' said I.

Ambrosia appeared carrying a tray that held eight dishes of

flan, each with a flourish of whipped cream on top. She set them all carefully in place. She said, 'Your guests are gathered in the waiting room, sir.'

'Then, by all means, send them in!'

I was most interested to meet these mysterious guests. Presumably they were at least part-time residents of the island, and it occurred to me that if only I listened carefully to their conversation, and was just a little artful in my own conversation, I might latch on to valuable information about this island, and what went on here. The door opened. Excited voices in the hallway. Six monkeys swept in and, in a single breath, flew up on to their chairs and looked about expectantly.

'Welcome, gentlemen!' said Gurloch.

Three of the monkeys gave him a cursory salute. The other three looked confused, moved their lips in a weird monkey manner.

'Help yourselves, gentlemen,' said Gurloch.

The monkeys picked up their spoons and ate the flan, smacking their lips as they did so.

'They are quite well schooled in table manners, as you can see,' said Gurloch.

'They twitch a bit,' said I.

He laughed. 'But dukes and duchesses twitch even more.'

Ambrosia brought in a tray of mangos. She set two mangos by each plate.

'Help yourselves, gentlemen.'

The monkeys took him up on his offer, and grabbed mangos and began to strip them to the core with their active lips and teeth.

When they had nearly finished, Gurloch cried, 'Food fight!'

The monkeys began pitching fruit at each other, screaming, jumping up and down on their chairs.

I didn't ask. I began to think that I had stumbled upon a madhouse. Could even Holmes have made head or tail of all this nonsense?

After supper Gurloch and I left the monkeys to their fun – one seemed to be reading a book – and we retired to the pool room. He and I shot a game of eight ball, which I won easily. He was not much of a pool player. He then became confidential, told me he had an important meeting this evening. He asked me if I would be good enough to keep to my room. 'You have come at an inconvenient time,' he said. 'But if you just stay in your room, all will be well.'

I could only enthusiastically agree. Accordingly, after a few words of thanks, I ascended the staircase, found my room, closed the door, and sat down to write in my journal all that I had experienced.

SEVENTEEN
Under the Window

I had been writing in my journal only a short while when there came a soft knock at my door. Ambrosia entered, smiled. 'Hello, sir! Here is a little something to refresh you.' She set a tall iced drink on the side table. She bowed slightly, and disappeared, and the door closed.

Light was failing beyond the window. Tree frogs had begun to sing, a massive pulsing chorus coming out of the gloomy ravine that led down to the sea. At supper all had seemed normal enough – until the monkeys arrived, of course. But now again I felt as if I were in a strange world, full of dangers. I took the life-sensor device out of my pocket and pushed its little switch to '*on*'. I examined the small plastic pistol to make sure I knew how it worked. I slipped both back into my pockets and returned to writing my journal. I had not written half a page when the life-sensor began to chime, warning me someone was near. I presumed the lovely Ambrosia was returning. I watched the door . . . but the door did not open. I switched off the life-sensor chime. Then I heard ice clink in a glass. I turned. Behind me was the monkey with the bad ear. 'Charlie?' I said.

Charlie made a sound, tilted the iced drink to his lips and set about drinking it – a little awkwardly at first. He managed, however, to drink it up. He seemed amused when an ice cube toppled out of the glass and fell to the floor. Charlie began making strange croaking sounds. I assumed they were normal monkey sounds.

The glass fell out of Charlie's hands and thudded onto the floor and rolled without breaking.

Charlie wobbled as he walked back toward the window whence he had entered. He slumped to the floor.

The powers of Sherlock Holmes were not required to deduce what had just occurred. I hoped Charlie was alive. If he was dead, it meant they wanted *me* dead. I knelt by him. He was breathing. I pulled the little guy as gently as possible across the wooden floor and pushed him under the bed, letting the bedspread fall so he could not be seen. I then lay down on the floor near the fallen glass and the scattered ice cubes, positioning myself so that I could look out from under my forearm with one eye and see the doorway. I suspected that the thud of the glass falling, and the thump of Charlie falling, would prompt someone to look in on me to make sure that their concoction had worked. And I was right. I had lain there only three or four minutes when the door opened a crack. The young woman's face appeared. She came a few steps into the room. I hoped she would come no closer. She didn't. Evidently satisfied that I was out cold, she retreated, closing the door gently behind her. I heard the click of the deadbolt.

The sound of her footsteps faded away. I got to my feet and pulled the little fellow out from under the bed, back to the spot he'd fallen. He was breathing peacefully.

The long limb of the tree by my window tempted me. Surely that had been Charlie's route into my room. Sitting doing nothing is one of the hardest things in the world to do, and I've never been good at it. I did not intend to sit and await whatever fate Gurloch had planned for me. I gazed at the configuration of the dark tree for a long while. It was a tree with lots of limbs extending from the main trunk, limbs going all the way down to within seven or eight feet of the ground. I wondered how difficult it would be to get out that way. The problem with growing old is that one is liable to use what one has done in earlier days to judge what one can do now – which seems logical enough at first blush. But it is a method that invites miscalculation. I tried to take into account that my strength was probably not now as great as I imagined. Still, if I could get onto the window sill and step onto the nearest limb while holding onto the limb above with my hands, that would be the hard part. I could then make my way toward the trunk and go down in relative safety, one limb to the next, almost like descending a circular staircase, moving slowly down and down until I got to where I could hang and drop to the grass. I could then do a little exploring in the dark, and try to learn what was going on here. At some point in the evening I might simply walk back into the house as if nothing had happened. And the serving girl would be accused of having mistaken the monkey for me – impossible as that seemed. But what other explanation could there be? I would say that I had gone out right after she'd left the drink, and, despite my promise to stay in my room, had wandered into the dark to cure the claustrophobia which had been, I would say, a problem all my life.

Such was my murky plan as I stood up on to the sill of the tall window. I stepped out onto the near limb with a tentative foot, grabbed the limb overhead, made the move. In an instant I was free . . . I was committed to the tree. I felt my foot wobble, made a quick adjustment, soon was close to the trunk. I made my way down slowly, methodically, taking care always to attain a firm foothold before I loosened my handhold, and a firm handhold before I loosened my foothold. Down and down through the dark I went, feeling suddenly the charm of childhood – rough bark under my hands, stars scattered above me in black gaps of sky, tree frogs singing in the leaves, everything strange.

I reached the level of the window below mine. I paused to rest, and to contemplate my next move. Suddenly light flooded the window and a large sitting room appeared, as if a movie had been suddenly flicked on in mid scene. I heard voices, and an instant later I saw three men stroll into view.

'Jack, you'll need to return to London as soon as possible,' said Gurloch. 'I want you ready to act the moment I am charged with a crime.' He brusquely motioned toward chairs round the coffee table. The two men who had followed him into the room sat down as he directed. One was the man I had met on the patio of the Frangipani Hotel in Bequia, the tall, slender and slouching Dunstable Smith. The other was Bedford Brock, the barrel-chested man whom Holmes had ordered out of the dining room of the Dorchester Hotel.

'Do you think they will charge you, Gerald?' asked Brock.

'I suspect they might. And do you know, gentlemen, I almost hope they do?' He laughed.

'How you talk, Gerald!' Brock shook his head.

'He has a *plan*,' said Smith, 'and the plan is me.'

'If they charge me,' cried Gurloch, 'England will regret it mightily!'

'Don't be foolish,' said Brock.

Ambrosia appeared with a tray of drinks. She set the tray on the coffee table and then lifted off the glasses and set one before each of the men.

'Merci, sweet wench!' said Dunstable Smith.

'If they charge me with a crime,' said Gurloch, 'I will bring down, before the eyes of all the world, three of England's most honored symbols.'

'And what might those be?' asked Brock.

Gurloch took a sip of his drink, and smiled. He touched his cheek, as if being puckish. 'I will destroy first Sherlock Holmes, then Lord Nelson's column, and then the Queen.'

'You are either joking or mad,' said Brock, and he took a sip of his drink.

'Not at all.'

'Talk sense, Gerald.'

'And Jack, here, is my man,' said Gurloch, touching Dunstable Smith's arm. 'You *can* do it, can't you, Jack?'

'Hacking Jack Hawes never promises what he can't perform,' said Smith. 'The plans are in place. 'twill be quite easy. My hacking groups in Bloomsbury, Mysore and Moscow have arranged everything so that nothing can be traced.'

'I have an idea,' said Brock, and his face shone rosy beneath his red hair. 'Why not blow up Parliament.' He laughed.

'We have considered that,' said Gurloch.

'But it is too crude,' said Smith.

'I don't want to be remembered as Guy Fawkes the Second,' said Gurloch. 'I prefer, my dear Brock, to be unique.'

'You're serious, are you?'

'Quite serious. We will move like lightning. The day after I am charged by the Crown Prosecution Service we will destroy Sherlock Holmes. The day after that we will destroy Nelson's Column. And the day after that we will begin destroying the reputation of the Queen. It must be a one-two-three punch that is so clear, so concise, that no one will mistake the meaning of it all, or doubt who did it – though no one will be able to prove who did it.'

'You astonish me!' said Brock, and his burly body quivered as he got out of his chair and walked in a circle and paced to the end of the room.

'I had intended to use standard terrorist and criminal tactics,' said Gurloch, 'but Hacking Jack has convinced me that cyber methods are more certain, more subtle, more memorable, and more suited to modern taste. We will send Holmes whirling to his death in his Aston Martin, we will blow up Nelson's Column with a Queen Anne furniture van, and we will destroy the Queen with doctored email data that is so complete and so convincing that her reputation will never survive our attack.'

'We have hacked into emails of the Royal Family,' said Smith. 'By changing certain words, altering texts just a little, we have constructed a scandal that will be hard for her to disprove. She will, by the time we finish with her, be reviled by all but her most ardent supporters.'

'The first story about the Queen will come out three days after I am charged. Just a hint of scandal. But that story will build, will be followed by more stories in the days that follow, until most of the world cannot help but believe, absolutely, in her guilt – and the rest will have such grave doubts that the effect will be the same as if they fully believed.'

'And Holmes?' asked Brock.

'He must be the first,' said Gurloch. 'The death of Sherlock Holmes, the column vanishing from Trafalgar Square, the defaming of the Queen. That must be the order. If it takes a day's delay to eliminate Holmes from the face of the earth, so be it. But the rest must follow immediately – one, two, three.'

'*Eliminate Holmes* is easily said,' said Brock. 'But the doing is another thing. He is a clever man.'

'Hah! The cemeteries are full of clever men!' sneered Gurloch.

'Even the cleverest of men,' said Smith, 'are easily brought down by a proper cyber attack. I suggested making it look like suicide, but Gerald prefers that it be an obvious case of cyber-cide. So that is what we have arranged. When investigators look into the crash, they will see that a malware programme caused the brakes to fail. The coroner's verdict will be "Cybercide".'

'Cybercide?' said Brock nervously. 'Is that a word?'

'It is now,' said Smith.

'But can you really *do* it?'

'If I can't do it, my name is not Hacking Jack Hawes!' said Smith.

'Jack, you need to get back to London within a week,' said Gurloch.

'I'll be there, never worry. Count on it. In a week's time I'll be back on the poop deck, captain of my crew, hacking and cracking in Bloomsbury – and darting out for pub breaks at the familiar old *Friend In Hand*, and altogether enjoying my London life. But first I need a few more days of primitive living, with nothing but wind and waves, and nary an electronic device within leagues of me. Only that can refresh me.'

'You ought to at least have a radio on that boat of yours,' said Gurloch.

'I navigate as they did of old,' said Smith. 'I am a universal man.'

'I am sure you are . . . by the way, a man was wrecked here in the storm yesterday. He needs to go back to Bequia. Can you take him, land him there on your way north? Like to get him off the island as soon as possible.'

'I'm sure I can bear company as far as Bequia. Where is he?'

'Sleeping upstairs. We arranged for him to sleep very soundly. He won't awaken till morning.'

At those words, I dropped softly to the ground.

By starlight I made my way around the huge old house, and I found the white stone path that led down to the jetty. Matters had suddenly become complicated. It seemed to me I was now in real danger. Smith would recognize me as the man who was keen to go to Manchineel Isle. Bedford Brock could identify me as Holmes's companion at the Dorchester Hotel. And if Gurloch realized I was a danger to his plans, I would likely end up buried at sea in rather short order. I had arrived on the island as a poor wretch down on his luck, and I had caught Gurloch in a sympathetic mood. Why shouldn't he help me? But if I threatened his grand plans it would be another matter altogether.

I reached the jetty, glad of no moon. To the right side of the jetty was tied Gurloch's lovely eighty-foot motor launch, the *Squid* – so named, no doubt, because a squid squirts ink to confuse its enemies. To the left was tied the *Boa,* a rather sweet white sloop, nicely rigged. I wondered which I should steal. Whether my sailing skills of long ago were equal to the task, I did not know. But the prospect of sailing to Bequia seemed less daunting than that of getting the big motor launch started – which most probably required a key – and figuring out the controls, and how to run it, and doing all this before the sound of the engine brought someone running down from the house. Far easier to step aboard the sloop, cast off, and hope for a fair breeze. So that is what I did.

I stepped aboard, walked quietly across the deck. It seemed unlikely anyone else was aboard. But I could not be sure. So I opened the cabin door, intending to descend the gangway. Instantly the life-sensor began chiming. I then remembered that somewhere down there in the dark – if Smith could be believed – was a boa constrictor. I went back on deck and closed the door. I cast off. The breeze pushed me clear of the jetty, toward open sea. I pulled up the jib, leapt to the wheel. I had no idea yet whether I was getting on in the right direction, but at least I was getting on. I headed west by the compass, then tied the wheel and hurried to the mainsail, and winched it up . . . and the wind took hold and began to draw, and suddenly I was moving along at a pretty good clip, and the wood was creaking and yawning, for it was an old wooden boat. My plan was to steer for the lights of Bequia, when I could spot them. I would either try to drop anchor in Admiralty Bay, or just let her go with the wind beyond the harbor entrance, and drop the dinghy off near the beach and row ashore. The latter plan would have certain advantages, such as avoiding the possibility of smacking into someone else's boat in the crowded harbor, and also not having to account for myself if someone saw me sail in.

After half an hour I began to worry I might run aground on

Battawia or Balliceaux, for I could not see well. By and by I saw the outline of Battawia. I steered so as to miss her by a good bit. In starlight the sea was a bigger mystery than ever, just patches of darkness sparked occasionally by little flicking whitecaps. Far ahead I could see a sprinkle of lights, as if a patch of the starry sky had fallen down to the sea. I thought it must be Bequia. I modified course slightly. I was sailing in spanking breeze, the boat was smacking sweetly through modest waves, the air was warm. An occasional splash of spray rose from the prow. I felt confident, free, and quite happy as I steered for my island of fallen stars. Then the life-sensor began to chime its sinister chime.

I turned. A burly man loomed like a phantom. He held a bottle of rum by the neck, wielding it like a club. I darted away and as he swung at me he lost his footing and went sprawling on the deck. He swore, crawled after the bottle, which had hit the wheel but hadn't broken. He got to his feet, holding the bottle as a weapon, and he growled at me, 'What the hell is going on here! I am the mate on this vessel.'

'And I am the captain,' said I, and I pulled the plastic pistol on him.

'What is that!' He laughed. 'A water pistol! I'm going to break you, old man!'

The 'old man' made me lose patience. I shot the bottle and it shattered in his hand. He dropped it, lurched back a couple paces.

'Jesus H . . .!'

'Now you take the wheel, fellow. And steer for St Vincent. You know where St Vincent is?'

He nodded.

'And if you do anything but what I tell you, I will shoot you in the back.'

He took the wheel without further ado, and he steered as I instructed. And so the waves and the stars marched on and when at last we were a couple miles from the island I made him lower the dinghy from its davits, and I instructed him to climb down into the dinghy. And then I threw him the oars. I left him wallowing in the troughs, and I sailed on. I neared the harbor and managed to bring the boat about and set a new tack, heading her out to sea. It was risky, for the shore was sliding by only a hundred yards away. I jumped. I swam in to shore without much difficulty. When I crawled up on the beach I turned and could barely see the white sail of the *Boa* afar off in the starlight. She was now a runaway.

I did not feel in exactly splendid shape. But my passport, credit cards and cash were safe in their plastic bag, deep in a pouch pocket. I was on the island, and for the moment was out of the reach of Gurloch and his shadowy minions. I was tempted to go to a hotel and sleep, and then perhaps tomorrow go to the Aquatic Club where I had hung out forty years before, and where I had met a beautiful girl named Kathy Mercury – and then I should have liked to have gone to the other end of the island, and to have climbed the volcano that Kathy and I had climbed so long ago – our 'peak experience' as we called it, climbing up through the banana plantation. But I had no time. Instead, I went directly to the airport, tired as I was. The rising sun and the prospect of new motion revivified me momentarily. I caught the first morning flight out to Barbados. In Barbados I was lucky to get a seat on a British airline bound for Gatwick, leaving in an hour. Late that evening I was home in Dorset Square. I felt very odd as I got out of the taxi. My adventure had happened so quickly that it seemed almost a dream. I wearily climbed the stairs to our flat, opened the door. 'Holmes!' I called. 'I'm back.'

No answer.

It was late but I decided to wake him up. I opened his bedroom door. But he wasn't there.

I was so exhausted that I could barely stand, and I went to my room, took a shower despite my weariness, then turned back the cover on my bed. But before I fell into sheets and slept the sleep of the dead, I found pinned on my pillow this note, in Holmes's hand, in the violet ink he always used in his fountain pen:

My Dear Wilson,

    No electronic communication is safe. Write C/0 Hôtel Beau Rivage, Quai du Mont Blanc 13, CH 1201, Genéve, Suisse. I will await you there until July 3. I am booked in the name of David Garrick.

    S H

    P.S. Lancy is with Mrs Cleary for the week.

EIGHTEEN
Jeremy Bentham, 1789

I got an afternoon flight to Geneva, took a taxi to the hotel, and found Holmes in the bar talking to a young woman about his adventures in Switzerland in 1892. As we three enjoyed a second round of drinks, he went on to tell her about the present case. I thought this odd.

'I am now off to see one of the best computer hackers in the world,' said Holmes.

'Really?' said Martine.

'I am told he is an expert in stealing secrets. Naturally, that is of great interest to me.'

'But whose side is he on, Sherlock? Is he a good guy or a bad guy?'

'I hope to find that out.'

'Oh, I must go,' she said, 'or I'll be late. It has been so nice talking to you – I didn't know before today whether you really existed!'

'I have often wondered myself,' said Holmes.

She laughed, tossed her pretty blonde hair, rose, and Holmes and I rose with her. And then she was gone.

'You seem to have a way with young women, these days,' I said.

'Passes the time. But what did you learn in the Caribbean?'

So I told him all that had happened. When I had finished, he looked very sober. 'Matters have taken a serious turn, it seems.' He frowned. 'Gurloch's schemes are so grand as to seem the ravings of a madman, and yet he cannot be ignored. The man's life thus far has been almost a fairy tale of evil accomplishment.'

'There is no doubt that he believes he can do whatever he sets out to do.'

Over supper that evening Holmes told me that Andrew Swann had invited us to his chalet, near Martigny, to discuss his father's death and its connection to his mother's death, Gurloch, and the government.

'And how did Andrew Swann convey that invitation?' I asked.

'By email – I take your point, Wilson.'

'So anyone might know.'

'Might.'

'There are so many pieces to this puzzle,' said I, 'that I am bewildered.'

Holmes did not answer. Except to say, 'Dessert?'

'Just coffee for me.'

That night in our room he sat up late reading the book he had bought at Quaritch's.

'If I were to employ your own methods, Holmes,' said I, 'I might observe that the book you are reading both disturbs and intrigues you. I suspect you do not wish to believe Henry Salt's arguments on behalf of animals, but you are being forced, by their logic, to believe them. And this puts you in a bad mood.'

'How irritating!' he cried.

'Pardon me?'

'I have just realized that breaking into someone's mental processes can be most irritating. I have done it for years to you and to Watson, without realizing the effect it might have. And now you have just done it to me, and I did not find it pleasant. Serves me right.'

'People do like to have privacy in thinking their own thoughts,' I said. 'It is not altogether pleasant to be intruded upon.'

'Mind you, I don't promise to stop!'

'I could hardly expect you to change your habit of two lifetimes!'

'Thank you, Wilson.'

'But I take it, then, Holmes, that my reading of your thoughts on this occasion was rather accurate.'

'Perfectly so.'

'Would you like me to reveal my method of deduction?'

'Let me guess,' said he. 'You observe that I have been reading this book for days, that in reading it I frown much of the time and look uneasy, yet that I do not clap it closed and cry "Absurd!" as is my impatient habit when I encounter arrant nonsense.'

'That's about it,' said I.

He opened the book again. 'Henry Salt's arguments on behalf of animals' rights are eminently reasonable, and cannot be faulted as far as I can tell. But, I tell you, Wilson, adopting his point of view would entail overturning the world order, overthrowing the habits of millennia and subverting a founding principle of civilization itself.'

'Overthrowing the habits of millennia,' said I, 'sounds like the very definition of how a civilization advances. We no longer keep slaves, Holmes, though every previous great civilization did – the Romans, the Greeks, the Persians, the—'

'Salt makes that very point. He quotes Jeremy Bentham who observes that superficialities like color of skin are "no reason why a human being should be abandoned, without redress, to the caprice of a tormentor". And then Bentham asks where the line should be drawn that defines which creatures should have the same rights and protections that humans have given themselves. And I quote: "What else is it should trace the insuperable line? Is it the faculty of reason, or, perhaps, the faculty of discourse? But a full-grown horse or dog is, beyond comparison, a more rational, as well as more conversable animal than an infant of a day, a week, or even a month old. But suppose the case were otherwise, what would it avail? The question is not, Can they *reason*? Nor, Can they *talk*? But, Can they *suffer*."'

'I hope, Holmes,' said I, 'that you are not going to be demanding a change of diet.'

The following morning we drove past Montreaux and the Castle of Chillon and into the Valley of the Rhône, and we reached Martigny very early. Holmes tapped the proper coordinates into the GPS device. Soon we were turning off the main drag into side roads. We scooted up a sharp incline toward a chalet among pines. 'Finding an address is astonishingly easy with this device,' said he.

The car rolled to a gritty stop on gravel. Overhead black choughs squawked and sailed, and across the broad limb of a tree two squirrels skittered fitfully in their stop-and-start way. Several cars and a gleaming black motorcycle were parked in the drive.

Andrew Swann, alias Black Swan, opened the door to greet

us. He was wearing a white golf shirt, flip-flops, baggy hiking shorts. 'Come in, gentlemen! Welcome! And this is Jenny!'

The girl was even more perfect in face and figure than her sister Victoria, whom we had met at the pub in St Albans. Subtle differences between her and her twin made all the difference – a slightly slimmer jaw, a wider look of wonder in her eye, a sweetness to the movement of her upper lip that her sister lacked. Her hair, however, was identical to her sister's, long and red with a hint of auburn. Jenny wore a silky white blouse, very short red shorts, white tennis shoes, a simple blue band in her hair. 'Good afternoon Mr Holmes, Mr Wilson. We have been waiting for you with great anticipation.'

They gave us a little tour of the chalet, pointing out a photograph of Andrew's father in his Hollywood days, an antique piano that his mother had bought in Austria, and so on. We passed through a large dining room. The gleaming table was empty save for a single laptop computer which sat glowing white against the dark cherry wood. 'In that computer may lie the fate of a nation,' said Andrew.

Jenny laughed.

'The day is so nice that I thought we might take brunch on the patio,' said Andrew. 'Canyon and Victoria intended to be here, but he got called away to business in Prague, and Victoria decided to go with him. Oh . . . here is my sister Amy.'

Flip-flopping across the patio stones came a small dark-haired woman. 'Mr Holmes, I have read all your adventures – you frighten me,' she said.

'I hope not,' said Holmes.

'Your intellect is frightening to an average person.'

'Intellect,' said Holmes, 'is only a small part of a man – and perhaps not the most important part.'

I was taken aback to hear him say it. Every once in a while Holmes falls into these modest moods.

'Come this way,' said Andrew, 'and I will show you the nerve center of my Black Swan operation.'

He led us up to the first floor of the house and into a large room filled with flat-screen monitors, computer consoles, wires, disks, books. 'This is my hacking room,' he said. 'And this is my partner, Sanji Masani.'

I hadn't noticed the small young man behind a mountain of monitors. He stood up, full of smiles. 'How do you do, sirs!'

'In this room,' said Swann, 'we launch our efforts to hack into some of the most sensitive databases in England. Our goal is to save Britain from Big Brother.'

'Orwell again,' murmured Holmes. 'I must read that man.'

'Orwell was wrong only in his dates and details,' said Black Swan. 'In all the essentials his predictions in *1984* were perfectly accurate. Big Brother is here. The government is spying on us, watching our every move – surveillance cameras, computer tracking, wiretapping. But the larger point is that corporations are tracking the every move of every citizen . . . and corporations, of course, are running the government. Everyone knows this: it is common knowledge. But almost no one attempts to do anything about it. First, the toilet syndrome: sit in the stink long enough and you no longer notice. Second, sheer laziness. It is convenient to look up information on the Internet . . . though every time one does, a corporation takes note. It is convenient to have email programmes and services supplied free . . . but the corporations who supply them are watching you, so they are not free after all. Mention *skiing* in a letter, and the next moment an ad for a ski resort appears on your screen. Do a Google search, and Google is watching what you look for, building a profile of your predilections. You are *known* to them. Use a credit card and the credit card company can track you as you spend your way across the country and around the world. Every time you use the Internet, use a bank card, use a mobile phone, you are selling a part of yourself, selling your privacy, for your own convenience. And what allows all this? The computer, of course. The computer has weaved the Web, Mr Holmes, in which many of us now are inextricably entangled. Wiggle a little, and spiders come scurrying to analyse us and paralyse us and suck us dry. For convenience we have sold our souls.' He laughed. 'But I rant. I don't wish to become a bore on the subject. Life must be viewed as largely a joke, and we can only do our best to make the most of it.'

'A moral vision is what we need,' said Amy.

'Morality is not enough.'

'Andrew!'

'*Morality*,' said Andrew, 'is a word that is bandied about till it has become almost meaningless. Everyone talks about it, advocates it – which saves them the trouble of doing anything about it. What is *moral*? Whatever it is, it is not the easy and obvious road so many suppose, but a hard and difficult path that requires making a strenuous intellectual effort not to contradict oneself.'

'He sounds like your kindred spirit, Holmes,' said I.

'I would never imagine myself to be on a logical level with Sherlock Holmes,' said Andrew. 'But let me give you an example of the illogical madness that passes for morality in this country and America. There are large numbers of well-meaning people who oppose abortion, and think that killing four cells with a morning-after pill is grounds for a murder charge. They may be right; I won't argue about that. But they stand in the street protesting abortion of a fetus that by no stretch of the imagination can be called a sensitive being, and yet they have just come from MacDonald's where they have eaten hamburgers to fuel their anger and give them energy for their moralizing – hamburgers that cause real suffering to a real being. A full-grown cow is infinitely more self-aware, more intelligent, and more capable of feeling enjoyment and pain than is a fetus, or even a newborn, or even a child of six months. A cow is full of life, able to enjoy the sun, care for her young, analyze the world, communicate with her kind, feel comfort and pain, know the sweet smell of hay and the bite of winter's cold. And why do these people contradict themselves in this way? Because eating a hamburger tastes good, makes them feel good, and is their habit. They are moralists to a point, only.'

'They will answer,' said Holmes, 'that humans are superior beings.'

'But can you prove that humans are superior beings, Mr Holmes?'

'I cannot.'

'Checkmate! I have put in my "*Frankenstein's Diary*" a little piece from the Washington Post of several years ago – look here, I've just brought it up on this monitor so you can read it.'

'I can see it,' I said. 'But judging by the picture, I am not sure I want to read it.'

'You are not alone,' said Andrew Swann. 'All the world prefers to look away from horrors.'

'Nonetheless I'll read it,' said I.

And I read it.

I confess that I am reluctant to include any of that article in this narrative, since to do so may give the impression I am less a biographer of Holmes than a shock jock, less a historian than a polemicist. And to give that impression would be both unfortunate and false, for I have no desire to upset anyone or to convince anyone of anything. Yet to omit altogether a sample of the article that Andrew Swann thrust upon us that day would be to throw away, I think, a useful key to his character. It would also be to ignore that portion of human nature which so oddly and so often combines kindness with cowardice, and makes men and women rather look away from horrors they abhor than try to halt them. I omit the truly terrifying sections, but here is part of what I read:

> It takes 25 minutes to turn a live steer into steak at the modern slaughterhouse where Ramon Moreno works. For 20 years, his post was 'second-legger', a job that entails cutting hocks off carcasses as they whirl past at a rate of 309 an hour. The cattle were supposed to be dead before they got to Moreno. But too often they weren't.
>
> 'They blink. They make noises,' he said softly. 'The head moves, the eyes are wide and looking around.'
>
> Still Moreno would cut. On bad days, he says, dozens of animals reached his station clearly alive and conscious. Some would survive as far as the tail cutter, the belly ripper, the hide puller.
>
> 'They die,' said Moreno, 'piece by piece.'

NINETEEN
A Call from the Past

Marguerite, the Swiss housekeeper, brought us coffee on the patio. The air was fresh, the mountains high. Amy Swann and Jenny Gurloch sat across from me, looking very young and pristine in the morning light.

'I hope you can recover the painting by Stubbs,' said Amy.

'I know where it is,' said Holmes.

'You *know*?' said Andrew.

Amy looked startled. She took a deep breath, stood up. 'Pardon me. I have a horse to feed.'

She vanished.

My mobile phone buzzed and I excused myself from the table. I walked into the house, through the dim dining room where the lonely white laptop shone on the long table. I did not recognize the number on my phone display. As I stepped out onto the front porch I pushed the button and said, 'Good morning.'

'Mr James Wilson?'

'This is he.'

'You will be surprised,' said the voice, 'to hear from me . . .'

But already I had recognized the faint Swedish accent, so I was only half surprised when he said, 'This is Lars Lindblad. I hope you will forgive me for intruding like this, Mr Wilson. Do you have time for a short visit? I should very much like to see you.'

'*See* me? I'm not in London at the moment . . .'

'I know where you are. You are in a chalet a few miles from Martigny.'

'But how do you know that!'

'My dear Wilson,' said he, 'I employ the very best hackers in the world. My hacker boys – and they are, literally, boys – are far superior to Black Swan's group, or to the Hack Magic Group, or to any other hacking group that I am aware of. As a consequence, I know what is going on with anyone in whom I am interested – and I am, as you know, most interested in Sherlock Holmes. I have a very rare gift I'd like to give you. I'm at a little town called Les Marécottes, not far from you.'

'A gift!'

'I can assure you, Wilson, that my gift will not only delight you, but will enhance your reputation, add luster to the reputation of Sherlock Holmes, stun the *literati*, and please the whole world. Do listen carefully. Go to the Martigny train station. Take the *Chamonix Express*. The first stop is Salvan, the second is Les Marécottes. Get off at Les Marécottes. Climb up from the station into the village above, then walk uphill through the village until you come to a hotel called *Mille Etoiles*. It will be on your right. Les Marécottes is a small village so you won't have any trouble. But you must come soon. Ask for me in the bar.'

I had encountered Lindblad twice before. He was the most wanted criminal in the world, and many believed him to be the world's most dangerous man. But toward me he had always acted as a gentleman, and I had no reason to believe that he had any reason to harm me, or that he would not keep his word.

'OK,' I said, speaking on impulse. 'I'll be there.'

'But there is a proviso, Wilson: you must not tell Holmes.'

'Why ever not?'

'You will understand when I see you.' He rang off.

Suddenly I wasn't sure why I was going. Yet it seemed the thing to do – if for no other reason simply to gain information about the elusive Lindblad. The man had twice in the last eighteen months escaped from Sherlock Holmes.

When I returned to the patio, Holmes and Andrew had disappeared. Jenny said they had gone to see the stable. When Jenny heard I needed to get to the train station, she said, 'I'll take you.'

'Very good of you.'

A few minutes later I was sitting behind her on the Harley. When I asked if I was sitting correctly, she reached back, patted my hand, and she turned her cheek to me and said, over her shoulder, 'Just hang on – trust me.'

'I'm in a trusting mood today,' I said.

Soon our hair was full of wind as we throbbed happily along the river road toward Martigny, *sans* helmets. At the station she told me where to get my ticket. 'Call me if you need a ride back,' she said. She gave me her mobile phone number, which I programmed into my own phone.

'Better take this,' she said.

She pulled a collapsible umbrella out of the saddlebag.

'If Holmes asks,' I said, 'would you tell him I'll be back in an hour or two?'

The cycle revved, shot away like a black bumblebee . . . leaving only a strangely empty street.

I hurried inside, bought my ticket, boarded the train. Soon we slid out of the station and I began to rise out of the valley toward Chamonix. Never had I ridden a train that tilted so steeply. The angle of climb was such that I might have been on a roller coaster. I was pressed back into my seat. Scarcely had we started upward than the skies clouded and it began to rain. I looked back into the blurry valley, surprised at the altitude we had already achieved. When I got off at Les Marécottes the rain was slashing down, runnelling in the dirt. I opened Jenny's umbrella and hiked upward past slate-roofed buildings, upward along the flowing street. I found the Thousand Stars just where I expected it to be. As I reached the door the rain stopped and the sun came out, blazing in a clear sky.

I asked at the bar of the Mille Etoiles for Lars Lindblad, and the girl nodded and hurried away. A few minutes later he appeared, striding with catlike grace into the bar, wearing a white cashmere sweater over a blue shirt, light tan trousers, a pair of easy leather shoes that complemented the rest. He smiled, and we greeted each other. His left hand glowed with two gold rings, one on his pinky and one on his middle finger. In that hand he carried a large, floppy leather case. I knew he had undoubtedly ruined many lives, had outsmarted Interpol for forty years, had recently served up two humiliations to Sherlock Holmes, but he was undeniably charming.

We sat down and we both ordered tea. He was about to explain what was in the leather bag when his phone began to sing *Quando men vo*. He opened it, said 'Ja, ja,' and quickly closed it. 'Never a moment of peace when you have as many enemies as I have, Wilson! Do you mind if we finish this conversation aloft?'

'Aloft?' said I.

'A bit safer for me.'

I shrugged.

'Good sport!' cried he, 'follow on!'

We hurried through the relative gloom of the bar and stepped outside into sharp sunlight that glistened wetly on every surface. Massive clouds sailed overhead like a flotilla of ships in a startling blue sea. I followed him through trees to a clearing where – to my considerable surprise – a large white sailplane lay sleek as a gull on the green grass. He waved me into the front seat, climbed in behind me, pulled the clear canopy over our heads.

'Buckle up, Wilson!'

Scarcely had I done so when I heard the rattle-banging *whuff whuff* of a helicopter. It descended on the far side of the clearing. A man jumped out, ran to our craft. He was hauling a thin cable that split into a Y. He hooked one fork of the Y to the nose of the sailplane, the other somewhere behind. He hurried back to the spinning helicopter, ducking to miss the blades.

'My own invention, this sailplane harness,' said Lindblad. 'Long cable so we don't get buffeted by the downdraft of the copter.'

The helicopter rose far overhead, and slowly the cable tightened . . . and then we were lifted away, we were swinging gently over trees. The village shrank beneath us. At 3,000 feet or so the copter began towing us forward. Lindblad said, 'Pull that little red lever to the right of you, Wilson!'

I pulled it.

The cables detached and the helicopter made its exit into the upper winds. We swooped, caught an updraft, began to rise over the Gorges du Trient. The sudden silence was enormous. Lindblad banked the craft in a tight right turn. We rose up and up, the altimeter spinning. We topped out at a splendid height, whereupon Lindblad tilted the plane and we sailed south, high over the Rhône Valley. Brightness, lightness, airy altitude, strange silence. Mountains were painted delicately on the blue horizon. Switzerland seemed of infinite volume but no weight, turning and turning beneath us.

'A beautiful world, from this plane,' I said.

He must have misheard me, for he replied, 'It is a production model, and it is fully aerobatic – loops, rolls, spins. I have modified it just slightly. I have put an ejection seat in front – a drop seat, rather. If I roll the plane, then pull this lever by my right hand, the front capsule drops out, seat and all, and the occupant has a quick trip to earth.'

'But what is the point of such a device?' I asked, unable to prevent myself from speaking this question.

'It is for people who insist on being difficult. The capsule is designed so that the occupant always lands on his head.' Lindblad laughed. 'It is just for my perverse amusement, really. I have discovered that when you get a man up in this plane, and when he realizes his life is in your hands, a strange psychological change occurs: he becomes more attached to you, more ready to do whatever you suggest. Even after he has landed and is safe, he is more apt to keep promises he might have made or implied – for he is thankful to you for not having taken his life.'

'Very astute,' said I, but I felt a flush of coldness in my heart.

'Here, I'll show you how the thing works . . .'

'You needn't,' I said.

But Lindblad already had put the plane into a shallow dive to increase air speed – and suddenly we rolled . . . I hung upside down as the distant earth slid under my head, and when the canopy slid back I felt a shock of fear . . . wind in my hair.

Then he rolled the plane back upright again, and the canopy slid back into place.

'Breezy,' I said.

'Enough fun for one day. I want to ask you something, Wilson. You've read Dr Watson's tales of Sherlock Holmes's cases.'

'All of them.'

'Do you remember a mention of *Cox and Company*?'

'I believe it occurs in a case called *The Problem of Thor Bridge*.'

'Yes. *The Problem of Thor Bridge* is one of the last sketches of Holmes that Watson ever wrote. And at the beginning of that sketch is a curious note about a tin dispatch-case. I have read that passage so often, over the years, that I have it by heart . . . "Somewhere in the vaults of the bank of Cox and Company, at Charing Cross, there is a travel-worn and battered tin dispatch-box with my name, John H. Watson, M.D., Late Indian Army, painted upon the lid. It is crammed with papers, nearly all of

which are records of cases to illustrate the curious problems
which Mr Sherlock Holmes had at various times to examine".'

'I remember that very well,' I said. 'Though I certainly couldn't
quote it from memory.'

'You may also remember that Watson went on to mention a
few of the cases contained in the papers of that dispatch-box,
such as the case of Mr James Phillimore, who, stepping back
into his own house to get his umbrella, was never more seen in
this world. Also the case of the cutter *Alicia*, which sailed one
spring morning into a small patch of mist from where she never
again emerged, nor was anything further ever heard of herself
and her crew.'

'You have an amazing memory,' I said.

'For what interests me, I do.'

'I wonder,' said I, 'if Holmes actually *worked* on those cases,
or merely examined and discarded them. He is very particular
about what cases he accepts.'

'I suppose he worked on them all,' said Lindblad, 'for the
cases fell, according to Watson, into three categories: those that
were failures and had no conclusion, those that could not be
written up for fear of embarrassing people still living at the time,
and those that were simply surplus. Watson often remarks, you
may remember, that he has more Holmes tales than he thinks
the public will care to read – and presumably far too many to
fill the slots available in the *Strand Magazine*.'

'I do remember him often saying he had to be selective.'

'But as it has turned out, Dr Watson was quite wrong. Had he
published three times the number of tales he actually did publish,
they still would not have been sufficient to satisfy the demand
of the reading public. Which is why we are besieged with so
many impostors – with Sherlock Holmes lookalikes that often
aren't even lookalikes.' He laughed. 'How odd that so many
authors and writers of screenplays think they can create two men
and simply stick labels on them – *Sherlock Holmes* and *Dr Watson*
– and get away with it, even though the two impostors are totally
unlike the originals. Odder still, so fanatical is the interest in
Holmes that most often they *do* get away with it! They cash
in on their modernized Holmeses and Watsons with the greatest of
ease. Much of the public evidently feels that a faux Holmes is

better than no Holmes! No wonder that the matter of the Cox and Company dispatch-box has aroused the curiosity of so many people who have followed Holmes's career. Everyone has wondered, does that dispatch-box still exist, and what exciting adventures might it contain?'

'Until recently,' said I, 'I thought that Cox and Company might have been a fictional bank, dreamed up by Watson to avoid making the real bank a target of criminals.'

Lindblad laughed. 'And then you saw the safe in the study of Sylvia Swann, and realized that the bank really existed.'

'Exactly. But how do *you* know about the safe in Sylvia Swann's study?'

'Dear fellow,' said Lindblad, 'you sent an email to your fiancée, alluding to that safe. I have a copy of your email. That is the only reason, in fact, that you and I are meeting today.'

Lindblad's voice was peculiarly real in the silence of the glider.

We turned and turned like a great white bird above the unreal earth. I heard only the sound of wind, and occasionally the flapping of an aileron – tiny bangs and thuds of the plane itself.

'I came upon that safe at an auction years ago,' said Lindblad. 'The antique dealer was unable to open it, but I knew an elderly Austrian who had done a lot of safe cracking in the old days. I was certain he could open it for me. So I bought the safe in the hope that it might contain the dispatch-box. Klaus Hauptman opened the safe . . . and there it was, the legendary dispatch-box. Pure luck, Wilson! The whole episode was pure luck, start to finish. I immediately sold the safe again, and gave the new owner the combination. A memorable combination it was, for it was the date of England's entry into the Great War, 4 August 1914. 4-8-19-14. A most appropriate combination for Cox and Company, who had been bankers to His Majesty's forces since 1758. That's when the Commander in Chief of British forces appointed his own secretary, Richard Cox, to pay his troops. Later, other regiments used Richard Cox as their agent for the same purpose. By the end of the Napoleonic Wars, Messrs Cox and Company were bankers to virtually the entire British army.'

'I knew you were versed in ancient history,' said I, 'but I had no idea you had such peculiarly detailed knowledge of British military history.'

Lindblad laughed. 'If it has to do with Holmes, I'm interested. The Cox bank headquarters were in Cox's house in Albermarle Street, across from what is now the Ritz Hotel. Later they moved to Craigs Court, Whitehall. In 1888 they moved again, this time to 16 Charing Cross Road, across from the National Portrait Gallery. And there they remained until 1923 when they were taken over by Lloyds. Not too long ago I walked down Charing Cross Road and found number 16. It is now a coin shop – appropriately enough. A large black sign with gold lettering announces "**Gold Coin Exchange**". I went inside to inquire whether this had once been the premises of Cox and Company. But the clerk had never heard of Cox and Company, and was unaware that the shop in which he was dealing coins had any connection to Sherlock Holmes.'

'Dr Watson was an army man,' said I. 'I suppose that is why he chose Cox.'

'Undoubtedly. It is likely that Dr Watson kept an account at Cox and Company while he was in Afghanistan, and that when he was demobbed he retained that account. It would, in that case, be quite natural for him to put his dispatch-box with Cox and Company for safe keeping. What happened to the box during the seventy years or so between the time Watson deposited it and the time I found it in the late seventies, is one of history's little mysteries. The important thing is that I have the box, and all the papers that were in it. And I want you to have them.'

'Good heavens, man! Why?'

'I have enjoyed the way you present Holmes in his modern adventures – and the way you present me.'

'I am astonished!' said I.

'I could niggle over small points in your renderings, of course. Your descriptions of me are not quite as flattering as they might be.'

'Many people have severely criticized me for painting a portrait of you that is altogether *too* flattering – you, an international criminal with blood and booty on his hands.'

'More booty than blood, you must admit.'

'I wouldn't know.'

'When I saw that allusion to the Cox and Company safe in your email, it occurred to me that you might be the natural heir to these papers. What an odd coincidence that Holmes should encounter a client who owns the old Cox and Company safe? I only ask, Wilson, that you agree to write up some of those old cases in the dispatch-box, and present them to the world.'

'It would be a delight to do so.'

'But do not tell Holmes.'

I felt mesmerized by the bright world, the silence, the landscape turning and turning below me. I scarcely realized we were coming down. The nearing earth began to flash by beneath us, faster and faster, fence hedgerow road field sheep (and then a blur of fast-approaching images) *streamchaletpondroadfieldhorsehousefence.*

In a green field we touched down. The brake made a sound. We stopped.

TWENTY
A Tin Box of Old Tales

The beautiful glider seemed like a large toy as we stood beside it on the strangely solid earth. Lindblad pulled the floppy leather case out of the small storage compartment behind his seat. He opened the case and drew out the antique tin dispatch-box. He opened the box and we knelt by it in the grass.

'This box is filled with notes and narratives that I hope you, Wilson, will bring back to life. But it will be a bad mistake if you show these to Holmes. He has vetoed them once – I don't want him to quash them again. You know how he is. Nothing quite suits him. Much as I admire the man as an enemy, he is lacking as a literary critic. His criticisms of Dr Watson's prose style I find, frankly, to be completely off the mark.'

'I must agree,' said I. 'Watson's talent for telling a tale has been somewhat obscured, not only by his own humble nature but, even more, by Holmes's constant disparaging accusations that he, Watson, sensationalized Holmes's exploits. To my mind, nothing could be further from the truth. Watson had the one prime talent required of every artist: he knew what to leave out.'

Lindblad drew from the tin box a typed manuscript titled *The Case of the Guernsey Bull and the Sussex Milkmaid*. It was dated 1890. Across the top of the typescript, in Holmes's familiar hand, was written a note in violet ink: 'Not this one, Watson. It is too sensational. It is my duty to solve sexual crimes of this sort in the public interest, but not my desire to be associated with them in the public mind.'

'If you write this one up,' said Lindblad, 'you will astonish the public and make Sherlock Holmes an even bigger name than he already is – which suits me, of course. For the bigger his reputation, the bigger mine.'

'You surely do not expect me to go against his wishes!' I said.

A cow *moo*ed nearby.

'Oh, come, Wilson. I expect you to circumvent him, politely. Sexual mores have changed. Ideas once properly taboo are now in the common knowledge of every schoolchild. Or look at this one . . .'

He slid another sheaf on top of the pile, and he held the paper in the faintly blowing breeze as I read the typescript's title: '*Notes on the case of the man who died in a hammock*'. And beneath this was a fountain pen instruction in Holmes's hand: 'You certainly have a knack for the macabre, Watson. This piece is exciting, weird, dramatic, shocking, and presented without your usual artistic exaggeration. But my methods are scarcely visible – I was little more than a bystander until the moment I leapt through the skylight and knocked the poisoned pomegranate onto the floor. Please do not use this one. It is frivolous.'

I shrugged. 'Holmes is a stickler for propriety and perfection.'

'A fatal combination. But see what you can do with them, Wilson. They are worth millions. There is a little sheaf of papers in here somewhere . . .' He thumbed through, and the breeze rustled the papers, and he could not find what he was looking for. 'Anyway, it's the Cushington murder case, in which a man was murdered in a haystack on a farm in Surrey in 1890, by his brother, who thereby inherited a large tract of land that should have gone to the murdered man and his family. Holmes never solved the case, but the queer thing is that he might be able to solve it today. DNA testing would be of assistance.

Read the case and see what you think. If he *did* solve it today, the land might be returned to its rightful owners, or their descendants.'

'But why give me the originals, Lindblad?'

'Because you will take care of them.'

He drew a black and gold business card out of his pocket. 'Give this to your friend Andrew Swann, in case he should like a little help. He is undertaking a rather large project, exposing the government and the police. I have resources that might assist him.'

I frowned, while trying to smile. One surprise after another was beginning to make me suspicious of everything.

'Why would you help him?'

'When the Metropolitan Police are undermining democracy, and denying justice to a whole society, they make my own little larcenies – stealing some statues here, some paintings there, some stashes of gold somewhere else – they make all this seem rather petty. I have a reputation to protect, Wilson! When the police become more dangerous to society than I am, where am *I*? Instead of pursuing me, they have, in effect, joined me.'

'You still have Holmes.'

'He alone makes my life exciting, infuses me with energy to get up in the morning. As a boy I dreamed of being pursued by the greatest detective in the world, though of course I knew – or thought I knew – that that was impossible. And then, miraculously . . . the glacier, the amazing Dr Coleman . . . and presto, Sherlock Holmes is back in the world, and is on my track!' He laughed heartily.

'Yes, no doubt you are a fortunate man, Lindblad. For the time being.'

'I am indeed. I have three dangerous gentlemen forever out to ruin me – what more could I ask?'

'Three?'

'Holmes, you, Lestrade. You are the threesome that is always on my track.'

'You view Holmes as an amusing opponent, do you? With whom to play the old crime game? I am not sure he views you in quite the same entertaining light.'

'I *hope* not,' he said.

He leaned into the cockpit and looked at the instrument panel. Then he slipped a pad of paper out of his pocket and wrote on it. 'Here are the coordinates of our location. You are very near the Swann chalet.'

I took the slip of paper. 'Tell me, Lindblad – where is your Grotto of Art?'

'Wouldn't Holmes like to know!'

'I don't mean the exact location, of course. Just the country.'

He laughed again.

'Serves me right,' said I. 'I hoped you might answer before thinking.'

'I'll show you my grotto someday, Wilson. You and Holmes both. When conditions are right.' He stood up and put the dispatch-box back into the larger leather case, and he handed me the case.

'I'll make copies,' I said, 'and deposit the originals in the British Library.'

'Brilliant idea. That way if ever I should want them again, I can simply steal them back.'

'From the British Library?'

'Not difficult if one knows how. I must tell you, Wilson, my first crime was a library robbery. The first crime of my life.'

'Always best to start small.'

'When I was eight years old I checked out a book of Sherlock Holmes stories. I didn't want to take that book back to the library. I told my father that I would not ever take it back. But he said I must. I simply lied to my father, kept the book, and I have it still. And I am very glad I do.'

'You don't really think you can escape Holmes in the end, do you? Be frank.'

'My dear Wilson, I am at an age when I no longer worry about such things. But if you ask me to bet on the question, I would bet against Holmes. It is most unlikely he will ever capture me, either dead or alive. Shall I tell you why?'

'Please.'

'Holmes is the most rational man on earth, but his virtue is his defect. Rationality carries one just so far in this world. He lacks the emotional spark that inspires unexpected action. He is a bloodhound, and relentless. But I am Proteus, and frivolous. I change with every whim that blows through my mind – now a bear, now a bird, now a fish. He won't catch me, Wilson . . . but it will be a close-run race, thank god!'

'While we are being candid, I must ask you: have you murdered people? There seems to be some debate about that. Some say yes, some say no.'

He tilted his head a little, smiled a strange smile. 'I've *killed* people, Wilson. Which is rather a different thing. And since we are being candid, I will tell you that I intend to kill more. A good many more, perhaps. Justice, my dear fellow, often requires killing. A man of your age, I suspect, has already learned that truth – however much you may wish to avoid it.'

Seeing him standing near his white gull, a handsome man of sixty-something, his full head of gray-blond hair lightly fluttering in the breeze, his face faintly tanned, his smile broad and his teeth white, his manner genial, everything about him relaxed and in command – seeing this, I had to admit Lars Lindblad had an aura of invincibility. I felt quite certain that if he decided to kill someone, he would.

'How will you get the plane out of here?' I asked.

He leaned into the plane and pushed something: a propeller unit rose out of the deck behind the cockpit. 'Very slick, aye? It's self-launching. Oh, by the way . . .' He clapped his hand to his breast pocket, then felt into his pants pocket, finally found a flash drive and handed it to me. 'Give this to Holmes. It contains interesting files on a man named Nigel Greenwood. Andrew Swann may have similar files, but I doubt he has these. These will bring the roof down on Nigel Greenwood. There is also a video on that flash drive, just to make certain he cannot slip away.'

'Video?'

'Insurance. I had it made just two days ago, courtesy of a very beautiful and experienced woman friend of mine. Greenwood has a penchant for young dark-haired women.'

'I will do my best with the dispatch-box papers,' I said. 'And I'll give this flash drive to Holmes.'

Lindblad waved his fingers at me in a sort of aristocratic *toodle-doo,* and he climbed into his plane.

As I walked away across the field I heard a whirring behind

me. When I looked back a huge white gull was rising slowly from the field, seeming barely to move at all.

I stumbled into a grassy ditch, got back to my feet, brushed myself off. I climbed a wooden fence. When I looked back a second time the gull had shrunk into the western sky, was but a tiny scrawl of white.

I phoned Jenny Gurloch and gave her the coordinates. She found me with no trouble, only a few minutes later. I climbed up behind her and she whirled me back to Andrew's chalet – me clutching the leather bag full of priceless papers.

She stopped the cycle and kicked down the stand, and the silence swept in. As I got awkwardly off, and stumbled, she laughed, turned, quickly kissed my cheek. 'Be careful, silly,' she said.

I put the floppy leather case into the boot of the Aston Martin, and I covered it with my jacket. The flash drive I brought immediately to Holmes and gave it to him, saying, 'You will find this interesting, but you must not ask me where I got it. Lestrade's career may depend on it.'

As Sherlock Holmes held up the little metal info cache in his thin fingers, and squinted at it curiously, I had the feeling that already he was trying to trace the flash drive (by insignificant markings, circumstances, vibrations, indications beyond the ken of most men) back to its source. I had a feeling I would never keep my secrets from him.

TWENTY-ONE

Death in the Mountains

Black Swan suggested we have a late lunch on the patio. Marguerite, the Swiss housekeeper, had just taken our drink orders when Victoria Gurloch and her uncle Bedford Brock made an unexpected appearance. They had come up in Brock's car from Gerald Gurloch's house down the valley. Victoria explained that she had decided at the last minute not to go to Prague with Canyon.

'Surprised to see you here, Mr Holmes,' said Brock.

'The surprise is mutual.'

'My sister's girls, Mr Holmes, are my favorite people in all the world.' He laughed. He seemed, in this setting, altogether different than he had seemed in the dining room of the Dorchester Hotel or in the house on Manchineel Isle. He wore riding boots, tight trousers, a blousy white shirt that made him look like a cavalier, and he carried a riding crop which he tapped nervously against his left brown boot.

'Uncle Bedford is our protector,' said Jenny.

'Yes, yes – and a fine job I do of it, too. I try to protect them from the radical ideas that are so prevalent in this house, Mr Holmes – but I fail. Vegetarianism – ye gods, what next?'

'Do give it a rest, Uncle,' said Jenny.

'Your father owns slaughterhouses, grocery stores, and fishing fleets,' cried Brock. 'A shame to go against your own father, my lass, for a mad idea like that.'

'I would call it a healthy idea,' said Jenny.

Victoria looked sarcastic and sulky. She shook her head, as if she just couldn't grasp the situation, or as if she had just had enough. 'Jenny, you are a ridiculous case.'

'You cannot give me a single justification for eating some poor animal,' said Jenny. 'So do let us drop this tedious topic. We have gone through it all before.'

'No justification!' cried Bedford Brock. 'We are more intelligent than the animals we eat – *that's* the justification.'

Sherlock Holmes raised his index finger in the air. 'Then either I can kill you and eat you for lunch, Mr Brock, or you can kill me and eat me. For one of us, of course – by whatever test you choose – must be more intelligent than the other.'

'But we are humans, Mr Holmes!'

'What has that to do with the price of wheat?' asked Holmes.

'I like meat, Mr Holmes. That's the reason.'

'Ah! Meat is Right – *that's* the argument.'

'Very clever, Mr Holmes. But Might *is* Right. It's the way of the world.'

Victoria looked piqued. Moods seemed to flow over her like passing clouds across the sun. She glared at Jenny. 'What were you doing when you came home last night?'

'I wasn't home last night,' said Jenny.

'Yes, you were. I saw you. It was after midnight.'

'Yes, you are right – I did come home. Yes, I remember now. I forgot something in my room. A book. I wanted to read it, so I drove home, sneaked in, got it. I tried to be quiet.'

'I'll bet you did.'

'I did.'

'Yes, I'll bet you did *try*. But I saw you nonetheless. And sneaking out again.'

'I tried to be quiet. And I'll tell you something, Victoria,' she said softly, looking a little subdued. 'I don't like what I've been doing, and I shan't do it anymore. I will undo what I have done against Father.'

The meaning of this coded chatter escaped me completely.

'Come now,' said Brock, 'let us have a drink before lunch, and no more games. We are all civilized people.' He lifted his glass.

'Civilization is vastly overrated,' said Black Swan. 'But let us make the best of it. It is pleasant on this patio, and Marguerite will have lunch for us soon. Then let us drink to the happiness of all creatures on this earth!' He raised his glass.

Jenny and Victoria followed his lead, languidly lifting their glasses. All of us took a sip. The two girls looked equally beautiful in that moment – almost identical. And yet one sensed they were very different, these girlfriends of two brothers. Jenny was winning, and I liked her very much. Victoria was troubled, somehow, and not quite likeable.

'I think I will freshen up a bit before lunch,' said Victoria suddenly.

'Me too,' said Jenny.

They danced away together like blown leaves. How many times over the years (I wondered) had they whirled away like that together, two sisters, twins, lovely and in sync with each other as twins are always said to be.

'It strikes me there are two ways for a Black Swan to steal things,' said Holmes. He took a sip of his champagne. 'He may steal the virtual thing, or he may steal the actual thing.'

'True, Mr Holmes,' said Black Swan.

'I knew a London pickpocket named Sam Slipper,' said

Holmes, 'who was the prince of Fagins. When he picked a wallet from a pocket, he always replaced it with a phony, so that the poor victim kept feeling the pressure of what he supposed to be his own wallet, and only discovered his loss when he pulled out the phony.'

'Precisely right, Mr Holmes,' said Andrew. 'We have been stealing Gurloch's real computer regularly, and replacing it with a phony – but in such a way that he was, unlike Mr Slipper's victims, never able to discover the phony. And I now have all the information I need.'

'I wonder, Mr Swann, if you happen to have any damning material on a man named Greenwood, who is with the Metropolitan Police. Nigel Greenwood.'

'On Greenwood I have only some emails that will raise suspicion, nothing that will put him behind bars.'

'I say, Holmes,' said I, 'the flash drive I gave you may serve your purpose.'

'You lads will be getting yourselves in trouble,' said Bedford Brock. 'You do not know who you are up against – it isn't just Gerald, you can be sure of that.'

'No matter to me if I'm up against Gerald, the devil, or God almighty!' said Black Swan in his nasal voice, and he laughed recklessly.

'You would be better off to be up against God almighty,' said Brock. '*He* might have mercy on you. The chaps you are challenging won't. There are many ways to crush a man – and they know them all. Be warned!'

Marguerite emerged from the house with a tray. She set little fruit cocktails by every plate. 'I hope you will enjoy this!'

At that moment came a distant roar. I realized it was the Harley.

Holmes leapt from his chair. 'She's taking the computer!' he cried. And an instant later he was out onto the lawn, disappearing around the corner of the house.

Black Swan swallowed the last of his champagne, choking on it a little, and he raised a hand . . . 'It doesn't matter . . .'

I leapt in pursuit of Holmes.

The Aston Martin had already rumbled to life and was beginning to roll – and I do believe Holmes intended to roar away without me . . . but he saw me and the little car paused, like a bird in

mid flight, hovering silvery on the black asphalt. I jumped in
quickly – the acceleration threw me back hard.

The Harley was already out of the long drive and flickering
beyond the trees on the main road.

Holmes careened in pursuit.

We saw the girl on her cycle.

Lost her.

Saw her again.

She turned off onto a mountain road. Holmes was held up
behind a lorry. Finally he got around it. He accelerated steeply
up into the mountains. Landscape on either side blurred and
shredded in the corners of my eyes. I was not at all sure that
Holmes could hold it on the road at this rate. The smell of pine
hit me like a wall, we shot through a net of flickering shadows,
we were fired at by flashes of sun. I had about given up hope
that we were even close. Then I spotted the motorcycle, black,
strangely small, tilting round the next curve . . .

TWENTY-TWO
Feeding the Monster

S eeing a beautiful girl soar to her death was a shock – she
who an hour ago had kissed me so playfully on the cheek
as I had gotten awkwardly off her motorcycle. Her death
had the curious effect of making me feel utterly detached from
the world. I was numb when we arrived at the laboratory of Dr
Droon, numb and slightly sickened as we witnessed poor creatures
mindlessly tortured in the name of science – an incident which
I have already described, and about which there is nothing more
to say.

The memory of the cruelty at Droon's lab was bright in my
mind as we whirled back down toward the valley – Droon and his
cretin-like factotum, Klebbing Hackfelt, whipping and torturing
apes who were pleading with them.

We whirled down the mountainside and, despite the tragedy

of a young woman and three apes, the afternoon sun bounced merrily in the tops of trees as it always does, and the world rolled on as it had to do. Three ramblers in lederhosen waved at us, smiling. But the thought of the poor girl's death weighed on me more and more, and I kept wondering, *What was Jenny trying to do?*

I am not sure what I said, or did, or if it was just the expression on my face, but in any case Holmes broke in on my train of thought – as he so often liked to do – and said, 'It wasn't Jenny, my friend. Just her motorcycle.'

'What!'

'Last night Jenny stole her father's computer – as she has been doing for weeks. This time Victoria saw her, stole it back, and stole Jenny's motorcycle to return the computer to her father's house. It was Victoria who went over the cliff.'

Andrew Swann met us at the door of the chalet, stepping stiffly out onto the porch in his shorts and T-shirt and running shoes. He looked a bit done in. He raised a hand in greeting, smiled wanly. A police vehicle was in the drive, so we knew they already knew. 'Jenny is quite distraught over what has happened,' he said. 'She and Victoria did not get along well in recent years, but they were sisters.'

'The computer is in the water,' said Holmes. 'Perhaps it can be found.'

'No need.' Andrew touched the necklace around his neck. 'Everything is here.'

Then I realized the necklace was made of flash drives strung on a colored string, each one a different shade of blue. 'I have everything on disks, as well. Also on my server. It is all backed up.'

For the first time I realized how needless it had all been.

'You were stealing the computer itself, not hacking,' said Holmes.

'Both,' he replied.

Jenny glided out onto the porch, looking shocked, pale. 'I told Andrew I wasn't going to do it anymore. I did not like stealing from my father. Whatever crimes he was committing, he is my father. This would have been my last theft . . . and now, look!' She began to cry.

'It was the last we needed. We have all we need,' said Andrew.

'You used two computers, I suppose?' said Holmes.

Black Swan nodded. 'Jenny took his office laptop every other day or so – the computer on which he did all his work, wrote all his letters, gave all his orders, received all his emails. And she left an identical computer which had been updated with all his files as of the previous day. She took it at one o'clock in the morning, leaving the substitute, and usually returned it before five in the morning. Gurloch must have wondered how even his most secret memos – memos sent out coded, on the most secure networks – were intercepted. We were also hacking his companies, of course. But stealing the actual computer, which contained a record of his daily current of thought, made it easier to piece things together, to make connections we might otherwise have missed. We have all we need, Mr Holmes. We are ready to release a large body of material.'

'To what end?' asked Holmes.

'My plan is first to let the police, government officials, and Gurloch's employees know that they are in the cross hairs of Black Swan. Let them scurry for cover for awhile. Let them imagine they can escape. And then I shall begin plucking the real arrows out of my quiver, and sending them to their marks. One of the first targets will be the prime minister. I will show him what I have on him, and make a bargain not to reveal it so long as he sees to it that my father's animal rights legislation is passed in full.'

'Blackmail,' said Holmes.

'Double blackmail,' said Swann, 'for I have no intention of keeping to my bargain. I am not so foolishly honorable.'

Holmes frowned.

'I prefer justice to honor,' said Swann. 'A dog who, by its actions, promises love and fidelity, keeps that promise. Humans don't. And I am only human. You mustn't expect too much from me.'

'And then?'

'After the legislation is passed I will reveal all, and I will see that the PM is pilloried from one end of the land to the other. Not very nice? I see in your eyes, Mr Holmes, that you do not approve. But the prime minister – and all the others that I deal with in the same way – are counting on me to act honorably, to keep my word. But why should I, when they have been acting dishonorably, and have not kept theirs?'

'There might be reasons.'

Black Swan ran his hand through his thick black hair. 'If I, by acting dishonorably, can save a man's life, should I not save it? Or if I, by telling lies, can save the lives of innocent creatures, should I be so scrupulous that I let them suffer in order to preserve my own unsullied honor? Would not this be the ultimate in selfishness? I realize I cannot set myself up as the arbiter of all disputes, the holder of all truth. I cannot pretend to be a judge of others. And yet, I must take a stand somewhere. And the question only is how far I may go in defending the lives of the innocent before I have overstepped the bounds of reasonableness, and so, in trying to defeat madness, have become mad. For surely it is a madness that we see all around us, Holmes. We have become so used to the cruelty and torture that it scarcely makes us blink any more. For me, at least, we crossed the line long ago. There was a time when animals were killed for food, not tortured. Now the torture has become *de rigueur*, for without it *profits cannot be made* – or so the businessmen tell us. Now chickens in much of the world are raised in cages so small that their feet grow to the wires, so small that they can never stretch their wings even once in their lifetime. No longer is it a world where chickens cluck happily around the barnyard, pecking and preening till the ax falls in a swift death.

'Look at this article in "Frankenstein's Diary" about a gentleman from the architecture department of the Royal College of Art in London, of all places, who has seriously proposed removing parts of chicken brains so that the birds are not aware of their living conditions in those cramped cages on factory farms. He says, "As long as their brain stem is intact, the homeostatic functions of the chicken will continue to operate. By removing the cerebral cortex of the chicken, its sensory perceptions are removed. It can be produced in a denser condition while remaining alive, and oblivious."'

'But his proposal has,' said I, 'a certain chilling logic to it.'

'Let us not talk about this any more, please!' cried Jenny.

Later that night we sat on the patio – Black Swan, Jenny

Gurloch, Holmes, Amy Swann, and I. Overhead swam a thousand stars in a black sky. 'Canyon doesn't know about Victoria,' said Jenny. 'We haven't been able to reach him.'

A single dim light gleamed in a window far from me. Four pale faces floated near me on the dark.

'Where is your father now?' asked Holmes.

'He is flying back from the West Indies tomorrow,' said Jenny.

'It is getting cool,' said Amy.

'I think I'll get my sweater out of the boot,' said Holmes. 'Excuse me.'

'I'll get it, Holmes,' said I, and I darted away.

I brought back Holmes's sweater.

By and by everyone went inside.

We sat in the large living room. The blackness of night had made us all feel very close to each other out on the patio, but now in the closed room everyone seemed far away. Marguerite served us tea. Black Swan sat cross-legged on the carpet smoking marijuana. His ragged long black hair and necklace of flash drives made him look rather like a sixties hippie. He was probably more like his father than he imagined.

Somehow Jenny's youthful beauty – her lovely face, her red hair tumbling down onto her shoulders – made her seem very sad and lost. 'I really wonder if it is right, what I have done,' she said.

'Perfectly right,' replied Black Swan. 'It is one thing to forgive a criminal who has burgled your house, quite another to look away when he is literally destroying your country. There comes the time to set sympathies aside and do your duty.'

'And yet,' said I, 'the guilty ones are also the people themselves – the people who read and believe tabloids.'

'Quite right,' said Black Swan, floating on his inner cloud. 'That is the defense that Gurloch and his kind always throw up – that he is merely feeding the monster what it likes to eat – and it has some validity.'

'But he encourages their appetite,' said Amy.

'Quite so,' said her brother, and he exhaled luxuriously. 'And by feeding the monster, he makes it his own, comes to control it through its desire to be fed the rubbish that it craves and howls for – the rubbish that only he can provide.'

'Then the question becomes,' said I, 'whether the monster's own depraved appetites, or the man who feeds it, is more to blame.'

'By the way, Holmes,' said Swann, 'will we ever know how my mother died?'

'Of course,' said Holmes. 'The matter is plain. But I have a few small points to resolve. Meet me at your mother's cottage in three days and I will reveal all.'

'I cannot be there,' said Black Swan.

'Nor I,' said Jenny.

'I don't want to be arrested,' said Swann. 'I've taken too many chances already.'

'I can be there,' said Amy.

'I must now,' said Black Swan, 'turn my attention to Dr Droon. I am prevented from halting his experiments because I lack one piece of vital information – the exact times he conducts those experiments.'

'Then you are in luck,' said Holmes, 'for I can tell you that Dr Droon conducts his experiments twice daily, and always at precisely ten in the morning and three in the afternoon. He has made it an article of faith that his experiments will not succeed unless they are carried out on this rigid schedule. I fear, however, that you will have very little chance of breaking into his compound. It is well protected by gates, alarms, a wall, and by a servant who appears to have stepped right out of a gothic novel – one Klebbing Hackfelt.'

'No doubt Droon's compound is well guarded in conventional ways,' said Black Swan lightly, 'but it is not protected in the one way that counts.'

Silence hung in the room as this mysterious remark seemed to float from the lush brown carpet, where Black Swan sat, toward the massive timber ceiling beams overhead. Everyone stared at Swann . . .

Swann took a drag, exhaled smoke, and shrugged. 'Dr Droon has made the considerable error of connecting his laboratory computers to the Internet.'

Holmes was about to gesture with his empty briar pipe, but his hand froze in the air. His face looked suddenly strange. He seemed to realize something. He gazed at Swann. 'Good heavens, man!' he murmured. 'If you do that . . . you know what it means!'

Black Swan took another drag, and exhaled slowly, gloriously. 'I think it means justice,' said he.

TWENTY-THREE
Fantasies for Sale

We stopped that night in Nyon, on the shores of Lac Leman, a lovely little town with a castle floating above it. In the hotel lounge Sherlock Holmes sat reading the *De Rerum Natura* of Lucretius while I scribbled in my journal an account of the day's complicated adventures. Then I began to write a narrative account of my West Indies journey, working from my notes. The only other person in the lounge was an elderly lady of seventy-five or eighty who from time to time looked up from her book and gazed straight at me as if desiring conversation. I ignored her for as long as I could.

'I'm from Lincolnshire,' she said. 'I love Switzerland.'

'Wonderful country,' I agreed.

'Tell me what you think is wonderful about it,' she said brightly.

'Its sheer volume,' said I, 'and its utter silence.'

'How odd!' said she.

'In Switzerland I always feel I'm in a huge, bright volume of air. Far below are tiny roads, and all around are stupendous mountain peaks. And everything is silent and revolving slowly, like a hawk.'

'You are an odd fellow,' she said.

'I hope so,' I said.

'I am reading a mystery,' she said. 'I like mysteries, but not this one. Contrived. Nobody ever really does these things.' She tapped the book with the back of her fingers, dismissively. 'Do you know what I mean?'

'An intellectual puzzle, but not a tale?'

'Exactly!' she said.

'Like a man rowing a rowboat into a patch of fog and never reappearing – and the solution is that he had scuba gear and cement blocks in the bottom of the boat, and to vanish all he had to do was pull the plug in the boat, sink it in the fog, and swim ashore underwater.'

'That's it,' she said. 'It *could* be done, but no one would.'

'They are sometimes good stories, though,' I said.

'When I was a girl, I liked them.'

'Or a man walks into his shop, to which there is no back door. Neighbors see him go in but he never comes out. The solution to the puzzle is that he killed the postman who came to deliver the mail, put on the postman's uniform, dropped the corpse into a hole in his basement, then walked out of his shop carrying the postman's bag of letters and he drove away in the postman's mail van.'

The old lady clapped her hands. 'That's the sort of thing. Entertaining but totally improbable. You are a lively one, you are!'

Her enthusiasm spurred me on to yet another fantasy. 'Or a man is murdered by his brother in a haystack in Surrey, and the crime goes unsolved for a hundred years till it is solved today by the use of DNA.'

'That's more plausible than ten people stabbing a corpse on the Orient Express. That's what I'm reading now. Is that plausible? I *ask* you!'

'Entertaining, though.'

She glanced toward Holmes. 'That man looks like Sherlock Holmes.'

'He is an actor,' I said. 'Tomorrow he will make himself up to look like Charles de Gaulle. He does a different character every day.'

'How very odd!' she said, and she went back to her book, and became absorbed in it . . . and fell asleep in her chair.

At breakfast Holmes said he wanted to see Paris again, for he had not seen that lovely city of leafy green light for many years, not since 1914 when he had stayed there a few days during the last adventure of his old life. Holmes also wanted to take a spin up the Autobahn into Germany – just to see if the Aston Martin could do a hundred and ninety-two miles an hour, as advertised.

But we had no time for either adventure. We drove straight to Boulogne, crossed the Channel, and arrived very late at our flat in Dorset Square. I made sure it was I who grabbed our bags out of the boot. I retired to my room, leaving Holmes sitting in his easy chair reading Lucretius by lamplight.

The following morning when I got up I was surprised to smell the coffee already percolating and to find Holmes sitting in that same chair. On the table beside him was a large pile of paper sheets, each sheet neatly written over with lines in violet ink. 'Trouble sleeping, Holmes?'

'I am in no mood for sleep!' he cried.

He went to the kitchen, came back with a cup in his hand. 'I have been pondering the puzzling death of Sylvia Swann, the perverse case of Greenwood versus Lestrade, and the ancient case of the missing calf. I have settled on a course of action for solving the first two. The third remains elusive. You can see –' he waved his slender hand over the pile of written sheets beside him – 'that I have done umpteen drafts. And yet I am little closer to capturing Lucretius's calf than when I started.'

'Lucretius's calf?'

'I refer to the poem in *De Rerum Natura*, about the calf who is dying pointlessly on some sacrificial altar for some non-existent god or other – the "warm tide of its life" flowing onto the altar stones – while at that very moment its mother is seeing her child's cloven hoof print somewhere in a far field, and is filling the woods with groans and bellows of grief as she tirelessly seeks her child but finds only the empty stall. The poem has been translated often into Victorian English, but I thought it should be translated into modern English. That is what I have been attempting.'

'Anthropomorphism, Holmes.'

'I am sorry to disagree, Wilson. People who use the word "anthropomorphism" usually have not observed the realities of the world, or have some unscientific agenda to deny not only the *identities* but even the *similarities* between the behaviour of other animals and humans. If I see a mouse trembling as the cat approaches, I call it fear. If I see a baboon cuddling its child, I call it love. To call these exhibitions something else is to go to extremes to avoid the obvious – and one wonders why people do this. Anyone who cannot see the common element in a baboon caressing its child, a hawk feeding its young, a human kissing its child, a horse licking its foal, and a dog protecting its pup, is someone not to be trusted in matters intellectual.'

'Good heavens, Holmes! You are beginning to sound like an animal rights advocate.'

'Not at all. I am merely an observer.'

He sprang from his chair. 'And now, I think I will give up for the time being on Lucretius's calf, have a shave, indulge in a hot shower, and possibly take a short nap before making some calls to arrange a meeting tomorrow in St Albans with Lestrade, Sigvard Kipling, and as many of the Swann family as care to come – plus, of course, Nigel Greenwood.'

'In view of Greenwood's strained relation with Lestrade, I rather doubt he will come.'

'I tell you, Wilson, thanks to the mysterious little gift of a flash drive you gave me, Nigel Greenwood will not only be there, but will be there with hat in hand.'

Holmes disappeared into the shower.

A little later Lestrade arrived.

'What brings you out so bright and early?' I asked.

'Sad news, Wilson,' he replied. 'This morning I was instructed to clean out my desk.'

Holmes appeared in the doorway wrapped in a towel. 'Clean out your desk!' he cried. 'You said they had given you six-months' notice!'

'They have given me six-months' pay, but they want to be rid of me as soon as possible. I must be out of my office in five days.'

Holmes and Lestrade stood for a moment frozen, looking at each other.

Holmes quickly recovered himself, sprang away to his bedroom. He reappeared shortly, fully dressed. 'Cheer up, Lestrade. You have not a thing to worry about.'

'The police force has been my life, Holmes. They are taking it away from me much sooner than I had planned.'

'They *think* they are,' said Holmes. 'They are mistaken.'

'They have sent me the papers, all signed. It is a *fait accompli.*'

'Nothing is *accompli* until it is *accompli*,' said Sherlock Holmes breezily, adjusting his collar in the hall mirror. 'I will make you a wager, Lestrade, that you will still be in your office next Monday.'

'You will lose.'

'Just a small wager,' said Holmes. 'Say, six months of your salary – that would suit me.'

Lestrade looked at him. 'What are you up to?'

'By the way, what is Nigel Greenwood's private phone number?'

'It will do no good.'

'Are you ready to make the wager, Lestrade?'

Lestrade began to look hopeful. 'I can give you the number. But if he knows where you got it . . .'

'Heavens, Lestrade! I can get that number in a thousand places. Nothing is secure any more. Secrecy is impossible nowadays. Our secrets in this modern world are not remotely as safe as they were in older times, when people wrote secret journals and hid clandestine notes in crooks of trees.'

Lestrade slipped a pad out of his shirt pocket and wrote a number on it. 'You may be right.'

'Just put it on the desk, Lestrade – thank you.'

'What do you plan on telling him, Holmes?'

'I plan to instruct Mr Greenwood to meet us tomorrow morning at the late Sylvia Swann's cottage near St Albans.'

'He won't. I know the man.'

'Oh, ye of little faith!' cried Holmes. 'I tell you Lestrade, he will not only be there, but will be there in his most penitent mood. What sort of fellow is he? I'm curious. I always like to know a little about a man before I dismantle him.' Holmes put his hands into his pockets and turned to Lestrade, smiling, casual, and as calm as Holmes ever gets.

Lestrade's strained face relaxed a little. 'He is a young man, forty-eight or so, full of energy, full of himself, and ruthlessly adept at getting done what he wants done. He sees to it that underlings comply with his slightest inclinations.'

'Excellent!' cried Holmes. 'Then I shall take pains to make

him not only publicly penitent, but compliant. He is precisely the sort of fellow one loves to humiliate. This is going to be fun! Wilson is always telling me that life should be fun, and I think he may be right. So please, dear fellow, cheer up, and do not be a drag on me this bright London morning when my fettle is not only fine but almost flamboyant.'

Lestrade obviously found these outbursts from Holmes bracing, but also mystifying. He nodded. 'Must be on my way.'

'You'll be there tomorrow?' said Holmes. 'Ten o'clock?'

'Wouldn't miss it.'

'You have the address, I think?'

'I do. Cheerio.'

And he was gone.

A score of things weighed on my mind, not least of which was what I should do about the dispatch-box. Absently, I got out my phone and flicked through the pictures I had taken on my jaunt to Les Marécottes: the railway station, the valley, Lindblad sitting opposite me at a table with his hand on a tea cup, the gull-like glider lying tilted in a green clearing, an airy view out the window of the plane as we soared over the Rhône Valley. The images only brought the reality of my dilemma more forcibly back to mind. Should I tell Holmes that I had the box, or not? I had promised Lindblad I wouldn't. But what was the right thing to do, all things considered? According to friendship and long association, I owed Holmes. But by a gentleman's understanding and in gratitude for his gift, I owed Lindblad. I began to wish I had never heard of the Cox and Company dispatch-box. The dilemma was wearing me down. Should I tell Holmes, or not?

'You might as well tell me and get it over with,' said Holmes.

'For god's sake, Holmes!' I cried, startled.

The truth is that, as often as it had happened before – and despite Holmes's apology of a few days earlier – I was still not accustomed to him breaking in on my private thoughts, and I always found the trick a bit shocking and intrusive. The first time it happens one is amazed, the second time amused, but as a steady habit the trick wears thin. A man should have privacy in his own brain, surely. His own mind should be a private garden in which he can wander alone.

'Sorry,' said Holmes.

'I don't mean to be prickly, Holmes. But the next time you complain about someone hacking into your computer, your phone, or your Aston Martin, do remember your own habits.'

'My dear fellow, I was only hoping to be of help. I have noticed you anguishing for two days over this question, and I don't like to see you suffering needlessly.'

'What could you possibly presume to know about my anguishes?'

'Not much.'

'Good.'

'Just that two days ago you vanished from Black Swan's chalet for a couple of hours. I don't know the details of your excursion, of course.'

'I should hope not. Unless you were following me, you couldn't.'

'I only know that Jenny took you to the Martigny train station on her motorcycle, that you met Lars Lindblad somewhere and went for a ride with him in his sailplane, that he landed the craft in the Rhône Valley near the Swann's chalet, and that Lindblad then gave you the tin dispatch-box deposited by Dr Watson at Cox and Company in Charing Cross Road many years ago. Also it is quite apparent that you promised Lindblad not to reveal to me that you had the box, that you phoned Jenny, that Jenny picked you up on her motorcycle, that you rode home behind her while holding the box, and that when you got back to the chalet you hid Watson's old dispatch-box in the boot of the Aston Martin. That is all I know for sure. But to that I can add one speculation: Lindblad wants you to enhance my reputation – which will, of course, enhance his. He wants you to write up some of the old cases that I refused to let Watson write up. I suspect he advised you to do so without consulting me, for fear I will prevent their publication by objecting to them now as I objected to them then. And you must have promised him you would write them without telling me.'

'I don't understand how you can know all that without having . . . I don't wish to say it, but . . .'

'Without my having spied on you, or betrayed your trust? But my dear fellow, you have betrayed yourself! It is all quite obvious.'

'I am listening, Holmes.'

'Let us begin with your mobile phone. Before we left the Hôtel Beau Rivage in Geneva you cleared the phone of all its photo files – you told me you were doing it, and I watched you do it.'

'I remember.'

'Except for the time you were gone on Monday from Black Swan's chalet, I have been with you every minute of the last four days – and I never saw you take a picture with that phone. Ergo, when just now I saw you reeling through pictures on your phone, I knew they must be pictures you took during those several hours you were gone from Black Swan's chalet, and that you were recalling that secret adventure – how could it be otherwise? And when I saw you frown repeatedly, I surmised you were troubled. All this is obvious.'

'Yes,' I agreed.

'Jenny said she had taken you to the train station, and I was standing near Jenny when you called and gave her directions to pick you up. She returned with you so quickly that I knew she could not have gone the seven miles or so to the train station. She had picked you up very near to the chalet.'

'Easily deduced.'

'When the old lady in the hotel lounge asked you how you liked Switzerland, you gave a very strange description of the country – strange because the point of view from which you described it was not a normal one. It was not a point of view that allowed you to observe what nearly everyone else observes about Switzerland – the precision, the chocolates, the towering mountains, the steep hikes in lederhosen, the rides in gondolas, the boat rides on blue lakes, the raclette, and so on. Instead, you spoke of brightness, of volumes of air, of the whole country revolving like a circling hawk. Above all, you spoke of the over-whelming silence. Something had impressed you with this strange imagery, but what? Where could you have been that you were so impressed? Not on a mountain, for on a mountain the rocks and glaciers and trees and lakes are close at hand. And you could not have been on the valley floor, for you said roads were tiny and far below you. Where, then? In mid air, evidently.

'And how could you be in mid air in such utter silence? Not in a powered plane, obviously. In a balloon, then, perhaps – but a hot-air balloon does require occasional blasts of noise from the burner. And a balloon does not circle like a hawk, nor does the world seem to revolve around it. A sailplane, then – a glider circling round and round and rising in a thermal.

'The old lady next began discussing how she did not much care for contrived mystery stories, and you agreed with her, and then you gave two examples of contrived plots – not realizing that each of your examples was but a transformation of a plot mentioned by Dr Watson when he described the papers in his old dispatch-box. Watson's "cutter vanishing in a patch of mist" you transformed into a "rowboat rowed into a patch of fog". Watson's man stepping into his house and vanishing forever you transformed into a shopkeeper stepping into his shop and never coming out again. But it was the third example, the example of a murder committed a hundred years ago and solved today by DNA, a crime that involved a haystack in Surrey – this is the one that convinced me you knew the contents of Watson's dispatch-box, for that was none other than the Cushington case of 1890. And Dr Watson never mentioned that case anywhere in his voluminous writings! But I remember it very well and, indeed, I have often thought to myself that it is possibly a case worth taking up anew, in hopes of solving now what I could not solve then.

'So we have a dispatch-box, and possibly a sailplane. The question is who of your acquaintance might have two such items, and might be in a position to summon you so abruptly, and to swear you to silence. There cannot be many who answer that description. And I know from our previous encounter with him in the affair of the Shakespeare letter that Lars Lindblad is obsessed with flying and with Sherlock Holmes. And when I smelled on your person a faint whiff of English Leather cologne, I asked myself who uses that seldom-encountered old scent. And the answer, or course, was Lars Lindblad. He has worn that scent every time I've encountered him. Could it be that you were in a confined space with him for an hour or so, and that your wool sweater picked up that scent? In a sailplane cockpit, for instance?

'And, finally, there was the matter of the boot of the Aston Martin. Whenever I was about to go collect something from the boot, or put something into the boot, you quickly volunteered to do it for me. The third or fourth time this occurred, I realized that that was where the dispatch-box was stored. Knowing you had a problem, when we arrived in Dorset Square I allowed you to carry our bags up from the car. I confess, I glimpsed that old leather bag you hurriedly sneaked into your bedroom. In that large, floppy leather brief case, I suppose, is the dispatch-box. So you see, my friend, your dilemma is now completely solved and all is well.'

'Solved!'

'You promised Lindblad that you would not tell me about the dispatch-box, and you *haven't* told me. You also felt it was not right that I should be kept in the dark about the dispatch-box, since it was a thing so near my life and interests – and I'm *not* in the dark. So, as I say, all is well.'

'You astound me, Holmes.'

'And of course it was Lindblad who supplied you with the flash drive that will save Lestrade . . . It is a shame to owe a criminal so much, but there it is.' He shrugged.

Suddenly I was exhausted. I needed a break, called my fiancée and we met at the usual court and we played tennis for a couple of hours, and that calmed me.

Afterward we took showers at her flat – sweaty and exhausted as we were – and went to an early dinner. I told her the things that were weighing on me – Lestrade about to be fired, apes being tortured in a remote Swiss laboratory, my strange obligation to Lindblad to present to the world Holmes's old dispatch-box cases, the needless death of Victoria Gurloch, and the gloomy knowledge that Orwell might have been more right than any of us had imagined. Tabloids were running the country, politicians fearfully jumping to their tune, police working hand-in-glove with corrupt reporters, Big Brother watching us day and night in a thousand ways . . . and all of us willingly entangled in a hallucinatory cyber world where ferocious predators felt our every quiver through a trembling web, and scurried to feed upon us before we even knew we'd been stung.

How lovely it was to have a sympathetic ear.

And then we talked about ourselves, and we drank our wine, and we felt, for the moment, very happy.

* * *

When I returned to our flat in Dorset Square I found Sherlock Holmes playing his violin, his own arrangement of Liszt's *Liebesträum*. He then dropped back a couple centuries and flicked a Bach Gigue into the evening air, with the greatest of ease. And he concluded his set with a jazz version of *God Save the Queen*.

Grasping the Strad, Holmes sank into his chair, and struck a pose, his hand on his chin. 'And what shall I do the day after tomorrow?'

'You will do like all of us, Holmes – you will see what the day brings and make the best of it.'

He had already solved the present case, obviously – and was already bored. I had several times seen him eyeing the drawer where the emergency cocaine was kept, the supply authorized 'for emergencies only' by Scotland Yard.

'Not a single interesting new case in the offing,' he sighed.

'You seem to forget that Gerald Gurloch has made plans to kill you, blow up Nelson's Column, and defame the Queen – all by cyber methods. Surely those threats should be sufficient to rouse you from your *ennui*, and to occupy you for a few days.'

'Ahh! But all that will happen only if he is charged with a crime – and that may take weeks, months . . .' He flung his arm in the air, in a gesture of hopelessness.

'I confess, my dear Holmes, that I am beginning to lose patience with you. There *are* limits. The man who demands that life supply him with constant thrills and challenges is a man who demands too much.'

'What could be the harm, Wilson, if I took up my experiments with drugs once again? Not merely to ease my boredom, of course, but to add to knowledge of the subject. I should like to write a monograph titled *Drugs, Boredom, and the Criminal Mind.*'

'You used to be the world's most famous drug user,' said I. 'But since those faraway days we've had Timothy Leary, Aldous Huxley and numerous other experimenters with psychedelic happiness. I'm not sure the world needs more experiments of that sort, Holmes. Still, what do *I* know? But I don't think you wish to alienate Dr Coleman, do you? And I am certain he will strenuously object.'

'I need problems, Wilson! I need complexities on which my mind can work . . . or I'll petrify!'

'By which you mean you crave a constant diet of bizarre, unprecedented, extremely original problems, to satisfy your exorbitant tastes. If you are so fastidious, what can you expect? Try being realistic, Holmes! Is your meeting for tomorrow arranged to your satisfaction?'

'Quite so. I have even arranged a little lunch to be served.' He punctuated his remark with a little flourish on the violin that soared all the way up to its highest register.

'All shipshape and Bristol fashion,' he added.

TWENTY-FOUR
Sylvia Swann's Last Dance

We made quite a crowd in the study of the late Sylvia Swann – me, Sigvard Kipling, Amy Swann, Canyon Swann, Sergeant Drub, Chief Detective Inspector Lestrade, Nigel Greenwood of the Metropolitan Police, and Sherlock Holmes.

Kipling, tall and fresh and outdoorsy-sophisticated, kept tapping his index finger on his thigh as he stood by a window. Timid Amy looked small and dark and almost furtive. Canyon glanced anxiously from face to face. Sergeant Drub did not look happy, as if he sensed disaster. Lestrade was quietly reserved but obviously tense. And Nigel Greenwood – an imposing man in a fine suit and blue silk tie, and wearing black shoes that shone like mirrors – looked rather like a racehorse who has been harshly curbed.

'May I have a word with you, Mr Greenwood?' asked Holmes.

The two of them stepped out of the room. A while later we saw them conversing a little distance away in the garden, and we watched as we might watch a dumb play. Holmes stood stiff and almost unmoving, and evidently he was doing most of the talking; Greenwood nodded, then nodded some more. Greenwood shook his head, and held out both hands palms up, and he nodded his head, then shrugged. Greenwood seemed to be protesting something. By and by Greenwood nodded again. Holmes started for the house and Greenwood followed. A few moments later they re-entered the study.

'We're ready, Mr Holmes,' said Constable Drub, his dark thin face the picture of impatience.

'So am I,' said Holmes, 'but . . . ah, there's the bell. That will be Isabel Rocamora.'

Drub looked as if he'd been slapped.

Holmes ushered in the lovely Isabel Rocamora and introduced her.

'I have a warrant for your arrest, Ms Rocamora,' said Drub.

'There will always be time for that,' said Holmes.

'No time like the present,' said Drub, and he took a step toward the newcomer.

'Sir,' said Holmes, 'if you choose to wait a while, you will save yourself some embarrassment.' And then Holmes put on one of his acts, raising his voice a pitch or two, holding out his hands, vertically, as if he were holding a medicine ball, and crying, 'Still, if you insist, if you insist!'

'No, that's all right then,' said Drub, looking abashed. He put his hands into his pockets.

'Please carry on, Mr Holmes,' said Sigvard Kipling.

'Sergeant Drub's theory,' said Holmes, 'is that Isabel Rocamora, having several times fallen out with Mrs Swann – mainly because Sylvia Swann found her too obsessively neat – told Mrs Swann that she would not work past five o'clock on the day of Midsummer Night's eve. That was when the family traditionally celebrated the anniversary of Sylvia and David's marriage. Isabel also, according to Drub, decided she would kill her employer and steal a valuable painting that she, Isabel, admired – and, consequently, at a little before five o'clock, Isabel walked into the study, took the statue of Aphrodite from the top of the barrister bookcases and hit Sylvia Swann on the head with it, killing her. Isabel then, according to Sergeant Drub, went to the china cabinet in the dining room, got a gold and green damask tablecloth out of the lower portion, and a key out of the cabinet drawer, and then returned to the study and covered the body so that it could not be easily seen from outside. She took the painting off the wall, carried it out of the study, locked the study door. She replaced the key. She also flung her mobile phone toward the pond so her movements thereafter could not be traced. About that time her accomplice and boyfriend, Charles Bentley, came by in his car and collected Isabel and the stolen painting. They drove to Folkestone, says Drub, and took the ferry to Boulogne, and vanished into the vastness of Europe, where presumably they had a way to dispose of the painting for cash. Have I stated your theory correctly, Sergeant Drub?'

'Quite correctly, Mr Holmes.'

'Now I shall present my own theory, and I shall leave it to others to decide which is most likely correct. But first we must cast our minds back a little, and remember some family history. David and Sylvia Swann met at the famous Woodstock Festival that took place in upper New York state in the summer of 1969. She was twenty-one, he was twenty-one. Both had been traveling across the States to see the country. Numerous memorable things occurred to the couple at that festival, but perhaps the most memorable was what occurred at the end of the concert, on the third day: Sylvia, feeling in an oddly ecstatic LSD mood, jumped onto a deserted stage, began to dance, and pulled down the banner that was limply hanging overhead. While she was engaged in this performance, and while David was watching her at her tricks, someone stole her dog Toby, a stray English pointer that she had rescued in San Francisco and that had traveled with her across the country. Much later that evening David and Sylvia found Toby, and all was well. And the Woodstock Festival was over.

'A year later, on the day of Midsummer Night's Eve, David and Sylvia were married while ascending in a helium balloon over a horse farm in Kent that was owned by a very young Sigvard Kipling, who was Sylvia's brother. Toby the dog rode with them in the balloon, as did the clergyman who married them – and also Sigvard and his wife, who were witnesses – and also, of course, the pilot. Thus began the tradition of simultaneously celebrating the Summer Solstice and the wedding anniversary of David and Sylvia Swann. Each year, as part of that celebration, Sylvia wrote letters to all their closest friends, and wrote them on stationery designed each year by David, and made up either by Smythe and Son in New Bond Street or, in more recent years, by the Wren Press.

'This past December, David Swann had their 2012 Summer

Solstice stationery made up, and he placed it in this study together
with a note, which I shall now read. It is right here on top of
the desk:

> *Dear Sylvia,*
> *I hope to be with you for our next, but my heart beats oddly.*
> *I've ordered our new Summer Solstice stationery early, just*
> *in case – in remembrance of the golden days of wine we've*
> *known since first you danced for me at Woodstock, and tore*
> *down the banner in your delight. Accept also this small*
> *hidden gift, my love, for old time's sake. Hope you have a*
> *good trip!*
> > *Happy Anniversary –*
> > *David*

'Unfortunately, David Swann was correct. His heart failed. He
died. At the time, Sylvia was away at her apartment in the Rue
Jacob on the Left Bank in Paris. Notice the curious wording:
"*Accept, also, this small hidden gift.*" As if a gift were with the
letter. And a gift *was,* in fact, included with the letter, as I shall
demonstrate shortly. In the past he had given gifts of books and
paintings – one of them, in fact, the painting by George Stubbs
that seems to have gone missing from this room, a painting of
a horse standing under a tree with an English pointer that David
thought looked like Toby. Sylvia agreed the dog looked like Toby.
It was her favorite painting.'

Sigvard Kipling nodded assent at these remarks.

'At this point I think it best to re-enact the event, so that we
can all see what led up to Sylvia's unexpected death. Mr Nigel
Greenwood of the Metropolitan Police has agreed to help us
re-enact the scene. He will play the part of Sylvia Swann. Sit
down at the desk, Mr Greenwood.'

Greenwood, looking splendid in his fine clothes, sat down
awkwardly, looking as if he'd never sat at a desk before.

'Now take from the box a piece of stationery, and lay it in
front of you, and unscrew the cap of the pen, and write a line
or two . . . *Dear Agnes* . . . and then just write one line of
anything.'

Greenwood wrote '*etcetera*', and looked at Holmes.

'Now fold the letter, slip it into the envelope, lick the envelope, and seal it.'

Greenwood took up the envelope and licked it. Sealed it.

'Now write another and do the same thing. Lick it, seal it.'

Greenwood looked like a big schoolboy, following orders grudgingly. But he followed them. And licked the second envelope. And sealed it. 'Ohhh,' he said.

'Now, if you please, do the same thing once more,' said Holmes. 'Write a few words, then fold the letter.'

Nigel Greenwood wrote a line. 'I have huge thumbs,' he said.

'Most of us do not have terribly artistic handwriting,' said Holmes. 'Yours is not bad.'

'Ahh.'

'Lick it and seal it,' said Holmes. 'That's the lad. Lick it, seal it. Now address it to *Stardust* . . . Excellent.'

'*Stardust*. Am I finished?' said Greenwood.

'Thank you for your help. You are finished.'

As Greenwood got to his feet he inadvertently knocked the chair over. 'Sorry,' he said. 'I don't usually . . .'

'Not to worry,' said Holmes. 'Is the food ready, Isabel? Then let us repair to the dining room, ladies and gentlemen, for a bite to eat!'

The invitation to food had its usual effect, and our group herded itself into the dining room where for thirty or forty minutes we ate cucumber and tomato sandwiches, sweetbreads, pickles, raspberry tarts, and a selection of cheeses.

'What's Holmes up to?' Lestrade asked me. 'This seems an odd interlude.'

'I haven't the foggiest,' said I.

Sigvard Kipling slid into our conversation. 'Sherlock Holmes has a penchant for the dramatic. I suspect this little entr'acte is simply to build tension for the moment he springs the truth upon us.'

'It seems unnecessary nonsense,' said Sergeant Drub.

'I think you will find,' said I, 'that there is method, and a great deal of sense, in all Holmes does. There is a reason for this delay. It is not mere stagecraft.'

Nigel Greenwood stood admiring a small eighteenth-century Dutch painting, a night scene depicting cattle in a forest beneath a moon. 'The moon is god,' said Greenwood loudly, 'and stars are his minions. But this deceptive picture hides the stars. Jacob Van Ruysdael refused to go face-to-face with outer space.'

'It is not by Van Ruysdael,' said Amy Swann.

'Nevertheless! Nevertheless!' said Greenwood. 'I've made my point . . .' He began to sing, '*Twinkle, twinkle little star. How I wonder what you are . . .*'

'Excellent!' cried Holmes. 'The time has come to reveal the facts of this case. Shall we?' He gestured toward the study. We all filed into that room once again.

'I do hope we can get on with it, Holmes, and learn what you might have discovered,' said Kipling.

'We shall move directly to the solution,' said Holmes.

'Outer space is the place to be.' Greenwood held his arms out and ran a few steps toward the windows, as if he thought he might be an airplane.

'Are you all right, Mr Greenwood?' asked Isabel Rocamora.

'Beautiful you,' said Greenwood. And he sat down on the daybed and leaned back, bracing himself with one arm. 'Whoooo,' he said.

'What's going on, Holmes!' said Lestrade. 'The man looks ill.'

'I suspect he is on a journey caused by LSD,' said Holmes. 'If so, let us hope he is having what they called in the sixties a "good trip".'

'Whooo,' said Greenwood. He fell back on the daybed and stared at the ceiling.

Isabel Rocamora hurried out of the room and came back with a damp warm towel and a glass of cold water. 'I'm not sure which he needs,' she said. She sat on the edge of the bed and touched his arm.

Sherlock Holmes walked to the windows and turned to us, and said, 'Eleven years ago David Swann bought a set of the complete works of Robert Louis Stevenson, had them bound in full blue Morocco, and put them on the lowest shelf of his barrister bookcases. On the bookplates he pasted in, he recorded the date he bought the books, August 2001, which was some years before he gave up eating meat and buying leather. During most of the year, that set of books is in shadow. But at midsummer the sun has moved to its northernmost point in the sky. Then, when the sun sinks toward the horizon in late afternoon, it casts its rays into this room and lights up the books in the bottom several cases.'

'Interesting, if true, Holmes,' said Drub. 'What are you leading to?'

'To the fact,' said Holmes, 'that Miss Isabel Rocamora's father is a well-known bookbinder in Zurich.'

'That he is,' said Kipling, nodding his massive and handsome head.

'How interesting,' said Drub.

'You will now grasp what I am suggesting,' said Holmes.

'I'm afraid I don't, Mr Holmes. You seem to be rambling into a thicket of nonsense. I fail to see any point to your observations.'

'The point, sir, is that Miss Rocamora knows books, and how to care for them.'

'I have no doubt she does,' said Drub.

'And one who knows books,' said Holmes, 'knows that books should be kept out of direct sunlight – particularly books with blue leather bindings. Red leather and green leather fade, but fade relatively slowly. Royal blue Morocco, such as these books are bound in, fades quickly.'

Miss Rocamora's head nodded very slightly as her eyes glanced hastily toward Holmes, then back to her patient.

'Also, it is a fact known to all that Isabel Rocamora is a very fastidious housekeeper – in fact, Sylvia Swann was often irritated at her maid for being too enthusiastic about cleaning, polishing, straightening. It irritated Sylvia Swann, for instance, that Isabel could not resist straightening every picture in the room that was even a millimicron off dead center.'

'That is true,' said Isabel. 'I am Swiss, I am particular.'

'And even more than merely particular,' suggested Holmes.

'That is true,' she said.

'And when you saw those blue books in the shine of the midsummer sun,' said Holmes, 'you were disturbed. So you took the matter into your own hands, did you not?'

'I didn't think they should be unprotected,' she replied.

'So you went to the china cabinet and from the lower shelves you took a green and gold tablecloth, and you carried it to the room where Sylvia Swann was trying to write her letters. You weighted the tablecloth at the top of the bookcase by setting the statue of Aphrodite on one corner of it, and by setting a book on the other corner, and you let the cloth fall down over the front of the case to protect the books from the sunlight.'

'Yes, I did.'

'And I suspect,' said Holmes, 'that Mrs Swann was irritated at you for doing this, perhaps even asked you to leave the room.'

'Exactly right,' said Isabel. 'I hurried out. I heard her lock the door behind me.'

'It was to be expected,' said Holmes. 'She wanted to be alone to write her letters undisturbed. You had irritated her enough for one day. So she locked you out.'

'I shouldn't have been fussing so much,' agreed Isabel.

'What happened next,' said Holmes, 'was that Sylvia continued writing her letters. She had written five, and had slipped them all into their envelopes, but she had not sealed the envelopes. She sealed them sometime after the moment she locked Isabel out of the room – what time was that?'

'I think about 4 o'clock,' said Isabel.

'Between then and five o'clock she licked the envelopes one after another,' said Holmes, 'and sealed them. And by then she was well on her way into some other realm – for only a very small amount of LSD is required to send a person into orbit. In the sixties it was common to put LSD on a stamp, and lick it off. David Swann, prankster that he was, and always keen to do something to surprise someone, had given her the gift of an LSD trip. He had put LSD in the gum of the envelopes. Perhaps he had saved it from forty years ago. Or perhaps it is possible to obtain it even today, though it was outlawed long ago. In any case, it was his anniversary gift to her, in memory of the LSD trip she'd taken at Woodstock.'

'Typical of David,' mused Sigvard Kipling. 'I sometimes think he was daft. Animal rights, balloons, heaven knows; and in politics he was slightly left of Karl Marx.'

'Fantastical theory,' said Drub.

'Fire your retro rockets!' cried Nigel Greenwood.

'Fantastical drug,' said Holmes. 'The short of it is, that the gift of a surprise from her dead husband caused her to take a trip. His note reminded her of the Woodstock days, and her trip followed his suggestion, and she was taken back forty-four years ago to a time of joy for her, and she no doubt began to dance on stage, as she once had done, and she pulled the banner down – only the banner this time was the gold and green tablecloth protecting the books. The statue of Aphrodite toppled, hit her on the head, and the tablecloth tumbled onto her slumping body. And the book fell, as well.'

'Turn on the stars!' cried Nigel Greenwood.

'All very clever, but not very convincing, Mr Holmes,' said Sergeant Drub. 'You have forgotten an essential fact: the painting is missing.'

'Is it?'

I glanced at the empty space on the wall.

So did Drub, Kipling, and Amy.

'It certainly *appears* to be missing,' said Drub.

'Ah, appearances!' said Holmes. He strode over to the big safe with '**Cox & Co.**' written on it in gold letters. 'Look how this lace tablecloth on top of the safe is skewed,' he said. 'The skewing must have taken place after Isabel Rocamora was locked out of this room, for it is not psychologically possible that she could come into this room and tolerate this lace, bunched up as it is, without stopping to straighten it. Her character would not allow it. She could not pass by this disarray.'

'Turn on the stars!' cried Nigel Greenwood.

'That's all right,' soothed Isabel Rocamora, and she stroked Nigel Greenwood's forehead with the warm cloth.

'Sylvia Swann was back at Woodstock,' said Holmes. 'That was where she lost Toby. She did not want to lose him again. So she took Toby off the wall, pushed the lace tablecloth back so she could open the door of the safe, and she put Toby in a place where nobody could steal him. She then began dancing, and pulled the statue down on her own head, as I have described. Not to make a mystery of it, the Stubbs painting of the horse and the Toby lookalike is in the safe. Mr Kipling, would you be good enough to open it for us?'

'I cannot,' said Kipling. 'I don't know the combination.'

'Then I'll give it a try,' said Holmes. 'In the old days light-fingered Harry Shelton taught me the trick of opening these old safes. He made his living that way.'

Holmes knelt, began spinning the dial. Time passed. He pressed the lever. The safe did not open. He tried again. Again the safe did not open.

'Let me try it, Holmes,' said I.

'You?'

'Shouldn't be too difficult,' said I. And I knelt down and put my ear against the cold steel door. 'I have delicate fingers and good hearing,' I said.

I spun the dial several times, pretending to listen intently. Then I spun it to 4 August 1914 – right 4, left 8, right 19, left 14.

I pulled the lever.

The safe opened.

I was gratified to see a look of amazement on Sherlock Holmes's face.

Sigvard reached into the dark cavity and pulled out the painting and held it up, a beautiful picture of a bay horse and a mostly white English pointer beneath a spreading green tree. 'I am very glad I hired you, Mr Holmes!' said he.

'Man the ack-ack guns!' cried Nigel Greenwood. 'I'm almost out of range!'

'What are we going to do about him?' asked Kipling, jerking his bushy brows toward Greenwood.

'Shoot me down, please!'

Amy said, 'He'll come down on his own, eventually. Not to worry. I've taken LSD.'

'*You*?' said Kipling.

'Father let me try some a few years ago. Orange sunshine, Daddy called it. Quite exhilarating.'

'Coming down *eventually* may not be soon enough,' said her uncle.

Greenwood began pounding on the wall and crying, 'Woodpecker! Woodpecker!'

Kipling and Drub pressed the increasingly violent Greenwood into a chair, held him there, and advised him to 'calm down'.

'A word with you, Holmes?' said Lestrade, quietly. 'And you, too, Wilson.'

We three walked out into the garden. Lestrade looked concerned. 'The Grosvenor Square Furniture van, Holmes. It was near Lord North when he died, also near David Swann when he died. Yet you have not mentioned this to the family. Surely that van seems in some way connected to the deaths of those two men.'

'Quite right, old friend – but I cannot prove it. What I suspect – and cannot prove – is that Gerald Gurloch killed both men by hacking their hearts. Lord North had an artificial heart, David Swann had a pacemaker.'

'Cybercide, as Hacking Jack Hawes so pleasantly calls it,' said I.

'In addition,' said Holmes, 'almost surely it was a monkey trained by Gerald Gurloch, or by one of his people, who scaled the drainpipe of Lord North's house in Clifford Chambers, and stole his laptop computer – it was Gurloch's real-life re-enactment of Poe's *The Murders in the Rue Morgue*, which was his favorite tale as a boy.'

'The child in the green hat,' said I, 'running by the river . . .'

'Was a monkey, yes,' said Holmes.

'Then Gurloch has again gotten away with . . . in this case, with murder,' said Lestrade.

'But justice moves in strange ways,' said Holmes, 'and we shall see what we shall see. I thought it best not to burden the family with more anguish at this point, by voicing mere suspicions.'

'Very right you are, Holmes.'

We went back into the house. I helped hang the painting back in its place.

'Is it straight enough, Isabel?' asked Kipling.

'I say nothing,' she replied, smiling.

Lestrade shook Holmes's hand. 'Thank you, my friend.'

Holmes smiled. 'I will put Greenwood's performance today, and Lindblad's flash drive, to good use – you will soon be very glad, Lestrade, that you did not take me up on my bet regarding your future employment.'

Holmes turned quickly to Sigvard Kipling. 'I say, would you mind if I take along with me a few of those envelopes from the box of Summer Solstice stationery?'

'By all means, take the whole box,' said Kipling. 'But why do you want them?'

'Scientific experiments,' said Holmes.

TWENTY-FIVE
The Pub Called A Friend at Hand

I n Bloomsbury, just round the corner from the Celtic Hotel, and not far from the litter and bustle of Russell Square tube station, hangs the sign of A Friend at Hand, the only pub in Britain with that name – or so Holmes told me. He asked me to linger there whenever I had time, to see if I could spot Hacking Jack Hawes, otherwise known as Dunstable Smith, for every day it looked more and more like Gerald Gurloch would be formally charged – an event which would set in motion Gurloch's mad plans for taking vengeance against the whole of Britain by killing Holmes, blowing up Nelson's Column, and slandering the Queen. If I spotted Smith I was to follow him and learn the location of the Bloomsbury branch of the Hack Magic Group of computer hackers.

I was never keen on wearing disguises, but I took it as a challenge to try to find a new pleasure this late in life. Wearing a wig and a pair of horn-rimmed glasses was uncomfortable at first, but turned out to be a bit of a lark. These little additions changed my appearance amazingly, and in a strange way freed me from conventions I never knew I'd been a slave to.

The first afternoon I popped in beneath the welcoming painted picture of the big St Bernard – a huge dog carrying his keg of cheer to the lost – I struck up a parley with the jolly bar girl. I told her I was Jarky Harwing, ex of the Welsh Fusiliers, late of India, now a full-time denizen of Bloomsbury who spent his time writing poems.

'It don't pay,' said Marcia.

'But it don't cost,' said I.

I sat nursing beers and listening to the bounce and bubble of Marcia's banter as she greeted one customer after another. The crowd was eclectic and intriguing. Next to me, two young and smooth-shaven men in sports jackets with open collars stood talking earnestly about computer systems to a young woman who apparently was duly impressed. Her lovely young face made me sorry she had no better topics to discuss. In the middle of the bar sat an angular old woman in a purple dress with a red hat out of another era. Every now and then Marcia would say, 'Another, Dearie?' whereupon the old woman would nod and reply, in a cracked voice, 'Does me good!' Next to her slouched a burly working man in a dark jacket who just stared and occasionally uttered a gruff laugh as if an invisible friend had just told him a joke. In short they were the usual characters one encounters in pubs. I had sat there scarcely an hour when Dunstable Smith appeared at the end of the bar. Marcia greeted him. 'Hey there, Spider – I won't even ask.'

'Merci, sweet wench!' said he. 'You always take care of me.'

She pulled him a beer. It foamed as she set it down. 'You still tracking creeps through inner space?'

'It's a child's task, but it's all I know.' He grinned.

'Get a real job,' she said, laughing.

They came, they went. The old lady made her way unsteadily across the floor, bumped into Smith, dropped her long umbrella, retrieved it, and hobbled toward the door. Three hooligan-types with loud voices almost trampled her as they came in, but they were solicitous when they realized she was old and apparently could not see well, and they held the door for her, and also for the old couple just coming in. Such are the little scenes of kindness and clamor one sees in a pub, scenes that reveal the many sides of human nature.

After another half hour I noticed that Smith was looking about in a nervous way and seemed about to leave, so I paid quickly. When he vanished out the door, I followed. He had already reached the corner of Guildford Street when I emerged, and I barely glimpsed him as he turned. I am not practiced at moving fast while looking aimless, but with a bit of luck I stayed with him, despite traffic and stop lights, till he arrived at a white four-storey row house near Russell Square, a house long since converted to offices. Black iron railings. I noted the address but, for fear of being noticed, I did not attempt to read the brass plate by the door. At the first opportunity I stepped into an alley, pulled off my wig and glasses, put them in a bag, and then I walked toward Dorset Square with a jaunty step. I was very pleased that all had gone so well – almost as if scripted, I thought. I looked forward to astonishing Holmes with the good news.

But when I got home, he was gone.

I found only a note, carefully laid at my place on the dining-room table and weighted with a spoon:

> *Wilson,*
>> *I must return to Switzerland on urgent business. Taking the Aston. Carry on at your end and we may yet prevail. By no means contact me electronically in any form. Follow my words not my example.*
>> *Yours,*
>> *Holmes*
>> *P.S. I never believe what I read in the newspapers.*

This peculiar note left me at a loss. Why would he need to go to Switzerland? I could not imagine a reason, unless it were that Black Swan had new information that could not be safely communicated except in person. That seemed barely plausible. But why so cryptic a note to me? Clearly, there were things Holmes did not want me to know. *Carry on at your end and we may yet prevail.* I had new and important information, and the only thing I could think to do with it was to convey it to Lestrade. But I dared not email Lestrade, or phone him – dared not communicate with him in any way except in person. Walk to his office in New Scotland Yard, perhaps, and beckon him out onto the street?

I sat in my chair and gazed out the window at the trees of the square. I became aware of light shifting slowly toward evening. To feel that someone might be watching one's every move, might be aware of one's every thought, might hear one's every spoken or written word, quickly becomes oppressive. I felt rather as if I were in chains. I broke out of the chair and took Lancy for a walk in Regent's Park, and I felt for an hour quite free. I hoped, as I talked to the dog, something would occur to me. Every day it appeared that Gurloch was closer to being charged by the Crown Prosecution Service.

That evening I dined with my fiancée in her flat. 'I'm afraid Holmes has left me in a bit of a quandary,' said I.

'Whatever else happens, surely you must tell Lestrade where the Hack Magic Group is located,' said she.

'And Holmes goes off to Switzerland in that car, when we know almost for a fact that its computer systems have been tampered with in some way, and that Gurloch has proposed to kill him – and has killed others already, probably, by tampering with their cars. I can't understand what Holmes is thinking!'

'I am certain he has a plan, James!' she said soothingly. 'Holmes is a big boy, and clever. You must trust him. Meanwhile, I think you must somehow tell Lestrade.'

'Yes,' I said.

The following morning I did as Rachel suggested – and I did it almost without effort, for Lestrade came round to the flat, unannounced. 'I don't dare phone anymore; I scarcely dare speak,' said he.

'I know what you mean,' said I. 'It is a strange world in which we find ourselves. But I am going to tell you straight out, Lestrade, albeit in a soft voice – Holmes has gone off to Switzerland.'

'Again?'

I showed him the note.

'The man is entirely unpredictable. I should almost say irresponsible.' Lestrade shook his head.

'But some good news, Lestrade: I have learned the address where Hacking Jack Hawes keeps his nest of hackers – the London Branch. It's right here in Bloomsbury.'

'Is it!'

'There are also branches in India and Russia. But we can't do anything about those, of course.'

'No.'

'What can we do about this one?'

'I am thinking, Wilson . . .' He held up a finger, he frowned. 'Today Gerald Gurloch will be formally charged by the Crown Prosecution Service. I've just learned this. And if what you discovered in Manchineel Isle is correct . . .'

'Yes. Things may start happening soon. For as soon as he is charged, his plan is to kill Holmes, blow up Nelson, and sully the Queen – in that order. Hacking Jack Hawes seems at the center of Gurloch's schemes. If we neutralize him, we may defuse the immediate problem.'

'Agreed.'

'Then, how to proceed?'

'I should have liked to have had Holmes's thoughts on this topic,' said Lestrade.

'But that is not possible.'

'No.'

'Time is short.'

'I fear so.'

'Here is the address.' I handed him a card.

He gazed at it, pondering. He walked to the windows. He turned to me. 'Wilson, I have a plan that requires only a few trusted men. It may not be legal, but it appears to be necessary.'

'Can you get the men?'

'I can. But tell me, have you heard from Holmes since yesterday morning?'

'Not a word.'

At that exact instant my mobile phone blared forth its flourish from my bedroom where I'd hidden it, announcing the arrival of a text message. And the message was from Holmes. 'I am baffled!' I cried. 'Holmes has given me strict instructions not to communicate with him electronically, in any way . . . and yet he sends me a text message. He says . . . "*Arrived Lausanne. All well. On to Martigny. Back in two days.*"'

Lestrade shook his head. 'There is no figuring the man out. Does this mean you can communicate back to him?'

'I think the answer is that I had better not.'

'Then we must carry on, on our own,' said Lestrade.

'Tomorrow, then?'

'I'll collect you at ten – if you want to be a part of it.'

'I do.'

'Danger could be involved, Wilson. And illegalities.'

'Count me in.'

'You're in.'

We parted at the door. He half-turned on the landing, raised two fingers in a farewell salute, then hurried away down the stairs and vanished into the street.

I could not help but wonder if he was being followed. I looked out the front window. I saw no one suspicious. Lestrade hurried away in the direction of Baker Street. Evidently he'd come via Underground or cab.

That evening on the BBC all the focus of the news was on

the formal charging of Gerald Gurloch, his editor Maureen Gripp, and three of his aides. Maureen Gripp was confidently outspoken in front of the cameras. She said she was angry at being charged, was outraged, and was astonished that such a decision was possible in this country, a decision based on what she called 'two parts rancor and one part flimsy evidence'. She said the charges were totally false, utterly baseless.

Reporters tried to get a response from Gurloch. 'Have you nothing to say to these charges, Mr Gurloch,' called a clear-voiced young woman reporter.

Gurloch turned toward her and he said softly but firmly, 'England will regret this.'

More shouts from reporters. 'What do you mean by that, sir!'

Surrounded by burly bodyguards, Gurloch was hurried through the crowd. Umbrellas everywhere. He ducked into the black limousine. The car pulled away in the rain. I was reminded, for a gloomy moment, of a hearse.

The large headline on the evening newspaper was '**England will regret this!**'

I was one of the few in the world who knew what those words meant.

The night ticked away very slowly. I did not sleep well. Little did I realize that my worst fears were about to leap up before me when I opened the morning newspaper.

TWENTY-SIX
Tabloid Shock

Very early every morning Mrs Cleary walks her dogs, purchases three different newspapers in Baker Street, and carries the newspapers back to Dorset Square where she lays them on a small table in the lower landing vestibule as a favor to her favorite man, Sherlock Holmes. That is where I found them on that fateful morning in July. I carried them upstairs and dropped them on the couch, not intending to read them right away. But the bundle opened as I dropped it, revealing this headline:

Sherlock Holmes Dead at Age 158
Spectacular Crash
In Swiss Alps
Takes Life of England's
Greatest Detective

I sank onto the sofa. I couldn't believe it. Didn't believe it. Refused. Yet the evidence was overwhelming. As I read the story it seemed there was no way out. The story had been broken by *Le Matin*, the Lausanne newspaper, and the world press had instantly picked it up. Everything was there – the time of day, the exact place on the road where the crash occurred, the name of the reporter who filed the story. In addition to everything else, a videotape of the event had gone viral on the web: a tourist had been standing at the edge of the cliff taking a video of the water-filled gorge below, and suddenly Holmes in his Aston Martin had flown by her and soared into the water. According to the story, the number plate of the car was plainly visible, and the GB sticker, and the blurred image of Holmes himself at the wheel. I hurried to my computer and brought up the *Le Matin* website, and there was the video. I played it several times. It certainly looked like Holmes behind the wheel, and I recognized the number plate, and the car.

From that moment on, the world changed round me. I walked as if in a dream. Nothing at all seemed real. Lestrade arrived. He said only two words, 'You've heard?'

I nodded.

We said no more. There was work to be done. We were determined to do it. Had we been younger men, less buffeted by life's vicissitudes, perhaps we would have been sicker. Perhaps we would have been rendered momentarily useless by such a devastating turn of events. As it was, we had both experienced similar slaps of Fate before – not often, perhaps, but often enough – and had been numbed to their full effect. We went onto automatic pilot. We did what needed to be done. We got into a taxi. 'Herbrand Street, A Friend at Hand public house,' said Lestrade. 'Just off Guildford Street, Russell Square.'

'I know the place,' said the cabby.

We went into the pub and sat in a far corner. I faced the wall, obscuring myself in the unlikely event that Smith should come in.

'At eleven thirty we will leave here,' said Lestrade. 'We will walk to the address, you and I. The thing has been arranged for eleven forty-five sharp. Other men will be walking there from other directions. They will be dressed in ordinary clothes, as I am. I know them all. They are a tough lot. We will clean up this nest of Bloomsbury hackers this morning, Wilson – that you can count on.'

'How do we get in?'

'One of the lads will be bringing some tools.'

'Then it is settled.'

'We have been watching the place for the last two days, ever since you gave us the address. We don't know what floor the computer hackers occupy, but we do know they are in the building. The brass plaque claims it is the Bombay Jewels Trading Company. A very private company, it appears, for we have found it listed nowhere. Two of our men have been assigned to search each floor as soon as we enter. We believe our suspects are on the first floor, most of them. That is where you and I will head.'

'Anything else.'

'After we have arrested them, all is uncertainty.'

'Any suspicious activity in Trafalgar Square? Strange objects at the base of Nelson's Column? A Queen Anne side table?'

'Nothing but the usual. Tourists and pigeons. We have men stationed there. They have been watching.'

'Your superiors are unaware?'

'I did not involve them. This is Lestrade's operation. I am taking a rather large risk, as are the chaps with me.'

'"England expects that every man will do his duty."'

'And these lads will – for they are as patriotic as any a sailor in Nelson's fleet!'

At 11:30 we left the pub and turned left, walked to Guildford Street, turned right, made our way across Southampton Row, then walked diagonally through Russell Square where dogs sported on the green and children played by the fountain and ladies sat on benches and everything looked quite normal. A four-minute walk brought us to the address. Lestrade nodded at me significantly, and jerked his head toward a man fifty yards away who carried a long iron bar. We three converged on the steps.

At that moment an old woman in a red hat and purple dress pressed ruthlessly by us from somewhere behind. She hissed at Lestrade and at me, 'I lifted his key, stay back!'

Instantly I knew that it was Sherlock Holmes – although I knew quite well that it could *not* be Sherlock Holmes. Such a thing was impossible. For a moment I thought I was hallucinating. I seemed to see Holmes's profile beneath the brim of the red hat.

The old woman hung her umbrella on her arm as she leaned to extend the key toward the brassy and shiny lock. The door opened easily.

'Is it you, Holmes?'

'Of course!'

In a moment all ten of us had gathered in the foyer, men of every description, men in workman's clothes, in suits, in running shorts and running shoes.

Holmes lost his hat as he skittered up the stairs. We rushed up after him. No one in the house seemed to be aware of us. Not a sound could be heard in the building other than the soft rush of our own feet on the carpeted stairs. At the top step Holmes tore off his wig and dropped it. Other men continued upward. Lestrade and I followed Holmes along a hallway. Holmes paused at the first door, listened, then pushed it open.

The men at the computers were surprised but not startled. They looked up as if maybe pizza had arrived.

But then they began to realize.

Dunstable Smith, otherwise known as Hacking Jack Hawes, turned, and his dark eyes and thin face were amazed, then angry. 'What's going on here!'

On the monitor overhead I saw a green furniture van pulling into Trafalgar Square and somehow driving right down to the base of Nelson's Column. Tourists were moiling, pigeons whirling. Even the pigeons seemed to realize something was very wrong.

Smith smiled a contemptuous smile. 'I'm afraid you are too late, Mr Sherlock Holmes,' said he. 'You are in the wrong century, and quite out of your depth.' Smith laughed and turned hastily back to his keyboard.

'I wonder about that!' cried Sherlock Holmes, and with a sudden move he leapt across the room in the stiff and upright manner of a swordsman, his umbrella at the ready. With a single lunge he thrust the long metal ferrule of the umbrella into the computer terminal, smashing the screen and knocking the entire computer onto the floor, and knocking down Hacking Jack Hawes. Holmes whirled, jabbed a man at another computer, who cried out and fell from his chair, whereupon Holmes smashed his computer as he had done the first – and now he was looking rather like Douglas Fairbanks in a swashbuckler movie. Holmes leapt about the room like a Fairbanks kangaroo, and served three other computer stations as he had served the first two, jabbing their operators viciously and causing them to howl in pain before he gave the *coup de grace* to their computers.

Smith got back to his feet and pulled out a mobile phone.

'None of that!' cried Holmes, springing again like a rabbit. With a single sword thrust he smacked the mobile phone dead on, causing the device to fly out of Smith's hand and across the room where it hit the wall. 'Arrest them and cuff them, Lestrade!'

By then the rest of our force, having heard the commotion, were pouring into the room. The four men and Smith were soon in custody. A number of our chaps then set about collecting computers and storage disks and storage devices. The monitor high on the wall was intact and still recording events in Trafalgar Square. Lestrade was on his phone – heedless, at this point, of who else might be listening. I watched the monitor with interest as police swarmed into Trafalgar Square, cordoned it off. By and by two men, presumably bomb experts, approached the van. I kept thinking about those Hack Magic groups in India and Russia, wondering if they had the ability to set off the van. Evidently they hadn't. Or else they were unaware that plans had gone awry in London. I suspect that if Holmes had not smashed the mobile phone out of Smith's hand, the other groups in India and Russia might swiftly have been informed and taken a part in the conflict, and the result of our effort would have been much different. As it was, the van was towed away within an hour, no harm done.

Lestrade was all business. When the office had been cleaned out, and the confiscated materials loaded into a large lorry, he walked up to Holmes and me and said, 'Now, gentlemen, I must instantly initiate part two of my plan.'

'Part one was brilliant, Lestrade,' said Holmes.

'With thanks to you, Holmes.'

'It is kind of you to say so, but you orchestrated it beautifully. What is part two of the plan?'

'To save the Queen – her reputation, that is. We now have captured the trove of doctored materials designed to sully the Queen. We will send it to one of the few reputable papers in this town, and perhaps also to *The New York Times*. I want the story of the planned deception made so public that Gurloch's lies will have no chance at all of coming to life, or of deceiving a single soul in the world.'

'Excellent, my friend!' said Holmes.

'And speaking of deception,' said I, 'you have a little explaining to do, yourself, Holmes.'

'I do, indeed. But if you gentlemen don't mind, first I'd like to slip out of this frock and into something a little more comfortable.'

Lestrade laughed.

We descended the stairs and watched the prisoners being loaded into the police van. In the heat of battle I hadn't really noticed, but now it occurred to me that Holmes did look a sight, standing there in the street in a purple dress, his hair mussed, his angular body leaning cavalierly on his umbrella, as if it were a cane and he about to do a soft-shoe routine.

'You know, Holmes,' said Lestrade, 'you've had three deaths in Switzerland, all of them false. In the 1890s you deceived Watson with your supposed death at the Reichenbach Falls. In 1914 you encountered death in a Swiss glacier, which modern science and Dr Coleman proved also to be a deception. And now you have deceived us with a supposed death in the Gorges du Trient. Enough's enough, my good fellow. Switzerland is a fine country, but I'm thinking we had best keep you away from it.'

'Touché, Lestrade, a distinct touch!' cried Holmes, and he brandished his umbrella like a sword.

At that moment a man came up to Lestrade and said, 'Ready to go, sir.'

'Be right with you, sergeant.' Lestrade glanced at Holmes. 'Shall we meet tomorrow, then?'

'By all means,' said Holmes. 'That will give me time to freshen up and recover. The Celtic is a good little hotel, but there is no place like home for comfort.'

'The Celtic?' I said. 'Is that where you have been staying these past few days.'

'Yes,' said Holmes. 'It was quite by chance that I emerged from the hotel this morning just as you and Lestrade passed the corner.'

'So you followed us.'

'Rather be lucky than good!' cried Holmes, and he brandished his umbrella-sword yet once again, made a few feints and passes with it, then pushed the button and it opened in my face.

'Holmes,' said I, 'you are sometimes a most annoying creature.'

TWENTY-SEVEN
Three Dangerous Gentlemen

Sherlock Holmes sat in the streaming light of the morning window, his pile of three newspapers by his side.

'Breakfast?' said I.

'No sausages this morning, please,' said Holmes.

'Bacon?'

'More in the mood for kippers.'

'Had kippers yesterday.'

'Baked beans on toast, then,' said he.

'My dear Holmes, I do hope you are not going vegan on me!'

He picked up the first newspaper, snapped it open, stared at it in astonishment. 'My heavens, Wilson! Gurloch's tabloids are good for something, after all – surely only he would print a picture this ghastly! How grisly! How gruesome! How perfectly composed!'

Holmes held up the newspaper. Large on the page was a full-color photograph of a decapitated individual lying in a large open doorway, with mountains in the background. Klebbing Hackfelt's blue-handled hatchet lay on the ground in a pool of blood between his decapitated body and his perfectly recognizable head. His eyes were squinched closed and his lips twisted as if he'd just tasted a lemon. A thrill of horror ran through my body. After Holmes had read the article he handed the paper to me. The headline filled much of the page:

MAD APES MURDER SCIENTIST
Blood and mayhem at secret Swiss mountain laboratory
Authorities blame computer failure

Dr Jan Droon, world-renowned psychiatrist and animal researcher, was found dead in his laboratory this morning, evidently the victim of his own laboratory animals. Police say the gorilla that Droon used for his research broke all Droon's limbs and then strangled him to death. Droon's laboratory assistant, Klebbing Hackfelt, was found decapitated, with a hatchet lying nearby. Bloody prints on the hatchet suggest that the murder was committed by one of the two chimpanzees that were also used for research by Dr Droon. In the past, Droon has testified that chimpanzees are unable to use tools in any meaningful way, a claim this sad episode seems to disprove.

All three research animals escaped into the mountains, and were last seen crossing a snowy ridge.

Dr Droon used computers to control his animals by stimulating electrodes implanted in their brains. Authorities are attempting to determine what went wrong with Dr Droon's computer programme that allowed this tragedy to occur.

Holmes briskly clipped out the article for his scrapbook. 'Let us not mention Andrew Swann's hacking activities to Lestrade,' said Holmes. 'Our poor chief inspector, scrupulous as he is, might feel obliged to report them.'

'I'm a little surprised to hear you say that, Holmes.'

'Surprised?'

'A cybercrime has been committed.'

'Or has justice been served?'

We left it at that.

'I always enjoy sensational fiction,' said Holmes. 'That is why I never start the day without a morning dive into the London scandal sheets.' He turned a page, clapped his unlit briar pipe betwixt his teeth. 'Why, see here, Wilson. On page two we have even more international news – "Chinese Rooster Gives Birth to a Mouse".'

'The crass culture of the modern age has captured your imagination, Holmes. I begin to suspect you are simply enticed by the tits and bum on page three. May I pour you another cup of coffee?'

'Thank you. Very good brew this morn – My heavens, Wilson!' He threw his head back a little. 'I certainly *am* intrigued by today's girl on page three.'

I glanced over his shoulder as I poured his coffee. 'I can see why. A glimpse of her would raise a man from the dead.'

'But I *know* her, Wilson . . .'

'I am sure you do.'

'I do. It is Jill Bliss, one of the girls I took for a ride.'

'Jill . . .?' I sat down, buttered my toast, took a closer look. 'Yes, I see you are right. I was distracted. I did not recognize her face – at first.'

'You never know who you are going to meet in a tabloid.'

'You'll soon be meeting yourself,' said I, 'when word gets out that you did not die.'

The baked beans on toast, the fried tomatoes, and the spicy fried potatoes were excellent, and we finished with fruit cocktail consisting of fresh pineapple and grapes. Holmes picked up the second newspaper, paged through it impatiently, threw it aside. Then he grabbed the third. On the front page were the words:

POLICE SCANDAL SPREADS
Officials Resign

He held up the paper so I could see.
'Success!' he cried. 'Listen to this, Wilson!'

> Assistant Police Commissioner Nigel Greenwood resigned Friday night. It is expected that charges will be filed against Greenwood, but their exact nature has not been revealed. Said Greenwood, 'I feel a great sense of relief that I am off the force. I have seen the light: LSD has set me free. I wish to thank Mr Sherlock Holmes for sending me into orbit, thus cutting me loose from the ties that have bound my real nature for so long, and that have restrained my desire for justice. I have been mired in the habits of getting and spending, I have allowed time and circumstance to draw me into quicksands. Whatever happens now, a new way is open for me.'

'Bravo!' said I.
'I expect Lestrade should be here shortly,' said Holmes.
Scarcely had he said the word than the chief detective inspector appeared in our doorway. He looked very dapper in his civilian clothes. 'I'm back on the force, gentlemen,' said he.
'We had guessed it,' said Holmes. 'Have some coffee.'
'Thank you. I confess I have come by to learn the trick by which you were resurrected from the dead.'
'It is easily told,' said Holmes. 'To go back a little, you will recall that Gerald Gurloch was adamant when instructing Dunstable Smith – otherwise known as Hacking Jack Hawes – that the first three steps in humiliating England must be to kill Sherlock Holmes, to blow up Nelson, and to defame the Queen, in that exact order. I realized, then, that he must think me dead before he would proceed with steps two and three. I knew how

he intended to kill me, for twice while I was driving the Aston
Martin a green furniture van had paced me for a while, and I
later came to realize that someone in that van had undoubtedly
been programming my brakes to fail when I reached a certain
speed – I realized this only when Wilson came back from the
West Indies and informed me that this was Gurloch's plan. If
Gurloch thought I was dead, he would move to steps two and
three. So I set out to appear dead, and I enlisted Black Swan
and Sergeant Drub to help me.'

'Drub!'

'Yes. A good enough fellow. Very keen to be of help. I have
noticed, Lestrade, that a man who loves dogs can generally be
trusted.'

'I suppose you are right.'

'I arranged for Drub to take my mobile phone and my Aston
Martin—'

'You mean the *company's* Aston Martin . . .'

'Quite so. To drive it to Dover, where engineers from Aston
Martin met him. They reset the computer system in the car. With
the car no longer a danger, Drub crossed the channel and drove
to Switzerland. I suspected Gurloch would be tracking my phone,
also hacking it if he could. So I had Drub send a text message
from my phone to Wilson, from Lausanne, to make Gurloch
certain I was there. And the rest was done by Andrew Swann. A
cyber illusion, he calls it. He took video of Drub driving on a
mountain road, massaged it with his computers, and created the
video of Sherlock Holmes flying his Aston Martin through thin
air and plunging, yet once again, to his death in Switzerland.
Swann sent the video to *Le Matin* in Lausanne, and then hacked
into one of their reporter's computers and wrote the story for
him . . . and away the lie whirled into the world.'

'And now,' said Lestrade, 'Gurloch has been charged, arrested,
and released on bail – and so has his chief editor, Maureen Gripp.
I wonder what that means for the future of this country.'

'Hard telling if it will mean anything at all,' said Holmes.

'Whatever it means,' said Lestrade, 'I would be very grateful
if you two gentlemen would let me buy you dinner tonight, in
celebration, and in thanks for saving my job.'

'I accept with pleasure,' said I.

'I also,' said Holmes.

'Then it is settled,' said Lestrade. 'The truth is, Mr Sherlock Holmes, you have kept the Lestrade family afloat in the police detective business for a hundred and thirty years – wasn't it a hundred and thirty years ago when you met my grandfather?'

'Something like that,' said Holmes.

'I know a small restaurant,' said Lestrade, 'where they serve the finest roast beef in London – and I know how you love your roasts, Holmes! Roast beef, boiled potatoes with parsley . . .'

'To tell the truth,' said Holmes, 'I feel rather more in the mood for fish tonight, if that would suit you, Lestrade – perhaps Scottish salmon.'

'Sheekey's, then?'

'Excellent.'

'Aha!' I cried. 'Holmes wants fish because they swim free. And he prefers Scottish salmon because they are not farmed.'

'What's this?' said Lestrade.

'I have suspected for some while,' said I, 'that Sherlock Holmes is drifting toward becoming a vegetarian.'

'I cannot believe it,' said Lestrade.

'Don't believe it,' said Holmes.

'But how can you avoid it, Holmes?' said I. 'You have been arguing the logic of that position for the past several weeks – and doing it so brilliantly that I doubt you can undo your own arguments by answering them. You are in the position of a man who has won a chess game against himself, and now wishes to pretend he never played it.'

'There is more to life than logic,' said Holmes. He walked to the wall by the fireplace and looked at his own face in the mirror. 'There is the matter of habit, and that is my weakness.'

'Bravo!' said Lestrade. 'We have come at last to the weakness of Sherlock Holmes. I am very glad, my friend, to see you have one.'

'An Italian restaurant might also be nice,' said Holmes. 'In Soho there is a rather good—'

'Holmes!' said I. 'You are fooling no one. Now it has come down to Eggplant Parmigiana!'

'I will pick you gentlemen up at seven,' said Lestrade. 'I believe light rain and fog is forecast for this evening, so bring umbrellas.'

'The last time I was taken to dinner by a policeman,' said Holmes, 'we rode in a hansom.'

'I'll not offer the elegance of a hansom cab,' said Lestrade, 'nor the chic of an Aston Martin. I shall arrive in a black vehicle, roomy and stately and sedate, with a motor that quietly purrs.'

'A London cab carrying three old friends into an uncertain future on a foggy London night,' cried Holmes. 'What more could one ask!'

When we were seated at the restaurant that evening, the head waiter came to our table and quite unexpectedly set down a bottle of Dom Pérignon. He handed a square envelope to Lestrade. 'I was asked to deliver the champagne to your table, sir, and this note to you,' said he.

Lestrade slipped the note out of the envelope. It was not handwritten. It was engraved. He read it with a delighted frown, and then passed it around.

Congratulations, Inspector Lestrade!
Three Dangerous Gentlemen
are back in the game
and this calls
for a toast!
Skål!

'But who could it be from?' asked Lestrade, genuinely puzzled.

I thought it best not to mention my theory on that subject.

Quickly our waiter brought our menus, uncorked the champagne, poured three sparkling glasses.

Holmes proposed a toast. 'To our future adventures, gentlemen – may they be strange!'

'Hear, hear!' cried Lestrade with uncharacteristic exuberance.

Whereupon Holmes opened his menu, scanned it quickly, and proclaimed, 'Now, gentlemen . . . time to decide!'

9016593500